Cadence of the Moon

aflame books

Aflame Books
2 The Green
Laverstock
Wiltshire
SP1 1QS
United Kingdom
email: info@aflamebooks.com

ISBN: 9780955233937

First published in Spanish as *En Clave de Luna* by Uruk Editores, Costa Rica

Cover design by Zuluspice www.zuluspice.com

Printed by Guangzhou Hengyuan Printing Co, China

Óscar Núñez Olivas

Translated by Joanna Griffin

1

Juan José Montero, the editor, had a sense of smell as sharp as his nose and, as soon as he heard the first reports, he scented a major story. A front page splash, he said to himself mildly excited, abundant material for one or two pages inside, and a special print run for the vendors. In the best-case scenario, the story could even be stretched to leave behind some mystery, perhaps enough for two or three editions, but that would depend. Above all, it would depend on choosing an outstanding reporter who knew how to handle stories of blood and terror without succumbing to the temptation of peddling cheap sensationalism. He had it: this reporter was a woman and her name was Maricruz Miranda. Young, intelligent and bold, she seemed the ideal candidate to cover the story, although you might well say she was not ideal for the same reasons. So impetuous and fresh was the professional passion of Maricruz that she often had to be stopped in her tracks. On the other hand, his neck, as well as the virtue and prestige of the newspaper, among other imponderables, might be on the line. The point was that in the news section there was no other journalist who could the match this girl's eagerness, even if there was one with more experience or another who was slightly more malicious – so the editor hesitated no longer and summoned her to his office.

The whole thing began, Juan José explained to her, with a casual passer-by who – lured by the unmistakeable stench of death – discovered the corpse of the fourth victim, which for a week the police had sought frantically and in vain. The guy had decided to cross the park with the simple aim of taking a short-cut and took the least used route, although he might easily have gone another way, as he later told the police, the press and anyone else who would listen. He had known something was amiss because he had stumbled across a pile of human guts long before he came across the body or even smelt its stench.

To tell the truth, he confessed, all that he saw was a woman's hand, poking out rigid and solitary from a mound of rock, the ring finger bearing a gold ring and the long, polished fingernails still with traces of the red varnish that the police would find in the bag lying next to the girl's lifeless body. One of the officers who assisted in removing the corpse from the scene would tell the television reporters (on condition of anonymity) that nothing had moved him as much as the image of this hand frozen in what he saw as a pleading gesture. But another officer saw in it 'a gesture of farewell' and a third speculated that the gesture had not been made voluntarily by the victim, but was a consequence of the haste and gruesome nature of the crime. Time would confirm the logic and importance of this last appraisal, but in the heat of discovery, conclusions came thick and fast.

"That is more or less all we know," said the editor.

"Nothing else? Are you sure?" the reporter insisted.

Juan José Montero shook his head weakly and paused to contemplate the intense eyes, the luscious, full-blooded lips and Maricruz Miranda's short, boyish, chestnut-coloured hair. But he said nothing.

"Well...," she insisted.

At that moment, Montero weighed up her nervous tension, that eagerness which his many years of professional experience had taught him to detect in someone who might be called 'a congenital successor', 'one of those guys or girls who have the taste

8

for blood in their genes,' by his own definition. He could almost feel the tingling that must be running through her body and knew then (although he had known before he had called her) that she was, indeed, the ideal journalist for the job.

"According to what they're saying," he spoke at last, indicating a white sheet of paper marked with firm, twisting lines, "the body was found in this section of the Parque de la Amistad. Here, about 500 metres north, a week or so ago they found the body of her presumed companion buried on top of the corpse of another man who disappeared in December, the boyfriend of the first victim. Do you remember?" The girl nodded her head, opened her eyes and slightly parted, in an unconscious demonstration of her innocence, those luscious, red lips which the editor had an urge to bite, forcing him to compose himself hurriedly in a gesture of patient expectation.

"A very tangled affair," Montero emphasised as he settled his considerable bulk into the ramshackle frame of what passed for his executive chair, pulled a cigarette from his pocket and took all the time in the world to light it and exhale his first puff of smoke.

"So? Let's see," he continued, waiting for her reaction with a kind of feline curiosity. "We have a total of four corpses: those of a man and woman who disappeared together in mid-December, those of another man and woman who disappeared in mid-February. To recap, two couples murdered in the same place two months apart. However, the men's corpses seem to have been buried on top of each other. What does that suggest to you?"

He took a couple more puffs on his cigarette, smoothed his hair with the palm of his hand and went back to scrutinising the reporter's features. Now her face reminded him of a famous actress whose name escaped him.

"It suggests that the four must have been murdered by the same person. That's what seems logical. But, let's see, give me some more details."

In Montero's gaze there was a triumphant sparkle and a sarcastic grimace underlined the square contours of his jaw.

"You're really interested, aren't you? I'll give you the details in exchange for a kiss, just a little one."

The reporter went on the defensive, pressed her lips together and tensed her face in an eloquent gesture.

"What will it cost you?" he insisted.

"You don't need to give me the information. I have my own sources and I assure you they're better than yours."

"I believe it, but your sources cannot assign the story, which is the only thing that really interests you. The only person who can do that is the editor," he said, pointing at his own chest with his index finger. "If you want to cover it, I'll give it to you but the price is a little taste of those goodies." He indicated her lips by pursing his own, musty, nicotine-stained ones.

"You idiot," Maricruz blurted out. "If you don't assign the story to me, I'll sue you for harassment."

Juan José responded with a confused laugh tinged with the bronchial cough of a lifetime smoker. He was very tall, had a broad forehead and chin and long and distinct extremities, and although he was always laying claim to some ailment (a duodenal ulcer, hypertension) he was still the country's most abrasive columnist and not a few recognised his instinct for news.

"For God's sake," he exclaimed, still chuckling. "This rag is really the kingdom of shortages. Not enough telephones, not enough computers, not enough journalists or photographers, or cars, not enough of anything... and, on top of this, we're losing our sense of humour, the only thing there was in abundance."

"I don't lack a sense of humour Juan José, what happens is that some people confuse it with vulgarity."

The news editor looked at her closely from above his glasses and swapped his cynical smile for the look of a lovesick puppy.

"You're the only woman in this newspaper," he whined, "in this city, in this whole damn world, who treats me badly and in return all you get is tenderness, consideration, and perks. At least, give me a smile, a simple, basic smile."

"Are you going to put me on the story, yes or no?" Maricruz dug her heels in at the door of the office, pretending she was about to leave.

"Let's see, let's see. Have I ever refused you anything?" said Juan José opening his arms. "I am the slave of your desires."

"Don't be a fool."

"Okay, okay," he shrugged his shoulders. "Come, come and sit down, the story is yours."

The reporter smiled and a pair of dimples appeared at the corners of her sweet mouth. Not for a minute had she doubted that the story was hers, as long as she went along with this game of Red Riding Hood and the Big Bad Wolf, which was not always amusing, but harmless enough, repetitive but necessary to keep the boss eating out of her hand. He's a strange guy, thought Maricruz, delighting so in his self-image of coarseness.

"What I told you is practically all that we've got," said Juan José. "The body was found this morning by a passer-by, about 500 metres from where the men were found. My source tells me the same killer is responsible for both crimes, but he didn't want to give me more details."

"You said the body was mutilated."

"That's what I understand, as with the other woman."

"What kind of mutilation?"

"I don't know. As I told you, my source barely wanted to mention it, but it's obvious the police are hiding important information and your mission is to get hold of it. I want a complete story that's different to what the other media are running, for tomorrow. Agreed?"

"Agreed."

Maricruz smiled and Juan José responded with a triumphant look.

"Do you realise? At least you gave me the smile I asked for... and twice."

"Alright, it's fine if you're happy with that."

"I know who you look like," said the editor as the reporter was about to leave. "That famous Swedish actress who played Anastasia. What's her name?"

"You mean Ingrid Bergman?" said Maricruz.

"Yes, like her."

"Perhaps, but I'm more beautiful," declared the reporter.

It was 10am and the newsroom looked like a scene of devastation.

It was a kind of storeroom with a carpet, a vast windowless, tastelessly decorated cavern in which a mortal heat ruled 24 hours a day, 12 months of the year. Depending on its mood, the air conditioning either did not work or emitted an icy cold so that common sense dictated it was best to keep it switched off and wear socks rather than suffer these extremes. Each journalist had his or her own small cubicle lined in three long rows. In each there was the screen and keyboard of an ancient computer, a telephone, papers and the reporter's personal belongings. Most had gone off to hunt for news. Maricruz sat alone and more disoriented than ever. All she had been able to get out of the police spokesmen was what her boss had already told her, and she would not achieve anything by running back to them in search of more. She leafed through her contact book in search of a probable source, a name that would switch on a small light in the darkness in her mind. She made a few calls to colleagues in the business to sound out how much they knew, but all seemed as clueless as her.

She had almost given up hope when, just before 11 o'clock, Pedro turned up sucking on a peach and munching on a chocolate covered doughnut, and looking, as usual, as if he had had a heavy night.

"Junk food," he said, waving his breakfast under her eyes until Maricruz told him to stop. "That's what the much-trumpeted practicality of the bachelor comes down to."

The reporter pulled a face of disgust.

"I have a problem. I insisted so much that he gave me the story and now I don't know how to get out of it."

"Problems?"

"Just one, but a very difficult one," said Maricruz.

"Remember that phrase of the immortal philosopher: 'The road to eternity is paved with difficulties'."

"Which philosopher was that?"

"I don't remember. The immortal philosophers have some really strange names. But cheer up, Double M, there's a solution for everything."

"Pedrito, what I need right now aren't philosophical maxims but a good contact in the homicide department."

The society editor sat down beside her, took out a cigarette and lit it with a pensive air. "Let me guess, they've assigned you to this slaughter they're talking about on the radio."

"You got it."

"Congratulations. You've always wanted to be at the cutting edge. You're right in your pond... of blood."

"It seems the police are hiding very important information. If I don't get something from the inside, we're going to come out tomorrow with the same story as all the other papers, it will be the ruin of me, the end of my career," declared Maricruz.

"Sweetie, don't get histrionic on me," said Pedro. "There's a solution for everything. The solution is here," he added, gently raising the reporter's skirt.

She looked at him intrigued, offering no resistance. "Those beautiful thighs will be your salvation, sweetie. You're going to need a top that shows to the world that little belly button and the shortest and tightest lycra shorts in your wardrobe. At lunchtime we'll go to the Sabana and, with a bit of luck, you'll get what you want."

"What's this about?"

"The best contact you've got right now," Pedro said. "You're lucky to have friends so well connected."

The homicide chief was a man familiar with death. He had spent eight years looking at corpses and it had been a long time since he had been shocked by anything he saw in the mortuary, however brutal. He imagined that in his job astonishment or any other emotion was no longer possible, just a few cold and concrete recordings: a victim, an identification (if this was possible), an approximate age, details about the corpse's colour or degree of rigor mortis. On very rare occasions, the face of death retained an inkling of the human condition (pain, complacency, a final rage) that was capable of impressing him, but even in such circumstances, his unease was ephemeral and could be controlled. He focused only on rigorous observation of the details, the physical circumstances that almost no one noticed. The temperature of a made bed, the contents of a rubbish bin, a trace of perfume on the languid hand of a victim, all contained universes of information which his methodical mind was capable of placing in the gaps of the investigation until it formed a scrupulous hypothesis. With one look, for example, he could anticipate the forensic expert in establishing the cause of death and he was rarely mistaken. "This one was killed somewhere else, with a blow to the head, and then they brought him here to make it look like an accident," he could say with certainty after close scrutiny of the victim or the scene. Or "This one looks more like a suicide than anything else, although the weapon has vanished." Deductions that, at the end of the day, came from an astute judgment. He did not possess some superhuman skill, it was no different to the diagnostic power of a practising doctor, car mechanic, or one of those fortune tellers who say they can read our future in their cards but who do nothing more than search in our eyes for the torments of the heart.

So the homicide chief was the first to be surprised when the scene affected him so much that his solid legs, accustomed to running marathons, began to shake and he had to vomit up the breakfast of hotdog and coffee he had eaten shortly before he was told about the corpse. He felt a kind of inner weakening, of pain and disgust at the human condition and, for the first time in many years, he regretted the damn luck that had propelled him into a police career when he could have been, for example, an excellent technical worker with a peaceful life, a stable marriage and a bigger salary.

The duty judge, Aurelia Carranza, did not even dare to look. She kept her distance, leaning on a eucalyptus tree, her arms across her chest. She expected the police to take the photos, collect any possible clues and call it a day, without even reading the description of the crime scene written on the police forms. She threw the documents in her briefcase and ordered them to pick up the body.

"Have they finished yet?" She approached Gustavo with an air of suspicion that the homicide chief instantly recognised.

"In a couple of minutes," he answered.

She was a woman somewhat over 30, with a chalky whiteness

and air of abandonment that might have had something to do with the thickness of her glasses or a certain adolescent candour hinted at in her easy smile. The officer observed her out of the corner of his eye and, in spite of her spectacles and formal clothes, she seemed to be a beautiful woman. So she had seemed since she had arrived to work in the legal section two years before and their work had brought them together. Her attractiveness was linked, perhaps, to the intense paleness of her skin or her frail presence, or something less physical that he could not put his finger on.

"Why didn't you want to see it?" the policeman asked.

"I'm not in the mood," said the judge.

To Gustavo her explanation did not seem professional, but he did not feel qualified to comment. He shrugged and tried to change the subject.

"I've been working in this for years, but I've never seen anything like it. Whoever did this must have been in the final stages of dementia. The girl is practically..."

"Okay," she interrupted him. "I don't want to hear the details, at least not today."

"What's up? You've never been shocked by gruesome scenes?"

"Perhaps they don't shock me, but they tire me. Last night I had a terrible migraine and today I've got a headache. I don't want to break a date I've got tonight."

"You've got a date!" Gustavo exclaimed in the voice of someone announcing the arrival of aliens.

"Yes, is there something wrong with that?"

"No nothing, who's the lucky guy?" he asked, and immediately regretted doing so.

That look of hers is telling you that you're an idiot, he thought at that precise moment, but Aurelia just smiled enigmatically, from the depth of her black eyes.

"Don't be indiscreet Gustavo," she said softly, "someone who's not blind."

Gustavo spent that morning with his head spinning in confusion. The office was buzzing with activity and with all that commotion, people coming and going, telephones ringing endlessly, people shouting at each other, any idea of concentrating was an illusion. In his memory, the sinister scene of the crime alternated with the tender smile and freckles of Aurelia Carranza, and the surprising revealingness of her low-cut dress. But more than the woman's charms, what tormented him were her last words. "No one is blind." What the devil did she mean? The only blind one here was her (you could tell that from the size of her glasses) and it did not seem reasonable to presume that she was alluding to her own physical limitations. Although he was a good observer, he had never been very good at picking up subliminal messages. The only thing he knew clearly was that the judge had fired one at him and he did not know whether to translate it as a straightforward joke or a formal attack on his chivalry.

He shook his head to rid himself of extraneous thoughts and focus on the case. The important thing, he said to himself, was to carry on diligently before the usual police ineptitude began to erase any leads that did exist. However, nothing came to him beyond the same old formulas, which seemed inadequate for such unusual crimes.

He was just about to call off his lunchtime jog, the only routine that no sudden pressing work matter could interfere with, when he received the telephone call that changed his life.

"Prepare yourself," Pedro said, "I'm going to introduce you to the most stunning babe in the Costa Rican press."

"Come on cousin, I've been around far too long for this sort of stunt," he said in self-defence. "What you want is information for your paper. I swear I'd willingly give it to you if I had it, but there aren't even suspects... we're completely in the dark."

"In this case, you have nothing to lose and much to gain. I give you my word that my friend is absolutely gorgeous, a work of the celestial angels." He went on: "If I'm lying, you don't have to be my friend. You can disown me as your cousin..."

"Okay," Gustavo relented. "In any case, it would give me a chance to clear my mind, but tell your friend to be under no illusions. We'll meet at 12.30pm on the track at the south side of the Sabana."

Gustavo thought he was suffering an optical illusion when he saw Pedro accompanied by that girl who, for reasons that at first seemed obscure, seemed so extraordinarily familiar and so peculiarly attractive. She smiled at him from a distance and he felt as if he had waited an eternity for that smile. She approached and the vision was even more pleasing, but it was not until she held out her hand, touching the tips of his fingers, that it all became clear: Pedro's friend was just one of those reporters who meandered around the offices of the Judicial Police looking for information. But unlike other journalists, who did so frequently, she had neither asked him for an interview nor stopped him in the corridors to press on him urgent questions. Nevertheless, it was impossible not to look at her.

"Pedro told me that you also like sport," he said after a formal introduction. "And I see you've come prepared. Shall we do a few laps, or would you prefer to talk right away?"

"We can talk while we run."

2

Mr Grey hung up, inhaled deeply then breathed out, almost violently, before uttering in a barely audible voice the lengthy, furious "Shhiit", which was his particular way of expressing the annoyance, distress or revulsion that had been triggered by his small-mindedness.

"Majorie!" he shouted.

Majorie appeared at the door of his office on the count of six, which was the maximum time in which she was permitted to react, notebook and pencil in hand.

"Sir?"

"Tell Juan José to come here at once. I need to talk to him."

Normally, to wind up the gringo, the editor would have taken his time to respond to this urgent summons, even if he had had to improvise a way of doing this, but he had woken up that morning in an excellent mood and this time he answered the call almost immediately. That morning he felt overwhelmed by an unusual optimism, as if the world – those six billion fastidious people and their ill-fated organisation, as he liked to describe it – suited him better. Mr Grey was waiting for him, lounging in his executive chair, his arms folded over his chest and his body slightly reclining, with a long, penetrating look that was a bad omen.

"What's up?" said Juan José.

"Explain this to me," the businessman said, pointing at the main article in the news section. "The Psycho attacks again," Juan José read out the headline and shrugged his shoulders.

Without being asked, but out of habit, he sat in the seat reserved for visitors, directly opposite the director, executive president and majority shareholder of the newspaper *El Matutino*.

"What's wrong with it? I don't see the problem."

"The report is sensationalist, and I don't like sensationalism."

"I don't like it either,' said Juan José. "But I don't think it is sensationalist. I think it's a professional piece of work."

"The Psycho again?" the gringo waved the page violently and read out the part that shook him to the core. "'The police seem to be as confused as the rest of society. I don't believe that there exists a person who is qualified to carry out this investigation.' You have to be extremely wary of arriving at such a conclusion. What is it based on?"

He was a thin man whose black, bulging eyes, meagre grey hair and considerable arrogance lent his face an aggressive expression, like a rattlesnake about to strike. The same effect was caused by his restless hands and long fingers whose nails were gnawed to a stump, ravaged by his perpetual nervousness.

His mastery of Spanish, which permitted him to speak the language without an accent and almost faultlessly, his average height and sun-weathered skin meant that he was often taken for an ordinary Latino.

"And how do you know that this quote is exact?" the gringo insisted.

"Because I know who wrote the report," said Juan José. "I know the reporter very well and that's enough for me."

Bill Grey let out another long sigh, another "Shhit" between clenched teeth, and struck himself on the head with his hand several times, while the editor merely regarded him indolently.

"A few minutes ago I had a call from the press office of the Department of Public Security. They are accusing us of spreading alarm. They say, besides, that these theories are offensive to the authorities and made a veiled threat to withdraw our government advertising. Do you know what this advertising means to us?"

"No idea," said Juan José.

"Let's see," Mr Grey examined his papers. "Twenty-two million, five hundred and seventy thousand, four hundred and twenty *pesos* in the last three months. It's crucial for us, we need the money."

The day that the editor had imagined he would spend in an excellent mood suddenly turned sour.

"And as I have told you on other occasions, my responsibility is the news, not the adverts."

"But we pay you with the advertising that we sell," said Mr Grey.

"No, don't make a mistake," Juan José corrected him with growing disgust. "You pay the advertising sales people with the money from the adverts, perhaps the administrative staff. You receive the profits of the advertising. But the journalists are paid through the sale of newspapers, which is the result of the news that we write. That is our business and you should understand that for your own interest, and in the interests of the firm. Furthermore, without news there is no advertising."

The gringo shook his head, rubbed his hands, stood up and paced back and forth in the office, a spacious area with a carpeted floor and some elegant lithographs on the wall (Monet's *Water Lilies Morning*, *The Potato Eaters* by Van Gogh and *The Dream* by Rousseau). Was this a genuine passion for the Impressionists, a corner of aesthetic sensibility in that spirit moulded from metal, Juan José asked himself while he glanced quickly around the small gallery. Perhaps, but it seemed incongruous with his personality, he told himself. It was more likely that some interior decorator had put them there, and that the gringo did not really care what he had. On the other hand, however, one could not imagine the gringo paying for a service that was so unprofitable.

"Why can't we manage to understand each other," the gringo exclaimed after a long silence. "I have never been against incisive journalism, but what I ask for is moderation, balance and sobriety, that each word is backed up by facts."

"As far as I remember," said Juan José, "the only time that we have been sued because of false information was over something written by a friend of yours, which you insisted that we publish and took personal responsibility for. Do you remember?"

"You are impossible," Mr Grey unfolded his arms. "You'll use anything to contradict me. You can never just say 'Yes, yes, William, with great pleasure William, I'll try to please you.' You always have to create some problem..."

"That's not true. I don't have any problem in saying yes when you ask reasonable and coherent things of me. But one day you ask me to give some punch to the news and the next you ask us to tone it down, that we don't annoy the advertisers. Where does that leave us?"

"Did you read this?" the voice of Don Jovel sounded brittle as though someone was crushing eggshells underfoot.

"Yes, I read it," said Gustavo.

"Here, they are attacking us with a pretty outrageous statement. Don't you think? Who the devil do these journalists think they are to judge the competence of our investigation? They are undermining us with this, Gustavo. Besides, how do they know so many details about the crime? Here there are things that were not revealed at the press conference, detailed stuff. I would say that the journalist has come across a very big mouth in the department."

"The department is big, Don Jovel, and there are loads of big mouths."

"Tell your officers not to speak to the press, explain to them that this is a delicate matter, which might bring hassles."

The director of the Judicial Police spoke in two tones: the first was medium, like a trumpet player addressing a deaf person, and the second was low, like someone with a slight fever. A trained lawyer and policeman by profession, he suffered from a strange and stubborn illness, some polyps on his vocal chords which meant his voice was a chaotic, uneven mixture. However, he was not tormented by this problem because, rather than being inconvenient for his political career, it gave a distinct edge to his personality.

"What hassle are you referring to?" Gustavo asked.

"Well, you know how these things are. If we don't handle this thing well, the press is going to keep exploiting it until they create mass hysteria, the government is going to get uncomfortable, there will be people on our backs and we'll be under a lot of pressure. That wouldn't bother me if we had a few solid leads but you said yourself that we are searching for a needle in a haystack. We don't know how long it's going to take us to catch these killers," said Don Jovel, now lowering his voice.

"Killers, Don Jovel? Do you really think there is more than one?"

"What do I know? I wish to God I had a theory, but this is a mess and I admit I don't know the head from the toes. Did they really study the scene of the crime carefully? Are you sure?"

"Centimetre by centimetre."

"Then why isn't there a single clue? I find it hard to believe a murder can be so clean," the boss rasped after taking a long gulp of cold espresso coffee that he had been served an hour before. He made a sign of disgust and pushed the mug away.

"To some extent, I'd say that we do have some leads," Gustavo said.

Don Jovel's face lit up with an incredulous smile.

"The first is that in the last two months there have been two murders with similar characteristics. In both cases, the victims were a couple. The men were killed with a shot, with no other form of violence, but the women were subjected to bestial treatment, as we know. The procedure was so ordered that in both cases... I don't think this was the work of a gang, not even of two men together. There is one hand and one methodical mind behind these crimes."

"Or let's say it fits with that journalist's theory of the solitary psychopath," Don Jovel agreed.

Gustavo ignored him and continued his analysis.

"On the other hand, the fact that in none of the cases there are clues is a clue in itself. It suggests that we are dealing with someone who makes certain preparations, who knows how to manipulate the scene and who makes contact with the victim only at the moment and in the circumstances that he knows are absolutely safe. Don't you think? This creep is someone who knows what we need to start an investigation and he consciously avoids us getting it."

"Aha," said Don Jovel, "someone who knows our work. It's an interesting hypothesis, but..."

"It's something, and not without importance," Gustavo argued.

The boss gave a start, as if he wanted to shake out an idea.

"No, no," he corrected himself. "I don't like that idea. It's just one step from concluding that the guy is a police officer. We already have enough reasons to look for someone else. Besides, I'm not completely convinced by the idea of a lone killer, I still think it could also be a gang, which could plan the murders perfectly by agreeing on a modus operandi. Why not?"

"At a stretch," Gustavo said, "but I wouldn't bet ten *pesos* on that hypothesis."

"Have we got anything from ballistics?"

"We know that in both cases they used a 45 calibre, but it's not definite that it's the same weapon; they are investigating."

Gustavo paused and looked at his boss hesitantly.

"What else?" asked Don Jovel.

"I know it's not a good time to bring up the subject, but neither would it be responsible of me to ignore it."

"What is it?"

"The personnel, I need a lot of people to investigate this case, but I can't abandon cases that are pending."

Don Jovel scratched his head with four fingers and he smoothed down the few remaining locks of hair on his head, an unconcious reflex that he repeated in times of stress.

"Sacrifice something, take officers off a couple of old cases and I'll make an effort to get a couple of new places."

Gustavo went back to his office with the same feeling of despair he had had since the previous day, only worse. He had never felt so strongly that his hands were tied, that he was so lacking in resources to deal with a case. There were crimes that were not solved after years, but there was always a material clue, a suspect, a motive, some ground that was more or less solid on which to continue. This time, by contrast, there was nothing. Was there one or more killers? Were they killing for pleasure of revenge? Would this saga of terror end here or would there be new episodes? Any response was necessarily speculative and provisional, based on intuition.

"Society does not permit this kind of threat and, for society, the ones who are to blame for criminality are not the criminals but the police – the government and the politicians too, but especially us," he had told a small group of officers chosen to begin inquiries that morning.

After the conversation with Don Jovel, this became axiomatic. Someone was going to be made responsible for the collective insecurity and, sooner rather than later, this would be the organisation charged with discovering the killer (if it didn't discover him).

"It was brilliant," said Juan José. "They reckon the edition sold out at 10am, but the old bastard is incapable of recognising a good move. Do you know why he called me? To tell me that we are being sensationalist, that the government was disturbed by our use of the word 'psychopath', that they are threatening to take away their advertising and I don't know how much more bullshit."

"I don't understand," Maricruz put her hands on her hips. "If we do get involved, we lose – and if we don't, we also lose."

The meeting room was in a ruinous state and had no windows, the carpet was stained and the atmosphere forever impregnated with a stale humidity. The room had a table long enough for 12 people and an assortment of chairs, taken from wherever they were surplus. In this environment the journalists met each morning to distribute stories and plan the working day.

"He insists that he is very troubled by the balance of the reports," said Juan José, "but well, you only have to know the meaning of the word 'meanness'. Let's get back to work. What have we got for tomorrow?"

"In reality, very little. I doubt that my source in the police is prepared to give me more information. We interviewed relatives and friends of the victims: no one has any suspicions, no one saw anything strange before the murders. Neither did the owners of the farm and the neighbours see anything suspicious. Nothing occurs to me."

"We will have to think of something," Juan José pronounced. "We have to keep the subject going – for a couple of days, at least. Partly because of our readers and partly because I don't want the gringo to think that he scared us. Understood?"

Pedro cut in: "What happened with my cousin? Are you going to tell me that you're not capable of getting a little more information out of him?"

"Your dear cousin behaved himself very well, of course. After all, if it hadn't been for him, we would not have published that story today, but I feel we've arrived at a dead end. Either he doesn't know or isn't prepared to tell me any more."

"Maricruz, for God's sake!" Pedro exclaimed. "It was obvious he was bowled over by your beauty and Gustavo Cortés is a terribly solitary man – you don't know the power those formidable legs of yours would exercise over him."

"And that sweet mouth," said Juan José.

"I am not for sale, gentlemen," the reporter protested. "Why don't you offer yourselves?"

"Just make him think, with the subtle ambiguity that women know how to use, that he has a chance," said Pedro. "In chess, the threat of a movement can be more effective than its execution because it disorders the enemy. Sweetie, disorganise the enemy's hormones."

3

D eath was the raw material of his work and, over time, he had learned not to mix it up with unnecessary emotions, such as pain, fear or loneliness. In the presence of death he conducted himself with the cold objectivity of an anthropologist or a taxonomist, with the acute steadiness of the pin in the entomologist's hand.

Despite this, incomprehensibly, the atmosphere of the morgue provoked in him an uncontrollable sense of apprehension. Physically, this manifested itself like an allergic reaction, a rash that crept over his body each time he visited the enclosure that his work often led him to. But the physical aspect was merely an alarm bell ringing from somewhere deep within, an area ruled by ancient shadows. There, in this dark area of his conscience, death retained the grey and terrifying aspect it had had that morning when he had entered an office similar to this one, holding his mother's hand.

He was so small that he almost hung from his mother's arm. She was sobbing and, at her side Gustavo was circumspect because, in spite of being just five years old, he was aware that what had happened was both tragic and definitive. "Papa has gone to heaven," he heard her say on the way, an absurd phrase that did not bring relief but generated a silent and visceral resentment towards his father. And against heaven. In his memory there was a man in uniform sitting in the hall behind a small table. Behind him was a door with a small glass window.

His mother said something to the guard, handed him a piece of paper and then they passed along a white passageway towards a second door. "Wait here for me a minute, don't move," he heard his mother say in a shaky voice before she went into the depository of corpses. She did not realise that, in her clumsy attempt to close the door, she had left open a crack and she never knew that Gustavo had witnessed everything. From inside there came an unknown smell, something chemical that irritated his nostrils and imprinted itself forever on his tender memory, linked with the image of the silent, horizontal object that was pulled from the wall and had the face of his sleeping father. That smell was here, in this other building, more than 30 years later. There was no guard with murky eyes, no dimly lit passageway, but there was that inextinguishable smell.

"Doctor Meneses?"

"Yes sir, go through," said the receptionist. "He's in his office."

Gustavo breathed a sigh of relief. Occasionally, Dr Meneses received him in his dissecting room, a setting that seemed to exacerbate his macabre sense of humour. Not only did he not interrupt what he was doing, but he would continue to perform the most repugnant operations in front of visitors. Suddenly, he would take out a decaying organ and exhibit it with excessive enthusiasm as an example of some kind of congenital degeneration, or he would decide to share his astonishment about the size of a brain tumour and lift the flap of skin that had recently been cut from a patient's skull. And he did all this while smiling eagerly at the visitor as though expecting a round of applause. It did not shock Gustavo, but the pathologist's jokes seemed little more than obscenities, manifestations of a type of shameful necrophilia that was full of repellent humour.

"I was thinking how strange it was that you hadn't come to see me," the pathologist said.

"Why?" Gustavo was surprised. "Were you expecting me?"

"Well, yes, there's a lot to talk about. You must know that."

He was small and slender with bulging eyes and very pale skin that was covered with thick hair that sprouted everywhere but his hands, his nose, his eyelids and his wide, high forehead. The doctor invited the homicide chief to make himself comfortable and insisted that he accept a cup of tea accompanied by some Danish butter biscuits.

"A gift from a grateful patient," he smiled.

The office was like a bear's cave, with a haphazardly cluttered desk and a shelf stuffed with magazines. The wall was decorated with academic awards and certificates as well as numerous football flags from Real Madrid, Juventus, Racing, Manchester United.

"What I've got is really surprising. You're not going to believe me."

"I've seen many incredible things in this office. Why shouldn't I believe you?"

"Well, not many people take me seriously," the doctor sighed. "Most think because of my sense of humour that I'm a con man.'

"Aquila non capit muscas."

"Pardon?"

"The eagle does not hunt flies. It's Latin: a man with a strong character and proven intelligence shouldn't worry about the opinions of men with small minds."

"Wonderful!" the pathologist was delighted. "You also know Latin?"

"A dozen phrases," Gustavo smiled. "They come in very handy during arguments. As soon as you throw in a Latin phrase, few people dare to continue. It's a trick that I learned from my professors in the days when I had the deluded wish to study philosophy."

The pathologist looked at him with astonishment.

"You're a very unlikely police officer."

The pathologist made a note of the phrase. He liked to collect them and slip them into the lectures he gave at the Buenos Aires bar, where he was a regular visitor. He was such a regular customer that Cheo, the owner, made him feel quite at home. Dr

Meneses took off his spectacles and held them in his hand while he looked thoughtfully at the homicide chief.

"Do you remember the other girl, the one they killed in December?"

"Of course, I believe – no, I am sure – that there is a connection between this crime and the one involving the other couple."

"What kind of connection?"

"I'd say it's the same killer. I also think this is a lone killer. I don't believe in this theory about a gang."

"Hmm," the doctor indicated his agreement. "I would also say that this is highly probable. Doctor González performed the first autopsy and I performed the second and, when we were analysing the case today, we found similarities that left us cold."

The pathologist stood and began to pace the room in long awkward strides, dodging the piles of books, the boxes of documents and even his old Remington typewriter that was no longer in use and had also been relegated to the floor.

"I suppose you know the victims, particularly the girls, had been mutilated."

"I know."

"One of the things that is strange, Gustavo, is that their sex organs were removed and – know what – in both cases, the organs were intact."

"What do you mean?"

"Whoever took them out was careful enough not to damage them. I don't know if you understand me. The guy took out the entire reproductive system without making any mistakes."

The homicide chief stared into the pathologist's eyes. He detected no hint of sarcasm in his words, which meant that he was taking this matter more seriously than normal. "I'm no psychologist but I'd say the murderer has a serious problem with women, particularly with sex or female sexuality. That's pretty obvious, isn't it? But the most important thing is that the guy must have advanced knowledge of anatomy."

"Did he rape them?"

"There was no trace, no sign of penetration. Not a single pubic hair or drop of semen."

"How strange," said Gustavo. "What are we dealing with here?"

"I've no idea," the pathologist said. "But be patient, since I haven't even told you the most important part. When I performed the autopsy, what struck me most was the way in which the girl had been mutilated. It looked like the work of someone who clearly knows about human anatomy, but there was something else, something very disturbing. I assure you that, with my team and my 25 years of experience, I would find it hard to do a more precise job. Now, imagine, during a massacre with practically no light, with the nervousness you feel in these conditions... I don't know, I think it would be difficult, almost impossible for me, for any of my colleagues."

The homicide chief did not respond. He was weighing up something. This was clearly not one of those routine investigations, he thought.

"The strange thing is that the same thing happened with Dr González in the other case. He said he hadn't said anything about it because it seemed so strange to him. He thought it was just a coincidence."

"A coincidence?"

"Yes... I don't know, as if the criminal made a cut here and there without much knowledge and it ended up looking like professional surgery. But such a thing could not happen twice. I believe that what we're seeing is the work of a true expert."

"A surgeon, do you think?"

"I wouldn't discount it," Meneses said, "although I find it hard to imagine a guy who spends the day trying to save lives and the night mutilating women. It's a contradiction."

"It certainly seems contradictory," said Gustavo. "But we do know that some of the most famous serial killers were doctors or nurses. I remember the case of one who performed an autopsy on several of his victims."

"Don't look at me like that!"

"What about a butcher?"

"I don't think so," the pathologist said. "There are important differences between human and animal anatomy. A butcher would not be capable of carrying out an operation like this. Besides, to do so he would need the right surgical equipment and to know how to use it. It's not so easy."

"So?"

"What do I know?" he shrugged his shoulders. "You're the detective. Crack the code."

After a lengthy discussion that left more questions than answers, Gustavo left the building and returned to his office, wondering whether the case would end in spectacular success or failure. Lately, the police body had been populated by arrivistes, careerists, birds of prey incapable of striking a blow on their own as they flocked to devour the dead meat. You had to be as careful with them as with the bosses, who were under pressure from the political authorities and public opinion. That is what he was thinking when he entered the hallway to his office and bumped into Maricruz Miranda. She was wearing a short skirt and a tight blouse that hugged all her curves, each rise and fall of her body. Her red lipstick made her mouth appear fuller and more suggestive and her short hair, which gave her the air of an adolescent, was sensual in the extreme. At that moment, he felt like a dog. He would have been capable of hurling himself on the ground and licking her feet, but a kind of sudden insight, maybe a kind of police reflex, allowed him to see that this display of her charms had nothing to do with chance, and that the young woman had come armed with all the weapons she possessed as a journalist and as a woman on a mission of seduction.

"What are you doing here?" he said.

"I was waiting for you. Do you think you could spare me a couple of minutes?"

"Right now I'm very busy. If you'd like to wait, I'd be happy to talk to you."

In reality, he did not lack things to do but nothing was exactly urgent. What he wanted was to make her realise that the miniskirt was insufficient to crush him, or to demonstrate to himself that he did indeed possess the mental self-control he believed was a vital part of his public image.

He made her wait for almost an hour and, when at last he

authorised her to enter his office, the beauty of Maricruz Miranda was no longer as radiant. Her skirt seemed a little rumpled and her eyes looked tired. Her features were tense and betrayed resentment.

"I'm sorry I made you wait so long," Gustavo said.

"Don't worry," she said with false nonchalance. "In this job you get hooked on waiting rooms."

"Make yourself comfortable, please," the homicide chief invited her to sit on one of four armchairs that were available for visitors.

If she had been able to visualise what was about to happen, Maricruz would have refused his invitation and remained standing or improvised some kind of manoeuvre to avoid sitting, but all this became clear when it was too late at the moment when her body sank into the moving sands of a pile of cushions, her skirt rolled up her legs and all her privacy was laid bare. Tugging at her slip of a skirt only made things worse. Her cheeks reddened and she sprang to her feet awkwardly.

"Better to stand, thank you."

Gustavo smiled, walked over to his desk and reached for his office chair, which he offered to the girl with an indulgent gesture.

"Perhaps you'll find this more comfortable," he said.

Such humiliation had dented her spirit. She had come ready to test a new operational strategy: to lure him with the discreet insinuation of her physical charms (according to Pedro and her colleagues) and then strike with a tough interrogation all at once, just like they did on the television. But the only thing she wanted to do now was leave as quickly as possible with or without information. If she could have, she would have disintegrated into tiny molecules and recreated herself somewhere else entirely, just as they did in futuristic movies about space travel.

"So, tell me," Gustavo said. "How can I help you?"

"To be perfectly honest, I don't know," she said humbly, which had not been in the script. "I need to write the second part of my story about the Psycho and I don't have any material. I was wondering whether you could perhaps give me some more information."

"We have a similar problem," Gustavo said, folding his arms. "I need to solve a quadruple murder and I don't know how. I don't have anything other than what I gave you yesterday."

"Is there a suspect? Has anyone been arrested?"

"Hard as it is to believe, the situation today is even more confused than yesterday. We have received around 300 calls from people who think the murderer is all over the place. Some of these trails are interesting but then they cancel each other out. Others are absurd and even laughable. One woman called us because her neighbour howls like a wolf. There are many reports that you can't simply discard but neither do we have enough staff to investigate them all quickly."

"Do they know anything about the weapon?"

"The ballistics lab is working on it now. We'll have a report soon, but in any case we've asked the FBI for their analysis too. Their technology is more advanced than ours."

Maricruz began to feel at ease again, thanks to the friendly way the police officer treated her and the realisation that, in spite of everything, she was collecting worthwhile information.

"The director of the Judicial Police told me the theory that this is a serial killer has not been confirmed, that this is just mere journalistic speculation. However, yesterday you told me the opposite."

"I told you what I think. It's how I see things. I admit that it's my fault for presenting this to you as if it were the official version. But, no doubt about it, your report has caused me some problems."

"What kind of problems?"

"The boss suspects that you have inside information."

"Are you saying that now you don't want to help me?"

Gustavo decided that this was not the direction he wanted their conversation to go in for no reason other than raw physical attraction (although this did not usually influence his decisions). Before the girl had come to his office, he had not had the slightest inclination to treat her in a special way. In fact, finding her waiting for him this afternoon had irritated him and, if he did not send her away immediately, it was because she looked downright sexy. He chewed his bottom lip as an idea suddenly sprang into his mind.

"Let's put it this way," he said. "I'd like us to maintain a relationship that is mutually beneficial. I'll keep you informed about the investigation if you promise to keep quiet when I tell you to. Do you understand? There is certain information that cannot just be thrown at the public, for many reasons."

"I understand," said Maricruz. "But what do you stand to gain?"

"It's hard to explain in the abstract, but experience tells me that the publication of certain information at the wrong time can have a disastrous impact."

"In other words, you give me information, it's up to me how it is used, but you maintain some control over me."

"That's it – but you also keep some control over me. You follow the investigation and you guarantee that no one apart from your newspaper gets the scoops. It benefits both of us, and I'll go along with it as long as you do. What do you think?"

4

"You are swine," said Maricruz, pointing at each of them with her index finger. "Never in my life have I been so embarrassed...and it's all your fault."

"And why is it our fault?" asked Juan José, shrugging his shoulders.

"You got more than you wanted, no?" Pedro interrupted. "Which proves it: a woman's pretty legs have more traction than a team of oxen."

"Don't waste time on them, Mari, men have no sense of shame, they are genetically obscene," advised Diana, the economics editor, who – in spite of her supposed female solidarity – was struggling not to join in with the raucous male laughter.

"Worst of all, said Maricruz, is that he managed to get a date with me. It's the last straw!"

Juan José stood up, choking with laughter, raised his arms in the air like the wings of some prehistoric animal to indicate that he could no longer stand the heat and went to switch on the air conditioning.

"Don't get all dramatic," he said, (a wave of cold air swept over the table and relieved the stifling heat), "it's a very decent exchange – useful and abundant information for good wine and a delicious meal with a little pleasant company."

"I am a journalist,' said Maricruz, "not a geisha."

The conversation was suddenly and dramatically interrupted by Amalia, the cleaner, who entered grumbling as usual and tortuously pushing the vacuum cleaner, a heavy and loud Soviet contraption that was designed to work backwards and compressed the air. In fact, on a couple of occasions it had been used to paint the building.

"Pigs," she was saying. "That's what they are – a mountain of hogs. Of course, mummy never showed them how to use the potty and so you have to go round cleaning up trails of piss all over the place... they might even have syphillis. And all that for what? For the miserable 10,000 *pesos* they pay me because gringos are tight bastards when it comes to money. Yes sir, they are all pigs, this is a newspaper of pigs."

"Amalia," shouted Juan José. "Can't you see we are in the middle of a meeting? Are you blind?"

"What do I care about your meeting?" said Amalia.

Without waiting for a reply, she plugged in the vaccum cleaner and began to clean the carpet with a determination that disarmed the editor. The machine made an infernal racket that drowned out all efforts at communication, and the meeting was cancelled. The journalists took the chance to get themselves a coffee or go to the bathroom.

Once she seemed satisfied, she unplugged the vacuum cleaner, dragged it towards the door and, before she left, shot a disgusted look.

"Peasants," she exclaimed.

"If it wasn't clear that she was mad, I'd have had her hanged some time ago," said Juan José.

"Mad no," said Pedro, "a lunatic. There's an essential difference. A madman is an individual whose behaviour is erratic and unpredictable as with, let's say, our dear director. A lunatic is someone who is born under the aegis of the sinister moon and who lives subject to the tyranny of continual lunar changes. He or she can switch from the most elevated state of virtue to the most abject without even thinking about it. Today, she is friend-ly and sweet, tomorrow she's a madwoman."

Diana let out a loud laugh.

"Don't tell me you actually believe in your astrological waffle. That stuff is just for the readers, remember? They got you to write the horoscopes because of your literary talents and because the gringo didn't want to pay a real astrologer, if such a thing exists."

"You may mock," said Pedro. "One of these days I'll do your stars and perhaps you won't find it so amusing."

"Let's concentrate on work," interrupted Juan José. "The important thing now is to decide whether Maricruz wants to con-tinue with this assignment, which seems to be so difficult for her."

"I didn't say that," the reporter said in self-defence, "I was just telling you what happened to me, but I am not quitting anything. I have it under complete control."

"Agreed," Juan José curtailed the discussion. "The other pressing topic is the crime against the former security minister. I need Juan Fernando to monitor him while Maricruz continues to squeeze the police."

Maricruz passed the day in a state of anxiety that even to her seemed absurd. She was unfocused and unproductive, and spent ages writing a report on a traffic accident that ended up a mess. The rest of the time she remained cocooned in her cubicle, drink-ing tea, eating chunks of cheese, and trying to decipher what she felt. She was not overwhelmed by the size or complexity of the job. Nor did the pressure from Juan José cause her any stress, she was used to that. It did not make her nervous, either: it was nothing new for a man to try to take advantage of a work rela-tionship to get closer to her.

"It's as if he was proposing something," she confided to Juan Fernando, "but I don't know what."

"Sometimes it happens," he said in the tone of a wary man, "you feel a tingling in your stomach and you think it's a sign something is going to happen, but it turns out to be unimportant. Are you afraid of this police officer?"

"Absolutely not," Maricruz was sure. "He seems calm, respectful... serious, at the least he seems to be very professional.
Although... perhaps that's what intimidates me – I feel overwhelmed by his courtesy."

Gustavo chose a sky blue shirt he had bought on a trip to Spain
years ago, and which he had only worn on a couple of special
occasions; a dark grey English cashmere suit which he usually
wore on Sundays; and a red tie – Italian silk, of course, with blue
sailing patterns. As he applied a hint of Xeryus Rouge behind his
ear, he tried to convince himself that this reflected nothing more
than his conscientious approach, strictly nothing else. However,
he had lost his appetite and he felt a ball in his stomach the size
of a huge potato that had not been digested. An unmistakable
sign.

Although he thought of himself as a man with little luck in love,
the ladies at the office considered him the best catch of all and he
had even won, although he never knew about it, an informal male
beauty contest they organised in secret. His one metre eighty five
height contributed, as did his devotion to sport, which kept him in
excellent shape. In addition, he had a kind of intuition for good
clothes and the right combinations which, added to his diplomatic skills, bestowed on him an image of gravitas and elegance. In
spite of all this, his image of himself was completely justified by
the barren solitude in which he had lived for several years.

He would have preferred to call by to pick her up at her house
or at work, but she refused emphatically and warned that she
would only accept the invitation if she drove her own car. It
occurred to him that she did not want to feel as if she was being
fetched and taken home, as if on a romantic date. When she
arrived, Gustavo had been waiting for 15 minutes in the restaurant foyer, checking his watch every few minutes. She was a
radiant vision that competed with the landscape of neon lights of
the city below. She wore a light grey trouser suit, a see-through
black blouse and black high-heeled boots. To contrast with her
short hair, she wore clearly visible earrings of white gold, and
used a discreet red on her lips, which she rarely painted. There

remained little trace of the girl in the miniskirt of the day before, attractive but obvious. The girl who approached him now radiated less youth, although she was struggling to walk in her high heels and this made her unsteady in her step.

"Am I very late?"

"Fifteen minutes," said Gustavo, consulting his watch one more time, "but I assure you that you are the most punctual woman I have ever known in my life. The least punctual makes you wait for 45 minutes to an hour."

"Men complain a lot about women's lack of punctuality, but I have the impression that deep down they love to wait for us," said Maricruz as a waiter led them to a table by the large window with a flower arrangement, a candle and a panoramic view of the city. "Isn't that so?"

"Yes, to some extent. Expectation is a good dressing if used in the right proportion; if used to excess it can be indigestible."

"Are you speaking from personal experience?"

Gustavo observed her, surprised, and her olive-green eyes smiled mysteriously back at him from the other side of the flame.

"It's strange," he said. "I have never seen it from that point of view but now that you mention it, I think impunctuality cost me a marriage. In this case, I was the unpunctual one. I always arrived late for everything, dinner every night, our child's birthday party, our wedding anniversary and so on. Finally, I realised the damage I was doing and tried to fix it, but it was too late."

"Why were you always so late?"

"Work, always work. That's my big problem."

"Which can also be a virtue."

"I'm not so sure. Any virtue in excess is a fault."

"I love everything about you, even your faults," Mayela had told him in a sugary tone that sent a shiver down his spine. Those words were the detonator. He had just started at the Judicial Police after a year and a half of truncated studies at the school of philosophy at the University of Costa Rica. She was the inoffensive clerk of a penal court located in the building opposite.

Every day they met in the lift or at the water cooler and

exchanged a glance or a smile, until one day at lunchtime, he approached her table and asked her if she would join him and Mayela gave him a categoric yes that dispelled his doubts. They interrogated each other and made a date to go another day to the cinema, a week later to dance, and a month later to bed.

"A beginning of the most pedestrian kind, with no waving of a magic wand or anything like that," Gustavo added.

"I love everything about you, even your faults," she had declared a few minutes before he proposed marriage. A few years later, his faults had seemed so numerous and so difficult to bear that she would list them each day in a high voice so that it was clear how miserable her life was at his side.

"I've always understood that that's how marriage is," said Maricruz. "My Papa told me it's like a Malinche tree."

"And what does that mean?"

"That after so many and such beautiful flowers, all that remains are the pods."

Gustavo laughed.

"And do you believe that?"

"I can't comment, I'm a born spinster."

"Engaged, perhaps?"

"It depends on what you mean by engaged," Maricruz said with a tilt of the head. "Let's say that I have a good friend who until now has put up with my long days at work."

"Is he another journalist?"

"No, a systems engineer, something to do with computers. But he is also finishing his studies and doesn't have much time for me. I believe he's a bit more in love with software, but we generally get along."

"He's a lucky man," Gustavo said, and Maricruz felt startled by the direction of their conversation. She went on the defensive.

"I think we've talked enough about ourselves for today," she declared. "I'd like to talk about work if that's alright. Is there anything new?"

Gustavo felt offended by the brusqueness of the gesture, but tried to hide his displeasure.

"Of course," he said, "as you wish. At last we have the reports from ballistics and I don't know if the news I have is good or bad."

"For a journalist there is no bad news."

Gustavo smiled. "What we do know is that the weapon used to murder the first couple, an M-3 automatic, was the same that killed the second. This would confirm the theory of a serial killer: a single weapon, the same modus operandi. However, I assure you that this case has never been more confusing."

"How?"

"Something unexpected has arisen, Maricruz. Do you remember the crime at the Cross of Alajuelita?"

"Of course."

"Seven women slaughtered, sexual assault, drugs, alcohol, rivers of blood, a real criminal orgy," said Gustavo. "From the police point of view, the case was solved. We have four suspects, two dead and two more in jail, and more than enough proof to incriminate them."

"And?"

"Now it turns out that the weapon used by the Psycho to finish off his victims is the same one that killed the women at the Cross of Alajuelita."

"What?"

"The ballistics experts are completely sure. There's some kind of connection, although we don't know what."

"How can the ballistics experts be so sure? Couldn't there be a mistake? Forgive me, I don't know much about the subject but it seems so strange."

"It's difficult. The firearms are designed in such a way that they leave a trace characteristic of munitions, like digital tracks. There can be two that are similar, but not identical."

"So?"

"Seen from a technical perspective, the case has become more complicated because the crime at the Cross was tremendously chaotic. The killers left their mark all over the place and that helped us identify them. But the Psycho is a very stealthly killer who leaves no signs and runs no risks. What does it mean that there is a weapon in common? We don't know."

"Risk a hypothesis," Maricruz suggested.

"It's too risky," said Gustavo.

"What am I going to tell my readers?"

"Absolutely nothing," said Gustavo, "this information must not even come out. I am only telling you about it so you can store it in your personal archive, for now."

5

'Complicated' is a term that defines very mildly how this day has been, but no stronger or more precise an expression occurs to me to sum up the conditions of the lunatic asylum in which we survive. At 9am Mister Grey appeared, completely wild, shouting about all the mistakes that his neurotic eye had discovered in today's edition.

He carried an edition of the paper, defaced with arrows, underlined in red and covered in fluorescent orange circles. His jaw was set even more sharply and his eyes were even more bulging than usual. He wanted to destroy my day. As usually happens, the reasons for his torment were not more than occurrences, hallucinogenic effects of the poison that his wife must put in his coffee each morning to kill him bit by bit. What an excess of space for the parliamentary news, how over-prominent the photo of the shanty town that the police evicted in Purral, that this is not a communist newspaper – that this article is missing a business source... the same old wish to fuck with us. However, the combat took up several hours of my precious time, delayed the co-ordination of the section editors and, in general, the business of the day.

Immediately, he offered a lecture on Success, a mishmash of

all the manuals on how to be rich and famous in 24 hours, of which he is a compulsive reader, blended with high school sociology, sometimes organicist, sometimes functionalist, always rightwing and always badly edited. If he hadn't regaled me with the same speech 20 or 30 times before, I would have suspected that he was experiencing a kind of *delirium tremens*, so excited was he by his own monologue.

"The difference between success and failure is in being daring," he said. "He who dares might fail once, twice, three times but he always gets back up and ends up triumphant. He who dares nothing is a total failure, a permanent failure, a mediocrity beyond redemption."

Pretty words, I thought, but it all depends on the lips that speak them. Related by an Olympic athlete, for example, they are a hymn to the power of constancy: in the mouth of an old miser they reflect all the coarseness, the lack of style, the shameless brutality on which all the new light-fingered capitalism is based.

"That is the difference between development and under-development, a strictly mental problem. The people who work hard, without caring about the hours they put in, without pitying themselves, without so much protest, work miracles and the others go to hell. Look at the Japanese. Look at the Asian Tigers, the economic indicators that they have. And how, when 30 years ago they were poorer than the poorest in Latin America? With work, a lot of work."

And what, I thought, if a community prefers to live without electronic chips and economic miracles, or only with those that can occur without them having to sacrifice themselves; and what if a community prefers to protect its mental health and its natural resources at the cost of an internal product and modest per capita income? Why do we all have to chain ourselves to the hell of infinite growth? What obliges us to use up our short lives between the four walls of a factory or an office, dying of a heart attack at 60 or perhaps earlier, without having enjoyed the sea, the mountains, fine wine, agreeable friends, all because of some economic indicators? How much happiness is a car capable of bestowing on us, or a state-of-the-art computer so that it's worth trading in our own freedom? Finally, I dared to interrupt and I poured out all these questions in one go. He looked at me as if I was a lunatic, as if I was an alien, as if I was mentally retarded, like all these things together, but it stopped his waffle in its tracks.

"You Costa Ricans, Ticos, are loafers *par excellence*. Things turn out badly because you don't work hard enough, or willingly enough," he said by way of ending the conversation.

In spite of everything, Providence must have taken pity on us and bestowed on our distressed souls a drop of relief. Today the new culture correspondent started and, although it's too early to draw any conclusions, the first impression – which they say is the most important – is good, very good, more than good. She breaks with all the stereotypes of the sluts who usually do this job, I mean that she doesn't go around bragging (at least, not for now), or wear trainers with holes in or have orange streaks in her hair. She is a natural blonde, slim and with an enchanting smile. She has divine eyes and cold hands. I felt it when she was introduced to me. Women with cold hands have burning hot hearts, a certain fact that does not appear in biology or psychology textbooks. Cold hands – burning hearts. She said her name was Lidia.

Maricruz heard the telephone and did something impulsive. She lifted the earpiece convinced that she would hear the voice of Gustavo and said hello with a slight acceleration of her heartbeat, which changed the colour of her cheeks and made her feel childish on an adolescent scale. Her intuition was wrong.

"Miss Miranda?" asked an unfamiliar male voice.

"That's me."

"You don't know me," the voice seemed a little evasive, "but I have some very important information that might interest you.'"

"Who is this?"

"I can't identify myself now. Are you interested?"

"How do I know? You haven't told me what it's about."

"It has to do with the crime at La Cruz. It's very important," the strange voice insisted.

"I'm listening."

"Not over the telephone. We would have to meet in person somewhere."

"Why?"

"It is sensitive information and you know telephone lines aren't safe. Someone could be listening. I don't want to compromise myself."

"Frankly, I don't know," the reporter hesitated.

"There's no reason to be afraid. We can meet in a public place – if you prefer. You can come along with someone you can trust. I assure you that it's an explosive piece of information."

"I don't know what to say. We don't usually work in this way."

"Think about it for a while, if you wish," the stranger said. "I could call you early tomorrow so you can give me a definite answer. One day. I can't give you any more time."

Maricruz's first reaction was panic. It had not been 48 hours since Gustavo had told her all about the probable link between the crimes of the Psycho and the massacre at La Cruz, and someone she did not know had called her to offer her information on the subject.

It is true that newspapers attract all kinds of weirdos, paranoid madmen who wander through the streets looking for someone who will believe their delusions and help them along with their fantasies, but something told the reporter this was different. Was it a simple coincidence? But there's no such thing as a coincidence, she recalled an old saying. From this perspective, she told herself, she should presume that this was a situation that was potentially dangerous. On the other hand, that should not really bother her since journalism is a job with inherent insecurity – and adventure and risks excited her.

She had confirmed that a few months before, while working on a report in the border area of Nicaragua. Frustrated by a scarcity of information during her trip, she gave in to the temptation to cross the border, illegally, to interview the suspected contra guerrillas who were believed to be based on the banks of the San Juan River. For a few *pesos* she hired the services of a boatman who took her to the other side, showed her the road that led to the village and went back as quickly as he could with the promise that he would return in a few hours to collect her. She never found the village or the rebel camp, nor was she on time to meet the boatman: she had run into a Sandinista patrol who threw her in jail for a day and a half, interrogating her and making degrading remarks. She managed to get out of this spot of difficulty because there are people who come into this world under a star, and Maricruz Miranda was one of them. Everything was a chain of coincidences: a Nicaraguan journalist who was reporting in the area found out about her capture; a military friend of the journalist gave him details such as the girl's name and the newspaper she claimed to work for; a sense of professional solidarity made him call her editor, who then considered it necessary to inform San José. In this way, the crisis was resolved through the opportune and energetic mediation of the Costa Rican ambassador in Managua.

Returning to the routine at the paper, she had been in a high state of excitement. She seemed elated as she wrote the report, which had initially been intended to describe the peasant migration into the neighbouring country prompted by the war but which ended up as a taciturn report about child soldiers, a cry for their crushed innocence in that nauseating environment of barracks, minefields and unburied corpses. She had met three of them during her hours of captivity and all of them confessed, sooner or later, to have been recruited against their will. They boasted courage in combat, but there was fear in their clear eyes.

The report, which was serialised over three days, gained for Maricruz professional fame early in her career. She even won a Unicef prize for journalism about childhood issues. However, she never referred in personal terms to the ups and downs of her adventure. "I believe I was never in danger of being killed, but a few more minutes and they might have raped me and – worst of all – they were all beyond ugly," was the only disconcerting comment that she made to friends.

After that, what was there to fear? She asked herself. War reporters could be passionate but their expectations were rarely fulfilled. She had always dreamed of mysterious journalism (interviewing masked individuals in dark places, rummaging in the hidden corners of crime, putting together an impossible jigsaw puzzle and things like that). She imagined such things as the essence of her trade. And now that something came up, even though as a remote possibility, would she shiver? Would she run like some faintheart?

From another point of view, to have secret information, an alternative source to the man who was in charge of investigating the murder, was an attractive prospect. In fact, what she had feared from the start had begun to happen: Gustavo had started to reveal the most amazing scoops, but he had forbidden her to publish them. He delivered the information according to a supposed agreement to collaborate, which meant that she could not obtain it by other means and publish it. She was in the midst of a juggling act, conscious of being the victim of an unfair game that she had to get out of, but had no wish to get out of. Worst of all was that matters completely unrelated to her work were bearing down on her, obstructive and unwanted emotions that she had not summoned but were there all the same, making life difficult.

"How can you not?" Juan José had said. "What's the damn use of giving you information like this if he doesn't want us to publish it? Is he taking the piss?"

"I don't know. What do you want me to do? He said he would give me a signal when we could publish it, but at the moment it would really endanger the investigation."

"We can't work like that," said the editor. "That puts us in an unethical position. One can hold on to information while filling it out – if it is confirmed – or look for other sources, but to deny it to the public for the convenience of the police is something that leaves a bad taste. In the end, it's the same thing the gringo tries to do when he asks us to manipulate the material in this way or that because it affects the interests of the advertisers."

"It's not my fault. The decision to go on with the game was made by everyone."

"It's better if we get out of this and carry on working with other sources. What do you think?"

Terrible. It seemed dreadful to her but she found neither valid reasons with which to oppose his proposal nor the courage to formulate her own arguments.

For the first time, in spite of her internal resistance, Maricruz admitted to herself that Gustavo was attractive. She had begun to feel this from the day that Pedro had introduced him and, talking to him, decided that he was not an arrogant and stupid policeman but a sensitive man, intelligent and with basic humility that seemed genuine to her. While the attraction grew, she tried in various ways to disguise it, but there was no way to avoid the truth. If she broke the agreement, she would stop seeing him and that prospect plunged her into unexpected sadness. There remained only the possibility that Gustavo would take the initiative, that he would try some other way to get close to her.

"And why not you?" Pedro scolded her that afternoon after he heard her confession. "What's the problem? Women spend a millennium fighting for equal rights and at the moment of truth they let themselves be ruled by senseless modesty."

She put an end to the conversation. "Are you going to come with me tonight?"

"Where are we going to meet your mysterious gentleman?"

"In La Villa."

"We're all going to protect you, I promise."

Beneath a curly, blonde wig twice as big as her head, behind some myopic eyes virtually obscured by her spectacles and with the grin of a happy rodent, sits a girl alone at a corner table. She wears jeans ripped at the knees, tattered at the hems, a green T-shirt, a wide leather Guatemalan belt stamped with quetzals and a velvet waistcoat buttoned up.

At first sight, you might think that she has escaped from a psychiatric hospital, but those in the know are aware that she is a skilful and ingenious journalist. Her name is Diana del Valle, her beat is economy and she does as well in this field as she would in any other. She follows popular dance, alternative theatre, ecological painting and non-conformist texts. She would not hesitate to declare herself revolutionary and anti-imperialist if she had been born ten years earlier.

Pedro enters La Villa during the tearful rendition of *Alfonsina and the Sea*, sung in the inimitable voice of Mercedes Sosa. He signals to Tilín, who nods to indicate that he has understood that he'll have his usual tequila with lime and salt, then goes straight over to Diana, who greets him by flashing her wide, powerful teeth.

"Sorry for the delay," he said.

"No problem. I had a great time. I had three beers and shocked 10 or 12 guys who looked at me as if I was a prostitute."

"And Artemsia?"

Diana lifted her coat and revealed a four-year-old girl sleeping calmly on the floor.

"Poor girl," Pedro exclaimed. "Not only do you give her a dog's name but you treat her as though she were one."

"It's the name of a goddess."

Diana was greatly amused by the concern of her friend and let out an uninhibited laugh. She had a contagious and healthy laugh, it was the trademark by which she could be recognised in a crowd. Pedro took off his grey Nautica jacket, folded it and put it under the child's head, like a pillow.

The Argentinian diva was now singing 'Gracias a la vida, que me had dado tanto/me dio dos luceros que cuando los abro...' and at the next table a group of unattractive but highly made-up women, tipsy on myriad drinks, began to destroy the song by shouting out at different scales. Such was the din that Che Guevara's cigar fell out of his mouth for the first time in all the years that it had been stuck to the wall of that den of nostalgia.

"At what time is our distinguished ecology reporter arriving?" Pedro said in a high voice.

"Any time now. He told me he would arrive at 7.30pm and he is a punctual man."

The bar began to fill up with regular customers: the bearded sociologists who had spent 15 years looking for a truly scientific formulation about whatever social issue; the artists who on one warm day in the 1970s had left their muse sitting on a bench in the Rodrigo Facio university campus while they attended a march in solidarity with Vietnam (*jo-jo-jo-chi-min, jo-jo-jo-chi-*

min) and, on their return, had never found them again; the militants who carried on reading Lenin so as not to admit that Gorbachev was dissolving socialism, in cohabitation with the Pope. Dark and gloomy, one by one they made their way to the back of the building, where Tilín had constructed for them a 'wailing wall' with the photos of Marx, Engels, Fidel, Che Guevara, Camilo Cienfuegos, Sandino, Farabundo Martí, among other holy figures. The bar also began to fill up with the newest customers, the untimely youths, half peace and love, who let their hair and beards grow and who liked to listen to Silvio Rodríguez and Pablo Milanés and to wrap themselves in Havana Club, but not to commit themselves to anything, especially politics.

Pedro went to the bathroom and on his way gazed around the bar: the stained and torn fabric on the chairs; the virtually colourless paint on the old wooden walls; the dust covering the multitude of cards announcing deaths, nationalist crusades, triumphant revolutions; the works of Brecht and García Lorca that are often mounted in university buildings. He read the graffiti scrawled on the walls of the urinal. An anthropologist of the future could reconstruct a piece of 20th-century history by reading these scribbles, he thought: 'Che has not died, Sandino has returned', 'Let the whores rule since their sons don't know how to', 'Yankees, go home', 'The waitress is a good fuck'. He went back to the table with a pathetic expression.

"Mon Dieu! Nothing lasts in life, man is ephemeral and his dreams even more so," he sighed. "Have you read Kundera? *The Unbearable Lightness of Being*? 'What happens once is as if it never occurred. If man can only live one life it is as if he never lived at all'," he quoted.

"I don't know anything about this philosophy, Pedrito, but I assure you that there is nothing light about life," said Diana, her expression like something out of a Greek tragedy. "Much less with a phoney husband who waits for you at home and who never verbalises his anger, but just looks at you in silence with the eyes of a sad cow."

"I see that things are not going very well with Roberto," said Pedro. "Haven't you managed to evict him?"

"Not even by calling the emergency services, he is stuck to my life with suction pads."

Roberto, her second romance, had been an oasis of peace until the day he decided to separate from his wife and appeared at Diana's house, ready to install himself forever, with two suitcases full of dirty clothes, a box of books about turtles and an old, slow computer. Essentially, he was a good man, and she couldn't find a way to get him out of her house, although she had already begun to remove him from her life. Without much hope of love, she was secretly going out with Gabriel, the editor of the paper's ecological section, who enters La Villa and stops at every table to greet acquaintances.

"Isn't Maricruz here yet?"

"No," Pedro reached out to shake his hand.

"I love conspiracies," said Gabriel. "Don't you?"

He was older than Diana, an unrepentant conversationalist, possessed of an elephant's memory, which permitted him to offer an opinion about every possible subject, and of a genial invective with which he surrounded his more off-the-wall digressions, although this inclination had the tendency to drag him into ontological fixes.

"There's no conspiracy," Diana said. "It must be some dirty old man."

Maricruz arrived agitated, greeted them with kisses and sat down.

"Sorry for the delay," she said. "But the gringo bastard wouldn't let me go. He made me rewrite a story five times. One of these days I swear I'll kill him."

To recognise a gypsy at a ladies' cocktail party would have been more difficult, said Pedro when the interview had ended. Both knew it was him from the first moment, as soon as the thickset figure appeared in the doorway and cast a dark look around the bar. He was an individual of medium build, with a coarse complexion and closely knit eyebrows, thinning hair parted on the side with abundant gel, thin lips and an involuntary, linear smile. He wore designer jeans, a black leather jacket and finished off the look – in the way that a cherry tops a crème chantilly – with Texan boots with number five heels and steel toecaps. The only thing that did not quite fit with the vulgar impression was the file he carried in his right hand and which, from time to time, he swung back and forth – perhaps unconsciously – as if he had a great need to confirm its weight.

He must have also recognised Maricruz right away since he scarcely hesitated before walking straight towards her table.

"Miss Miranda?"

She held out her hand uncertainly. "Pedro Naranjo, society editor," she said, introducing her companion.

Maricruz felt her hand become enveloped in soft flesh and the grimace that formed on the man's face practically made her jump out of her seat.

"It's a pleasure." He greeted Pedro with a movement of his abundant eyebrows, a gesture that seemed almost scornful. "My name is José Manuel Sandoval. I imagined you to be older," he said to the reporter.

"Nevertheless, you had no trouble recognising me," she said.

"Because there's no one else here who has the look of a journalist," he said, as if he referring to a scar on her face or some other indelible mark.

Maricruz was lost at the ambiguity of his comments and she paused for a moment before the immutable expression on his face, but knew she had to say something relevant.

"It's strange," she fixed him with that olive-green look that could disarm anyone. "I also recognised you as soon as you came in, there's something unmistakable about you."

"Such as?" José Manuel Sandoval fell right into the trap, even permitting himself a smile; this time one that was broad and voluntary.

"The look of a dealer," she said, trying to disguise the offensive intention behind a gesture of understanding.

"To a certain extent, I am – but I am not going to sell you anything. If you want the information, it's a gift."

At that moment, Carlos Mejía Godoy began to sing his *Christ of Palacaguina* and, from a corner of La Villa, a lone boy strummed the notes with an old but well-tuned guitar.

"Excuse me but I don't believe in gifts. Before we do anything, I need to know what you would gain from the publication of this information that you say is so sensational, you or whoever else is interested in it appearing in the newspaper."

"I thought that the information would interest you, that's all. Isn't it enough that I give you proof?"

"No, it's not enough," said Pedro. "The interests behind a piece of news are part of the truth, sometimes they are even bigger than the news item itself."

The man seemed momentarily caught off guard. He looked around the bar and let his gaze rest for a few seconds – while he was thinking – on an ancient poster of General Omar Torrijos being pursued by a dark-skinned mob over some pictures of the Panama Canal and words that proclaimed: 'Panama for the Panamanians'.

"Perhaps you're right," he addressed Pedro in a respectful tone for the first time. "But there are diffuse interests. The only thing I can tell you with certainty is that this is a matter with political implications. Which? Those you will know without my having to say, once you have the information."

Maricruz gave Pedro an enquiring look, and he shrugged his shoulders.

"Alright," she said. "Tell us."

Around two years ago, he began his story with imprecision, he had been involved with a clandestine leftwing group of whose existence no one knew apart from the government's intelligence services. How he had got there, who he had contacted and why he decided to go along with such an association were not relevant. The important thing is that, after a few months, he began to climb through the ranks – not due to his knowledge or any special talent for conspiracy, he admitted, but thanks to circumstances that were more 'hormonal'. The leader, the general commander, had had her eye on him from the start, and took him as her lover.

"Yes, a woman, a brilliant woman – a woman with a gift for

leadership that would make you shudder. This closeness allowed me to get an in-depth knowledge of the strategy of the group, their tactics, operational plans, a privilege that few ordinary militants experience since the organisation has a very rigid pyramid structure. Each member knows just a few of his colleagues and no one – apart from two or three commanders – gets sight of the whole."

Maricruz and Pedro indicated their incredulity to one another with a brief glance, part of a subtle code they often used to communicate in secret.

"The ultimate objective of the Clan (that's how they identified themselves) is, naturally, to seize power, but what differentiates this group from others on the left are the methods they choose to achieve it. They believe in terror as a method of struggle."

"Terror?" Maricruz spun round in her chair, unsure that she had interpreted his words correctly. "What do you mean?"

"For them it is the violence with which ordinary people respond to the violence of the rich... kidnappings, bomb attacks, blowing up electrical pylons, executions, that type of thing. Terrorism, Miss." Sandoval emphasised the point by jabbing the hard, clean fingernail of his right index finger on the table.

"It's a bit difficult to believe. Costa Ricans are a peaceful people, terrorism is not our style."

"Most Costa Ricans are peaceful, but there are people who will do anything. Besides, not only Costa Ricans are involved in this. There are a lot of foreigners in the Clan and of course its cash and its ideological argument both come from outside."

"From where?" Pedro interrupted again.

"From Nicaragua, of course."

"It seems to me the Sandinistas have enough problems of their own without starting a revolution in Costa Rica."

"For them it's not a new problem but part of the solution to an old one. If the situation starts to unravel in Costa Rica, the government would have no choice but to remove support from the Contras of Eden Pastora in Nicaragua and reduce the military pressure on Costa Rica's southern front, so the Sandinista army could focus on fighting the national resistance in their north, which is a real danger for them. At least those are their calculations."

"And what does all this have to do with the crime at the Cross of Alajuelita?" Maricruz asked.

"It's the work of the Clan. They massacred the women."

The reporter shook her head in a firm denial. "None of this makes any sense. Why would an organisation with political objectives – one which calls itself the defender of the people – go and kill a group of defenceless girls? How is that going to contribute to the political cause?"

"The murder of the women was casual. They veered off the path looking for a place to pee. Apparently, they got lost and had the bad luck to bump into a clandestine unit of the Clan, who on that day were on the hill. It seems that they do or did some of their training there. On seeing the armed men in their military uniforms, one of the women was startled, screamed and tried to flee. They shot her in the back, thinking she would expose them. It happened very quickly without anyone planning it, but with one of the women dead, they had no option but to kill the others."

The man paused to take a long sip of the beer he had just been served, wiped his mouth with a serviette and confronted the incredulous expression of Maricruz.

"If you don't understand the logic of these people, you'll find it hard to find an explanation for many of their acts. For them, the 'people' is not a collection of persons but an abstract thing they worship as if it were an ethereal god. Johnny, Marie and Freddie are people and people are imperfect, the unfinished versions of the new man: they might be against or in favour of the cause, but in all cases they are disposable. There is sufficient justification in sacrificing one of the people if it is for the good of the people in the abstract."

"You'd think that any organisation seeking power would try to win supporters. What's the point of terrorising people?" Pedro asked.

"Why do terrorists anywhere – whether from the left or right – plant a bomb in a marketplace and kill 10 or 20 or 30 innocent people? Does that make sense to you? To me, no," Sandoval indicated himself. "But it happens. The Clan is convinced that people will eventually understand this sacrifice as a necessary evil, that people will have to arrive at the same conclusions as them."

"There are two men in jail, suspects of the crime and they are not members of any political organisation but common criminals with a long history. The police assure us that there is a lot of material evidence against them. Your version does not fit with the progress of the police investigation," said the journalist.

"Of course not, those two are scapegoats, I swear. The police are desperate to find the guilty ones and fabricated or coerced evidence. It would not be the first time they've done so. When it comes before the judge, you'll see how all this proof unravels."

"How do you explain the rapes? That does not square with any political strategy, not even with terrorism," Maricruz argued.

"Indeed, it does," said their informant. "The more violent the crime, the greater the terror. It's all about causing commotion, destabilising, creating the feeling that everything is out of control. Besides, it's easy to hide base instincts beneath an ideological justification."

"But didn't you say that the murder of the women was a chance event? How do you then define this crime as part of the campaign of terror?" insisted the journalist.

"The first death was incidental, certainly, but to do away with the other women was a decision reached by the leaders. If they had no option but to kill the others, to cover their presence on the hill, that presented itself as a golden opportunity to initiate a campaign of terror, and they started it."

Maricruz smiled, but it was a bitter smile, a sign of feeling sick. Then she softly rubbed her eyes as if the mist that covered the story was located in her retina and she wanted to dispel it.

"How do you know all this? From what you yourself have said, it seems that information within the group is very tightly controlled."

"In an intimate relationship, we all behave more or less the same, we let down our defences, we talk more, we share our most guarded secrets. Lucía was no different from anyone else, although she seemed like a woman of iron."

Maricruz began to feel suffocated. At moments the story seemed about to sink into its own contradictions, but the guy answered all her questions with astonishing speed and certainty: he tied up the loose ends without hesitating and he left his interviewers with a sensation of certainty which, nevertheless, they tried to resist. Besides, the idea that the crime had political motives, however absurd that seemed, had been suggested by various people before the start of the investigation, even to the police and the President of the Republic. On more than one occasion, while Sandoval was talking, Maricruz sneaked a look at Pedro's face and observed on it a kind of childish fascination and open incredulity, the same mood that the story provoked in her. Either the story was true or the guy was shameless... unless, although it was spurious, he himself was convinced of its authenticity.

"And what about the Psycho? The police think there is a link between the crime at Alajuelita and the murder of those two couples?"

Sandoval arched his eyebrows in an expression that indicated either surprise or suspicion. "I'm not sure about that, but I have thought that those crimes might also be part of the terror campaign. The same goes for the murder of the former security minister. Doesn't it seem too much of a coincidence? Excuse me, because I think that it's your creation, but I don't believe in the Psycho the media are talking about. I think it's an invention to explain something for which there is no explanation."

"I can see the political implications of that, or at least imagine them," said Maricruz, rising above the commentary that had attributed the conception of the creation to her. "What I don't see are the motives that made you decide to denounce your friends, nor do I understand why you have chosen to give me this information."

"A few months ago, when I found out about the massacre, I left the Clan. Until that moment the issue of violence had been all theory. It's one thing to say that the violence of the bourgeoisie confronts the violence of the people and all that baloney. It's something else to be involved in crimes like these, even if indirectly."

The man gulped down the rest of the beer at the bottom of the glass, looked around at the walls and smiled joylessly.

"On the other hand," he went on, "things were getting increasingly difficult for me in the group. From the moment the commander laid her eyes on me, I began to acquire enemies. Men and women, all of them wanted to be in this woman's bed and I was an upstart. They conspired against me relentlessly, they claimed I had ideological weaknesses that could not be overcome, they all pressured Lucía to leave me. In December, when the crime at Alajuelita occurred, I stupidly criticised the action. That was the last straw. The command met to evaluate my conduct and concluded that I was a danger to the organisation. They decided to do away with me. If it wasn't for Lucía, who warned me, I wouldn't be here telling you the story."

"And this is how you repay the favour? By spilling the beans on her and her organisation?" Pedro confronted him.

"Lucía is dead," said Sandoval with pathos. "She died in Managua two weeks ago, supposedly in a car accident. I am sure they murdered her, I don't know if it was because she helped me or for some other motive, but I am sure that she lost command and her own people murdered her. Something has to be done to stop these maniacs and the only thing that occurred to me was to go to the press."

"And why me?" said Maricruz.

"Why not? It could have been anyone. You have a reputation for being a good journalist."

"One last question – what about your own personal safety? From what you have told us, clearly you are dealing with very dangerous people and if this is published, you will be the first suspect. Aren't you afraid they will kill you?"

"To all intents and purposes, to them I'm a dead man. There's a sentence on my head, but I don't plan to let them carry it out. When this story is published – if you decide to publish it – I will be totally beyond the reach of the Clan."

He opened the suitcase he had seemed to guard so jealously, took out a file stuffed with papers and a cassette, and gave them to Maricruz.

"This is the first delivery. There are interesting documents that will confirm my version of events. If you decide to publish it, I'm in a position to give you more information that is even more incriminating."

"And why not all at once?"

"For the same reason that a dealer does not hand over all his merchandise without a guarantee of payment." There was a hint of reproach in his voice, or perhaps it was just irony. "It was you who said I had the face of a dealer," he added.

The interview had been brief and hugely disturbing. José Manuel Sandoval said goodbye to Pedro then took the hand offered by Maricruz and, in a moment of carelessness, permitted the reporter to scrutinise his eyes. His pupils were over-large and immobile and there was something in his gaze that seemed hollow, lacking in human intensity.

6

It seems that my first impression was right. Lidia is a competent reporter who knows her stuff. Active and thoughtful, she spends most of her time focused on her work, but if someone approaches her in the mood to talk, she responds with a smile and she makes friends easily. Apart from being beautiful and attractive, she has a particular sweetness. This morning she came dressed in a way that was quite disturbing: she wore a long dress of such silky material that it clung to her hips, her flat stomach, her round buttocks, cut in such a way as to leave bare the entire length of her arms and half of her back, her lightly tanned back, covered in a soft, fair down with the texture of velvet. She seemed more willowy and glossy and, on passing her, I couldn't resist the temptation to look at her, to look at her with such an absence of inhibition, with lascivious, longing eyes that seemed to neither offend nor shock her.

"Where's the party?" I asked her. From her lips there issued forth some smiling words, which seemed to me a provocation.

"It's private," she answered.

In the afternoon I received a terrible piece of news. The newspaper and our top sports commentator were being sued by the Football Federation. The gringo didn't summon me to his office as he usually does, but he turned up in my cubicle unannounced, gave me an acidic look and threw the letter from the court on to my desk without saying a word. I read it twice while I thought about how to come out of this mess more or less unscathed.

"This is a newspaper," I said finally. "It can happen to anyone and, in fact, it happens a lot. We have to defend ourselves. What do you want me to say?"

"And with what are we going to pay the lawyer? Would you accept it if we paid for it with the 'dirty' money from advertising?" He hurled the poisonous word at me. I shrugged my shoulders because I could not think of a smart answer although now, thinking back, I can think of a dozen sweet nothings to have crushed him. God damn it. Why am I so slow to think?

Manuel Serrano, the journalist, is the old man of the office. He is one of those reporters who doesn't ignore the risks of spreading too many rumours with his pen, but who thinks that their veteran status confers on them some kind of immunity. He permitted himself to say that the Federation's directors had fallen in love with the funds of the institution and taken them out for a stroll – without evidence, without any backing, an authentic fuck-up. And this happened to the sports editor. The truth is that I already saw the lawsuit coming, so it wasn't a surprise. But someone will have to come up with something because I will have to foot the bill for the gringo. That's the way it is.

Worst of all, Amalia wound the cable of the vacuum cleaner around a computer and brought it crashing to the ground. It was one of the few that half worked. The gringo threatened to fire her and the woman flew into hysterics in the middle of the newsroom. It was necessary to administer first aid and to take her off, sirens wailing, to hospital because she said she felt sick and had a strong pain in her chest. An hour and a half later, when Mr Grey's fury had given way to fear, Amalia reappeared as if there was nothing wrong. The computer lay in the room without hope of being resurrected, but she had saved herself from being fired.

On the day that Maricruz picked for lunch to give him what she promised would be new and highly interesting information,

Gustavo realised more than during any of his worst times in the police force that he had no friend whom he could ask for advice or, simply, with whom he could share what he was feeling. During the last eight years he had lost them one after the other until he was left completely alone. He did not miss them until his divorce severed his last connection with the outside world, the precarious bridge that linked the walled refuge of his office with the rest of humanity. So, when his solitude began to weigh down on him, he consoled himself that his work was sufficient to fill his life and cured himself of self-pity by plunging even deeper into the rigours of his routine. Now, dominated by excitement, with his soul and body out of control at the prospect of seeing Maricruz, he needed, more than ever, a good friend who would listen to him and tell him 'You're confused, Tavito, it's not that you're in love with a girl of 23 who could be your little sister, but that you're excited by this half secret relationship with the press; it's not that you feel an unstoppable urge to kiss that luscious mouth or to caress the taut flesh of her legs, but that her talent dazzles you a little; what you need is not some incandescent girl but a mature woman, understanding, sweetly softened by the ups and downs of life, who is capable of accepting you and working together with you.' The absence of this comforting voice obliged him to be his own interlocutor, but he repeated these and other arguments without conviction, only to return to the same dreams, to the same mental images in which she kissed him and whispered tender words in his ear, in a room at twilight, as he approached and removed her clothes over the slopes of her brown skin, while she urged him on in that slightly harsh voice that was exasperatingly sensual.

"Are you thinking of training tomorrow, at lunchtime?"

"I don't think I can," he said.

"How about if we meet for lunch around one?"

"Where?"

"The Imperial Palace. Do you know it? Do you like Chinese food? I love it."

Gustavo hung up thinking that he hated Chinese food, but to see her and keep her happy he was prepared to do anything, to eat a casserole containing dynamite. He had only spent a week away from her and that absence was gnawing away at his insides. Strangely enough, the call from Maricruz brought him no relief but only a kind of tingle that lasted for 24 hours. Even the brief period he slept that night contained a shock. In his dreams, the passages of the morgue appeared, becoming interminably longer, sunk in a sad and austere twilight. He saw his mother drifting into the distance down a passage as her face mingled with that of Mayela, who was grabbing the hand of a child who was both him and his son, and then he was entering a room where dissections were carried out and there were the disembowelled girls, alive and with their eyes open, on whom Doctor Meneses was performing an autopsy. He awoke agitated, sweating buckets and, after drinking some water and breathing deeply, he went back to sleep to dream some more of the same.

During the morning conference he was lost, he confused the cases they were studying and came up with irrelevant conclusions, which his inferiors listened to with bewilderment but dared not rebuff. This is serious, he diagnosed himself at 11.30am. He called off a meeting and went home to have a bath and change his clothes.

A diabolical bottleneck between the churches of San Francisco and Zapote made him 20 minutes late. He arrived terrified, bathed in sweat and with his mouth disfigured by the hundred curses he had uttered on the way. Maricruz had arrived right on time, but she had not left, as Gustavo had feared, but had sat waiting for him looking at her watch and shaking her head.

"So women are the unpunctual ones?"

"I'm sorry, I have let you down and made a laughing stock of the male species. But it's not my fault. I was stuck in a traffic jam."

"No need for excuses. The important thing is that you're here."

Almost without preamble and in graphic detail, Maricruz launched into her anecdote about her meeting with the informant, from the initial phone call to the farewell in the bar and the strange impression that Sandoval's 'dead' gaze had left on her. Gustavo listened without reacting, without asking questions and eating only when she paused to do the same, chewing parsimoniously, rather more preoccupied by the threat of the Chinese sausage against his digestive system than by terrorist attacks on the political and institutional system of the country.

When she had finished, he was silent for a long time before sharing his opinion.

"It's a very strange tale. Did you say that he handed you some documents?"

"Yes, supposedly from meetings in which they plan their terrorist attacks. There is a list of business leaders and politicians whom they call 'kidnappable'. A map of the nerve centres of San José, diagrams of public buildings, instructions on how and where to plant bombs, such as on bridges and main highways. There's a tape recording of one of these meetings at which four people identify themselves as sub-commanders. Among them you can hear the voice of a woman, which must be that of Lucía, I suppose."

"I'd like to see those documents."

Maricruz hesitated, moved her hands across the table nervously, and then fixed his eyes with a penetrating stare.

"I don't know," she said. "It wouldn't be inconvenient to collaborate a little with the police, but I would like a reciprocal gesture, if possible."

"A reciprocal gesture," Gustavo repeated with the slow pronunciation of one who does not understand something properly and is not sure he has heard correctly.

"I need to publish the news about the discovery that the killers at La Cruz are the same ones who murdered the couples."

Gustavo observed her with poorly disguised astonishment, trying to imagine how far this quest for an exchange might go, and just how intrepid was this girl who looked so harmless. He assumed a thoughtful expression and, after a calculated silence, pretended to capitulate.

"Publish it, but make it clear it's not a conclusive fact but a 'possibility' which is being investigated. And attribute it to a confidential source who requested anonymity or whatever it is you say in cases like these."

'That's how we'll do it,' Maricruz celebrated with a triumphant smile.

"I presume you don't give credence to this guy's version since you prefer to publish that of the police."

"I didn't say that," Maricruz drained the last drop of water from her glass and dabbed at her lips with a serviette. "A version of events is a version. There is nothing to stop us publishing it as long as we don't pass it off as the definitive truth."

"No, don't do it."

"Hold on a moment," Maricruz stopped him. "The information I obtain through my own devices does not enter into the deal. An agreement to co-operate is one thing, but a regime of censorship is quite another. You can't stop me from publishing anything."

"I was only going to suggest that you hold back a bit. I wouldn't dare forbid you to do anything, and I doubt there's anyone in the world who'd do that either."

"My father does sometimes, but less and less. The truth is that I'm not thinking of publishing any of this just yet," she patted him on the forearm. "First, I have to consider some opinions. Yours, for example. Do you think it makes any sense?"

"What can I say? There is at least one aspect I'm totally convinced is false and that's that we have fabricated evidence to incriminate the suspects. The evidence is overwhelming. About the rest, I couldn't say anything with certainty. That such an organisation as the one you describe exists would not be altogether impossible. A few years ago an organisation of this type was dissolved, with the same type of structure and similar ideas. All this time we have been following the tracks of the members and sympathisers who remained free, and there's no sign they are regrouping. We cannot discount that other people might go down the same path. Nor does it sound crazy that the Sandinistas might be backing a paramilitary group. Recently we found out about a military cell that was taking Contras hostage in San Carlos, it seems that there were a couple of skirmishes but nothing more. As regards the documents, we would have to scrutinise them at length to know how authentic they are. The point, Maricruz, is not to work out who are the authors of the massacre – that we know. The point is to know who is behind this...what's his name?"

"José Manuel Sandoval."

"Right, well what was Sandoval up to by telling you the story? That's what seems strange to me, suspicious, worth investigating. Maybe he's just a trickster but maybe, underneath, there's something else going on."

"What?" Maricruz lit up with the brilliance that is seen in the faces of adventurers, archeologists and taxonomists.

"I could speculate but I think it's better to investigate before venturing a hypothesis."

"Risk it," the reporter said. "I promise I'm not going to take anything you say as an absolute truth. It's just curiosity."

'Do you ever stop pumping for information," said Gustavo. "Maybe you stop now and then so you can do some work?"

"Of course," said Maricruz. "I have a trip switch that works wonderfully well."

"I'd like to see that."

"That's easy," she said. "We always see each other for work. Why don't you invite me for fun one day?"

Gustavo felt as if he was at the edge of an abyss. Not the abyss that opened from the terrace of a building 20 storeys high or the one that gaped from the door of an aircraft, but at the edge of an internal precipice from where he would tumble into an abyss of unexpected emotions. An emptiness far greater than us and yet one which inhabits us; that makes us feel vertigo and renders us defenceless. He found himself more tempted by this invitation than he had felt in years, and yet he was incapable of pronouncing a single word. There was no room for doubt, it was a crystal clear proposal, made with all the childish temerity of which Maricruz was capable, but he was floating in the void, seized by a tide of panic that prevented him taking control of his body. The reply was easy, a question of agreeing on a day and time and planning the details later, but the homicide chief was paralysed and could not utter a word.

Maricruz sensed the changed atmosphere; the silence was

growing and she began to wonder whether she had made a mistake. She imagined the attraction that she believed she exerted over Gustavo: perhaps she had put him in a compromising situation and he was trying to extract himself in a gentlemanly way without hurting her feelings. Shit, she thought, I've put my foot in it again. A sensation of heat began to run upwards through her body, and finally reddened her face.

"Don't worry," she said without looking at him. "It was a joke."

"Don't say that," Gustavo spoke at last, exhaling strongly. "It would be far too cruel a joke. You don't know how I have waited for this moment."

The newsroom had taken on a funereal atmosphere. A silence peppered with rumours, whisperings and sidelong glances ruled. Starting with Juan José Montero, the mood of the journalists was a cauldron of rage, rotten decorum, and a cocktail of insecurities. Overcoming his claustrophobia, the editor shut himself away in his office and did not go round hassling his staff even as the newspaper was being put to bed, when it was normal to see him wandering around, distributing insults among the stragglers, shouting as he corrected texts, and attempting intrepid physical advances on the female reporters, which they took as a joke and fought off with their elbows. Anyone who tried to see inside his office, through the window, would only have seen a face that looked pathetically resigned, on the point of becoming blurred by the residual smoke of a packet and a half of cigarettes.

In the newsroom, Pedro was typing irritably while Diana had chosen to go home early, leaving her work unfinished, after proclaiming and then demanding a strike that fell flat for lack of support. Maricruz, who had done enough work to fill a whole news page, did not even return until after lunch.

That morning Mr Grey had declared what he called 'an administrative intervention' which in simple terms meant the prior censorship of all articles. Adopting an expression of martyrdom, he told Juan José that from that evening he would be lengthening his working day by a couple of hours to look over the material going into the paper. That way, he explained, he could be sure of putting a brake on the blunders that were slipping through with increasing frequency.

"How strange! No?" he said, opening his arms in a gesture of pious sacrifice. "I have to be on top of this so that it works."

The surprise blurred Juan José's vision and made him lose control of his bottom lip. He snorted like a caged animal and, for a few seconds, tried vainly to articulate some concept that was sufficiently weighty, something with the forcefulness of a baseball bat that would smash the gringo's obstinacy. In the end, he merely expressed a desperate opinion.

"You can't," he said.

"Why not?" Mr Grey used the formal neutral smile he adopted for conducting business. "I am the director of this newspaper, am I not? Apart from that, I am the owner. I have the right to look after my interests."

"When I came to work here," the editor did a quick count on his fingers, "nine years ago, we agreed that you would continue to be the director in matters of representation, but that I would be the director in questions of information, that you would never interfere in my work."

"I never said never," Mr Grey waved his hand dismissively while he searched for a chair. "What has happened is that it wasn't necessary before, but now there are too many mistakes."

"I can't work like that."

"But what's wrong with you?" He smiled again, this time ironically, with a hint of perversity, it seemed to Juan José. "Your guys are bad, they are not practising good journalism, they have no standards and instead of reproaching you, who is responsible, I am offering you a helping hand. You ought to be grateful."

"Me, responsible?" Juan José got up from his chair as if on springs.

"Who else?" asked the gringo, keeping the smile on his face.

"That really is the limit," he exclaimed, tugging at his hair. "With a few respectable exceptions, the editors, three reporters and that's it, I have a collection of novices who earn what novices earn and therefore work like novices. And you know this

just as well as I do. You have always turned down my sugges-
tions to integrate a team of well-paid professionals. What do you
want? That a pile of virtual adolescents fresh out of college work
like veterans of the *Washington Post*?"

"Well... to be precise, what I want is that they learn how to
work. I am going to teach them."

Mr Grey claimed to have an impressive journalism CV: he
said he had covered various wars, including Vietnam, interviewed personalities such as Henry Kissinger, Muammar
Gadaffi, Fidel Castro and General De Gaulle, but vox populi
was in fact the nearest thing he had done to real journalism.
Before buying *El Matutino*, he had gone to Belize to edit a
tourist magazine that had a short life span and scant financial
success. Oddly enough, it was his wife, a perverse fifty-some-
thing Italian who suffered from cellulite but was as ardent as
the Mediterranean summer, who took on the task of deflating
the image in which her husband had invested so much fantasy.
"He knows as much about journalism as a pig knows about
astronomy," she confessed one day to one of the accountants
who, with religious observance, she took home to screw on
Thursday afternoons while the gringo was attending meetings
of the chamber of commerce, of which he was an executive.

"Is that final?" Juan José asked.

"Absolutely, although it might be temporary. When things
improve, I'll leave you alone with the guys again."

"I cannot work like that," the editor repeated.

"If you're thinking of offering your resignation, I warn you
that this time I'm not going to try to stop you. I'll say nothing
but that at your age it's a bit difficult to find work and that here
you're a member of a family, a pretty insolent one, but one of the
family nonetheless. Think hard before you act."

As he consumed a box of Rex cigarettes with suicidal anxiety,
Juan José Montero came to the same unfortunate conclusion.
He was not in a position to stop the manoeuvres of Mr Grey
who, as the owner, could make of the newspaper whatever he
felt like. Resignation was a dignified gesture but not a very
practical one if he took into account the need to eat, drink, dress

himself and spend the night with the minimum of decency. And the idea that some other newspaper would hire him at forty-something, with his track record of uncomfortable and head-strong journalism, was to pretend a naiveté that was almost touching.

'The problem," he told his subordinates before announcing the gringo's decision, "is that dignity has a price and I am so hard-up I can't pay it. If any of you are in the position to do so, and does so, you have my full support and respect, the respect of everyone – I believe."

But no one did. The strongest reaction was by Diana with her failed strike about which Mr Grey never heard because he had gone to a business breakfast. Some reporters made discreet and pointless telephone calls to rival media but as soon as they heard, "I'm sorry but not at the moment," they shrugged their shoulders and carried on writing.

As for the editor, what the whole mess damaged most was his self-image because he had always believed, and declared with the full width of that mouth of his that never knew when to shut, that he preferred to die on his feet than live on his knees. The moment of truth arrived when he was not strong enough to starve because of his pride.

It was not that Mr Grey had never intervened in editorial matters. In fact, one of the points of conflict was his frequent incursions into the territory of news, but those adventures had not been more than guerrilla raids. Sometimes, he had an idea about a report and did not stop pressing them until someone wrote it. Or he threw a tantrum for three days because the content of an article had ruined the sale of a page of advertising. Then, in furious rhetoric, he accused the reporters of a communist conspiracy and demanded rectification of the Bolshevik and anti-enterprise tendencies of the journalists. Juan José had learned how to fend off those storms with the skills of a circus ringmaster. He made a few concessions to distract the beast, and soon after was putting his snout back in the trough. The most recent incursion, however, went beyond all previous attempts: it was not just a simple guerrilla raid but a fully fledged occupation, a disembarkation of the Marines. That evening, he left early so as not to witness the humiliating entrance of his enemy.

7

Maricruz could not help revealing her astonishment with the way she looked at everything, with a half-open mouth and a transparent smile that Gustavo interpreted as easily as if she had spoken.

"Well... what do you think?"

"I didn't imagine it like this," she said.

"Like what?"

"It's so elegant, so clean, so full of well-positioned details. I thought police officers' houses were real pigsties," she said with raw sincerity.

"I suppose there are some like that, but not all of us police are the same, just as not all you journalists are the same. I always imagined that news reporters were, without exception, pot-bellied dwarfs who drank human blood in satanic rituals," Gustavo said in vengeful mood while he took the young woman's briefcase and coat and hung them on a peg near the front door.

Maricruz smiled. She walked towards the small living room furnished with a sofa and two armchairs covered in tartan, a coffee table with a vase full of daisies, a bookshelf, music system and television, as well as corner bar with high benches, and a mantelpiece full of sparkling glasses. Her attention was called to the balanced distribution of pictures on the walls. Then her olive eyes hit on a Russian doll and a child's face above the bookshelf.

"That's my son," Gustavo said to her back.

Maricruz turned and stared at him.

"You have never talked about him to me, you mentioned him once. Is he the only one or are there more?"

"Just one."

"And his mother?"

"She has nothing to do with me. She left, definitively."

"A few days ago when we were having dinner, you told me the reason for your divorce was impunctuality. Was it really that?" Maricruz asked, trying to compose her features in order to express harmless curiosity, although Gustavo did not miss the undertone.

He pointed at the sofa, waited until she had sat down and then sat next to her.

"Well," he said after a long sigh, "although I might not always seem it – I am a reserved kind of guy, perhaps a little standoff-ish. And I find it difficult to talk to people about my private life. I don't have close friends. I barely have close acquaintances left. We have just got to know each other and this is the first time it feels right to talk about things like this."

The girl nodded, chewed on her bottom lip and folded her arms across her chest.

"I divorced three years ago but the process of separating began about a year before that. What happened? What was the true cause of separation? Perhaps there was more than one factor, perhaps she had false expectations or maybe I just never really managed to fall in love. We could think of a dozen things, but the big problems were always to do with my work and that's why I never looked for other explanations. I was almost never at home. Often I didn't come home to sleep, I missed all the occasions that mean something to people, when I guess families should be together: Christmas, New Year, birthdays."

"A policeman through and through," Maricruz said ironically

Gustavo picked up the thread. "Policemen, or at least the good ones, lead complicated lives."

"And your son? Doesn't that bother you?"

"Since my divorce I have lived in constant conflict between my wish to spend more time with him and my work obligations. I promise things that I can't deliver and then I have to excuse myself and he just lowers his head and says: 'It doesn't matter, Daddy, don't worry.' This makes me miserable because I know deep down that he's just trying to hide his feelings. He's a good boy, very intelligent, and that's why I think it's not so hard for him to understand my situation despite his age. But sometimes I am afraid of growing too distant and losing him."

Maricruz stood up and went over to the bookcase and chose a book whose title she repeated to herself (*The Greek Gods*). "Is the problem in your office, or in your head?"

"I wish I had an answer as good as the question. Truthfully, I find no way to forget about work. I haven't had a relationship in all this time. I don't feel like a good papa, a good friend or a good lover. Nothing excites me as much as my work, with the exception of this," he pointed at the book. "But neither do I devote any time to that."

"Ancient history and literature," she exclaimed. "Excuse me, but I just can't imagine a police officer getting excited about such things."

"Sometimes I find it hard to think of myself as a police officer."

"How did it happen?"

"That's funny," Gustavo sighed. "You are the second person in a few days to ask me the same question."

Gustavo explained that eight years before, when his mother became terminally ill, he realised that the pension on which they were living and which, miraculously allowed him to pursue his university studies, was running out. For a few months he tried to get work but no one was interested in the deep knowledge of a student of philosophy who was ready to discourse at any moment in any forum. He had filled in piles of applications without getting a reply when a friend told him about a job with the Judicial Police.

"I took it thinking that it would be for a short time while I found something more worthy of my intellectual capabilities," he explained, "but I made an astonishing discovery – something that totally changed my life: I realised that there is a practical knowledge, which can put bread on the table, that has nothing to do with what we like."

"That sounds a bit tragic," said Maricruz.

"It is tragic," Gustavo assured her, "but I have to say that, over time, I began to take pleasure in my work. I became more absorbed in it until it became my only true passion."

"And is that what happened with your ex-wife? You exchanged one passion for another?"

"Something like that, it was like an inverse process, a gradual disenchantment. Our love was dying without us even realising it. At least, I didn't notice what was happening."

"That amazes me," said Maricruz. "The disenchantment, the idea that something beautiful is crumbling and that one does not realise, or that one does not realise to stop it happening."

She sat down again, took off her shoes and crossed her legs in the lotus position. She was wearing white corduroy jeans and a short, sleeveless, tight-fitting orange blouse. She rested her brown arms on the chair behind her in a move that made her blouse rise by several centimetres, revealing a tranche of toned stomach.

"I remember that when I was small my parents had a nice relationship, they treated each other tenderly and they looked after each other. He called her 'Cholita', gave her flowers on anniversaries and took her out for strolls. She called him 'Papi', made the meals he liked – they were a pair of lovebirds. Now they can't even look at each other. When they are not ignoring each other, they hurt each other for no reason and do everything possible to be apart. I never understood what happened and I don't think they do either. Once I asked my mother what had happened and she shrugged her shoulders. 'Nothing,' she said, 'What should happen?'"

"That's one of the worst risks of marriage," said Gustavo, "growing old with a stranger at your side, in circumstances where you can no longer fix your life."

Maricruz nodded. "Isn't there a vaccination against that?" she asked, fixing him with a stare from within deep green waters.

"I don't think so," said Gustavo as he went to the bar, "but perhaps it helps to have a few relationships before and not get married until you have developed a sixth sense, a kind of instinct for people."

He returned to the sofa and handed her a glass, then sat close to her and covered her hand with his.

"To a lasting love," he toasted.

"Or a timely divorce, if there is no option."

They drank and, with cold lips, their mouths sought each other. It was long, moist kiss charged with a sweet energy that began to get under their skin until it almost made their hair stand on end. A sensation that she had not experienced for some time, thought Maricruz; a sensation he never remembered experiencing, thought Gustavo.

"I am worried that I have not developed this sixth sense," she spoke in a hesitant voice. "Because my instinct registers no danger on the horizon."

"But mine does. It is always dangerous to fall in love."

"Are you in love?" Maricruz asked. Now her look was ardent, the colour of the sea crashing against the cliffs.

He carried on kissing her without answering, and his hand wandered under her blouse, over the tanned skin which was soft to the touch.

"Are you in love?" she asked again without taking her lips from those of Gustavo, undoing the button on her jeans, offering the hard, warm contours of her hips to the nervous hand that wandered up and down her back and was asking for more.

"I only know that I want nothing else than to be by your side. That's what I feel now, at this moment."

His hand sank beneath the material, slowly, almost timidly, until it reached the base of her spine. He found no resistance. He continued that nervous exploration until he found her round buttocks, compact and perfectly proportioned.

Maricruz moved a few centimetres away, gently, as if she was just taking a break to breathe.

"I don't know if I want to go to bed with a man who does not know how he feels about me," she said.

Gustavo stroked her hair, her naked shoulders and firm long arms.

"I like you a lot," he said hesitantly, "but I am not going to say something so important without being completely sure. I feel I am beginning to fall in love, but..."

"But what?"

"It's all too new. Don't you see? A few months ago, before I met you, I was convinced I would never want another woman again. I thought it wasn't necessary. But now," he rubbed his eyes, "I am not sure of anything."

Maricruz sat up and began to adjust her clothes.

"I understand," she said with an ambiguous smile. "Perhaps we should give ourselves a little more time to be sure of what we feel."

Gustavo was alarmed by her change of tone. He composed himself too, put his arms around her waist and searched for her eyes.

"I am only trying to be honest, Maricruz. If I told you right now that I was madly in love, like an adolescent, I probably wouldn't be deceiving you. But the day I tell you that, I don't want to have the slightest doubt."

She nodded and rested her head on Gustavo's chest.

"I appreciate your honesty, really I do, even though I feel frustrated," she said. "The truth is that I don't have a lot of experience in these things, I've only had two boyfriends in my life and I only slept with one of those. A couple of times, a couple of spectacular disasters."

"Why?"

"It would be more comfortable to admit that it was through the inexperience of both of us, but I have always thought that the main problem was that we were not in love. I am afraid of repeating that experience."

It was growing dark and the only light in the apartment was a small lamp next to the sofa, where Gustavo and Maricruz continued to find out about each other for hours, unlocking places deep within. This session of amateur psychoanalysis made them feel closer, as if they had in fact made love. They had almost managed to forget the outside world when the telephone rang. Gustavo was tempted to ignore it but he ended up giving in to that absurd compulsion that makes us answer the phone at any cost, as if our life or the life of a loved one depended on it.

"Hello?" the homicide chief then said nothing else for several minutes. "Are you sure?" he said at last. "Okay, yes, but it won't be until tomorrow."

"What's wrong?" asked Maricruz nervously as her journalist's intuition cranked up.

"Incredible," Gustavo shook his head. "Do you remember the woman they killed through a window two days ago, the one from San Antonio de Desamparados."

"Of course."

"The Psycho. It was the work of the Psycho."

Carolina had been murdered on the third and final night of the fiesta of Saint Antonio, just before 9pm. A 45 calibre bullet fired through her bedroom window snatched her from this world without anyone realising and without giving her time even to moan or realise that she was going to die. The next morning her relatives found her naked body stretched out on the bed, her head and neck supported by the wall, legs flexed and parted, her right hand on her chest – a position that indicated death had taken her completely by surprise. On the bedside table there was a Bible and a cup with the remains of coffee. Scattered around the room was religious material, pamphlets and flyers printed by a Protestant sect. Nicanor Morales, the victim's grandfather, told the police that at around 9 or 10pm the previous night he had heard noises at the back of the house, so he had approached a window and called out: "Who's there?" To which a voice replied. "Don't worry, it's the police. Open the door." But Nicanor Morales did not open up because he was suspicious. He stayed alert until the noises faded away. Finally, he forgot all about it and went to bed. No member of the family heard the shot, but they all remembered that on that night there were fireworks in the town square a block and a half away, which might lead one to suppose that the gunshot was confused with these noises. An inspection of the house revealed that the aggressor, to enter the property, had broken through the spiked wire fence, cut the telephone cable – and must have acted with extreme stealth since he left no tracks or signs of any kind that could lead to his identification.

8

Don Jovel would have preferred the typical agent from a television series: 1.9 metres tall, white as a turnip and dressed in a dark suit and tie. That would have inspired more trust than this Puerto Rican mulatto who had no qualms about turning up in a T-shirt and old canvas trainers, as well as the most distressed jeans he had ever seen in his life.

In spite of everything, the man had credentials from the Federal Bureau of Investigation and a letter that credited him as an envoy from Washington. His name was Aníbal Pedroso. In the letter, the FBI director said he was one of the officers with the broadest capability in the science of criminal profiling, and that he had solved some of the most difficult murders in the United States and other countries. It practically described him as a master, and Don Jovel decided that the dishevelled appearance of the recent arrival was not sufficient reason to discredit the recommendations of his colleague.

"It's a pleasure to have you with us," he said, extending his hand. "Have they already taken you to your hotel?"

"I've come from there," said the visitor, "and I'm ready to get to work, right now."

"Excellent news," said Don Jovel. "Would you like a cup of coffee or...?"

"No, no – let's get started," the agent insisted.

His attire might have been scruffy, but this guy had arrogant ways. A brief dialogue was enough to get a sense of his laconicism, and Don Jovel immediately refrained from ceremony, summoned Gustavo and they held a meeting there and then.

"The fact is that we have never had a serial killer in this country," the director said. "I have to acknowledge that we lack experience and need all the help you can give us."

Pedroso nodded. "I know, that's what we're here for. Please let's get down to it."

More than to start, he seemed anxious to finish: do what was asked of him and complete it as soon as possible. This was the impression made on Gustavo by the foreigner, whose expression seemed no less histrionic than his moderation. To acquaint him with the territory, he forced himself to deliver a complete summary of the crimes, without omitting a single detail. The FBI agent listened without asking questions, without altering the serious expression on his face, without making notes.

"The question is," the homicide chief concluded, "that until a few days ago we had a case that was difficult to solve but the premises seemed clear: we had to look for a solitary assassin, a maniac, and we just had to wait for him to make a mistake so we could trip him up. However, the ballistic studies have revealed something unexpected: the weapon used in the last three crimes seems to have been the same one used, a year ago, in the massacre of seven women on a hill near San José known as La Cruz. We believe it was an M-3 automatic."

"Do you mean it was the same killer?" Pedroso asked.

"Apparently not and that is the great unknown," Gustavo affirmed. "Two of the four suspects of the massacre of those women are dead and the other two were in prison when the couples were murdered."

"I need to have access to the complete documentation on both cases."

"Of course, I have prepared copies of everything for you," said

Don Jovel, passing him two thick files. Pedroso stood up, took the dossiers and left with the promise that in two or three days he would have his first conclusions. It was disconcerting. They had prepared for a first session lasting hours and the FBI envoy seemed satisfied with an exchange of words that barely lasted five minutes. Even worse, he was promising an initial report on the case in less than a week, with nothing more to go on than a bundle of preliminary enquiries, when they had had a headache over it lasting months.

"He must think he's the reincarnation of Sherlock Holmes," Gustavo exclaimed.

The director frowned and nodded his head.

"It seems you didn't like the guy much. Am I right? Well, frankly I didn't either, he didn't make a good impression on me, but he is what they've sent us and they reckon he is the eighth marvel in his field. Besides, gringos are not in the habit of offering experts and we should respect the fact that they're doing so with us. So, let's listen and try to learn what we can."

The FBI agent did not return in two or three days as he had promised but the following week. He sat down in the director's office with a resigned air without giving any explanation for his delay, and dug out a notebook buried in his pocket, which looked like the one he had had with him on the first day.

"Let's see," he examined his notes. "I have analysed the four cases and reached my own conclusions, but I would like to know the nature of your doubts in more detail, perhaps that will help me to refine some of my ideas."

Don Jovel scratched his head and observed the gringo in silence, as if trying to organise his thoughts. Then he gave Gustavo a look that suggested he wanted help.

"Alright," the homicide chief began. "The point is that in the four cases we have very strong coincidences, such as the murder weapon, the fact that the main victims were women and that the scene of the crimes was on a mountain. But, on the other hand, there are many differences. For example, the massacre at La Cruz was complete chaos in terms of the handling of the scene. We found objects of personal use, bottles of liquor, cigarette butts, trodden all over the place, several of the victims had been raped. Inside their bodies we found the hair and semen of the aggressors, even the imprint of one's teeth in the skin of one of the girls. All this facilitated a rapid identification of the criminals. In the cases of the couples, we found no single physical sign, rape did not take place, the corpses were moved and hidden but we found no fingerprints or tracks that gave us even a small lead. The latest murder is atypical: a shot fired through a window at a girl, there was no manipulation of the body, there was no trophy, the scene is totally different, but again we have the same weapon."

"Interesting," Pedroso said. "That means that the only strong argument that there is a connection is the trace of the M-3, according to your criteria. Haven't you thought of the possibility that the killers of the seven women – once they had committed the crime – sold the weapon to someone else and that he or she is the author of the other crimes?"

"Of course we've considered that," said the director, "but the hypothesis does not seem very reasonable. If you commit a crime – would you hide the weapon where it could not be found or would you put it in the hands of someone who, eventually, in one way or another, could inform on you?"

Pedroso thought about the question reflexively although he had formulated answers to such queries in his head often. Oddly enough, the ones who most often posed such questions were never novices, but the police and criminals.

"If I was the murderer, I would do the first," he explained. "It's what seems logical to you and me, but we know that the mind of a criminal does not always function in accordance with our logic. It hasn't occurred to any of us to murder seven defenceless women, but there are those who are not only capable of conceiving of this but also of carrying it out and it's even possible that these people sleep peacefully without the slightest twinge of conscience."

"It might be," said Don Jovel. "It's still a possibility."

"However, I recognise that your suspicions are well grounded. I also believe that there must be a link between the massacre at the Cruz de Alajuelita and the crimes that have been attributed to the one they call the Psycho because there are other coincidences, very important ones, which you do not mention. For a moment, let's leave aside the last victim and focus on the first three cases. If you observe closely the forensic reports, you will notice that these two women, whose deaths are attributed to the lone killer, were killed by a shot to the left temple. The victims at La Cruz received several bullets in different places in their bodies, but they all had a shot to the left temple as well. A common thread in all the murders and I don't believe that it's a coincidence. Rather it would seem to be the hallmark of a killer. Besides, look at this," he showed several photographs from the reports. "The seven women killed at La Cruz were found in the same position: lying on their right sides in a foetal position. The reports suggest the corpses had been moved post mortem, which indicates that this position is also not just casual. Someone must have placed them in that position for some reason that we cannot explain."

"Well, I have to admit that I had noticed such details but I didn't think they were especially important," said the director. "So where does this discovery lead us?"

"It's too early to say," said Pedroso. "But we can try to find an explanation."

The man stood up and went over the window offering a panoramic view of a large part of San José. He put his hands in his pockets and looked out in the fleeting, unconcerned way of a tourist.

"According to our observations over the years, there are two types of serial killer, one is what we call 'organised' – generally a very intelligent guy, methodical, obsessed with detail. He spends a lot of time planning his crimes and executes them with the least possible risk, which is why it's hard to catch him. Nevertheless, he is vain, conscious of his habits, the type of criminal that would want to leave a sign of his distinctive temperament, which could be the shot to the temple or placing the bodies in the same position. There is another kind who is 'disorganised', who acts by inspiration – he does not plan, he does not measure the risks or leave evidence at the scene. In the crime at La Cruz we find characteristics of both types of killer, a rather unusual mix, while the other two murders are typical of the organised type."

"All very interesting, but how do these theories help us to get to the bottom of things?" asked Gustavo in an unconsciously distrustful tone. "So far I just see more and more confusion."

"These discoveries have led me to elaborate a preliminary hypothesis, which I'd like to present to you," said the FBI agent. "I would say that more than four individuals took part in the crime of La Cruz, at least one more who has not been identified. He is the owner of the M-3 and is certainly who you are looking for in connection with the deaths of the couples. He is a white man between 25 and 30, middle class, university educated, possibly in the field of medical sciences, with some kind of military training, the son of an aggressive or very dominant mother."

"That's incredible!" Gustavo cut in. "How can you arrive at such conclusions with so few facts?"

Pedroso either did not pick up on the aggressive tone of the homicide chief or pretended to ignore it. He was used to the incredulity of amateurs, and it did not surprise him that at first they considered him a fraud. The results always – or almost always – ended up proving his analysis to have been correct.

"I said hypothesis, not conclusions," he said in self-defence. "The hypothesis is a guide, or an instrument to work with but it can always be modified along the way if an investigation calls for it. And, yes, as you say, it can be elaborated with very few facts thanks to the help of scientific theory. In this case, the broad brushstrokes of the profile can be explained easily, if you'll allow me." Pedroso returned to his seat, crossed his legs and leaned back in his chair as if preparing to launch into a long speech.

"The first thing I have taken into account," he said, "are the forensic reports which describe the victims' wounds. All the murdered women in the three cases received the impact of a bullet on the left temple, an identical mark. It seems that the killer wanted to say to us: 'I was here, they are my work'. That is a thread common to many serial killers. Some go to the trouble of leaving a card with a pseudonym and others go to the other extreme of sending messages to the police after every killing to take credit for the incident and in so doing demonstrate that they are more astute than their pursuers. Given that you have four suspects for the massacre at La Cruz, two of whom are dead and two in prison, there is just one possibility – a fifth man."

"It sounds reasonable enough," the director said hesitantly, cleaning his glasses with a cloth and then scratching his head while he attempted to formulate a question. "What I don't understand is what a lone killer – as you say this Psycho is – was doing taking part in a murderous orgy like the crime at La Cruz. Would you be able to explain that?"

"Probably. It is common for many serial killers to begin their criminal careers accompanied, even in groups. It's likely that the murderous fantasy has been incubating in them for a long time before they dare to take a step. Sometimes they associate with others to break through the last hurdles and take courage – once the first crime has been committed, the others are just added to it. Let's say it's a kind of help at the beginning, but the tendency is to continue alone. Normally, the serial killer enjoys the solitiude of his act, he wants neither observers nor participants, it's a matter between him and his prey." The agent paused, looked at his notes and added: "The rest is a question of common sense or statistics. I think he is white because the overwhelming majority of serial killers murder others from their own race, white on white, black on black."

"And the question of his age?" Gustavo asked.

"Let's see, there is also an explanation for that. Psychiatric science has established that this type of psychosis begins to develop in adolescence and it takes eight to ten years for it to manifest itself fully. So, presuming that the Psycho had his first experience with the women from La Cruz, he would be between 25 and 30. The rest is logical deduction. For example, the fact that he uses an M-3 suggests that he must have some military training – because we know it is a weapon designed for war which fires in bursts. To fire one shot again and again – as the killer seems to do – is something that requires training."

"Exactly," Don Jovel interrupted. "Considering this fact, we began to think the killer might be a policeman but we held back from this hypothesis because of public opinion."

"I understand," Pedroso smiled for the first time – a small incision in a stoney countenance. "It could be a police officer because in this country there is no army, so they tell me. But we shouldn't discount the possibility that it could be a soldier or guerrilla from a neighbouring country. It would be good to inquire whether there are any similar cases in any neighbouring country. As far as the other threads go, they can be deduced easily from the reports. The mutilations of the last victims indicate that the killer had advanced knowledge of anatomy – and that indicates a certain social condition, middle or upper class."

"That's clear enough," said Don Jovel, "and the mother? What does the mother have to do with all this?"

"We haven't been able to establish a causal link, but the vast majority of serial killers or mass killers whose targets are generally women have had mothers who were prostitutes, vicious or excessively dominant and aggressive. It could be that the sickness is there – genetically – in some individuals and that a frustrating or painful experience with the mother helps to unleash the criminal behaviour. We don't yet know this for sure, but the link exists."

Most surprising was not the coherence of the analysis but the absolute certainty with which Aníbal Pedroso strung it all together, thought the homicide chief. At least it looked like that – there was no change of mood, he was neither excited about his own discoveries nor was he troubled by the distrust his ideas might provoke. He began to recognise in Pedroso his own habit of observing facts in detail and formulating judgments that were strictly rational, but in the formulations of his colleague there was something more convincing, almost impossible to contradict.

"We left hanging the analysis about the last victim. How does that fit with the rest?" asked Gustavo, "because this case seems completely atypical to me."

"I don't see it as so atypical," said Pedroso. "The only thing missing is the dead boyfriend and a reproductive organ moved out of place. As far as the rest is concerned, we have a young victim, a female as in the other cases, a scene with erotic associations since, according to what I've read in the reports, the girl was naked, a known weapon, an absolute domination of the territory by the killer. A single perfectly executed shot from a gun that normally fires in bursts. They don't seem a few coincidences to me."

"Well," the director stammered, passing his fingers across his bald head, "seen in this way, I'd say you are right. But how secondary are," his voice broke a little and changed tone, "these missing details?"

"That there was no boyfriend seems the least significant to me. In the previous cases, by killing a man the killer has done no more than get rid of a nuisance. Do I explain myself? His real victim was not the man, he was just someone who had to be killed so that he would not interfere or would not recognise the killer afterwards. Why the woman has not been mutilated is a bit more difficult to explain because I think it was a significant element of the previous cases, but it's not completely incomprehensible. It could be that in her case the disembowelling was not a condition for the murder to take place. On the other hand, it is obvious that he wasn't in circumstances that were sufficiently secure. For that he would have had to enter the house and surprise the whole family and run the risk that the neighbours found out what was going on."

"Perhaps," said Gustavo, "that's why he asked them to open the door – I am referring to what the grandfather said."

"It's possible," Pedroso concluded. "It's also possible, though, that our man is not someone who takes unnecessary risks."

"What I don't understand," said Don Jovel, "is why he chose this woman and not another. Why didn't he look for a solitary couple like on the previous occasions?"

"Perhaps to take precautions," said Gustavo, "so as not to repeat the same procedure because he presumes that we are trying to set him a trap."

"Effectively," Pedroso backed up his opinion, "or because the press has made such a racket that there are not many couples left who go around making love in isolated areas."

Don Jovel nodded, but looked gloomy, his eyes wide open, his hair – or the little that remained of it – dishevelled.

"And now what? What do we do with this? There must be hundreds of people who share his characteristics."

Pedroso fixed his black penetrating eyes on the director, nodded his head and seemed to hesitate briefly before responding.

"Perhaps we should look for someone who has been a hunter, above everything else I have said to you."

"A hunter? What kind of hunter?" Gustavo asked.

"A sports hunter, one of those guys who live to shoot at ducks and deer. They are a very particular type of person."

"And why a hunter?" Don Jovel asked with sudden anxiety.

"Have you ever been on a hunt? Well, if you have, you will understand my reasoning. Let's say that a good hunter is someone who imitates the behaviour of a natural predator, he follows his instinct but remains under total rational control. The hunter does not allow his emotions to interfere, he is not hasty. In the hunt, the first step is patient observation, the dispassionate study of the potential prey. A true hunter can observe for a day or for three days just the same, without caring about the weather, his bodily needs, or the everyday life that he has left in the city or elsewhere. Next is the observation of the surroundings, the evaluation of risk, factors for and against, such as the eventual presence of an enemy who is stronger, the direction of the wind, the characteristics of the territory, many details. Third is the subsequent approach. The period of time in which the victim has to react. Fourth, certain attack, fast and without hesitation. That is how the feline behaves and that is what the human hunter does as well if he knows the job. Hunting is not about hiding in the woods and firing shots, it's a game of judgment, a mortal game of chess which has its own rules, a sport in which one bets his own life against that of another being. If we analyse this last killing, just like the two previous ones, you will see that the killer behaves with complete devotion to the procedure."

"I don't know," said Gustavo. "Too many things are coming together. We have a guy who hates his mother, who knows a lot about human anatomy, who has mastered some surgical techniques, who moves easily in the mountains. Now it turns out that he is also a hunting expert. Doesn't this seem too complex a personality to be real?"

"He would not seem real to me if he was too simple," Pedroso said. "In general, the human mind is complex, but the mind of a serial killer is virtually indecipherable."

The homicide chief shrugged his shoulders while Don Jovel observed one and then the other man with glistening eyes. The boss seemed governed by a state of growing excitement, scratching his head, moving his feet and rummaging through the papers on his desk.

"Your theory is interesting, fascinating," he said, "but if we wanted to apply these rules to the conduct of the Psycho? How would you do so?"

"It's a question of logic," Pedroso said. "For example, let's consider the cases of the couples. It's obvious that they weren't casual victims in the sense that the Psycho bumped into them and liquidated them there and then. A meticulous murderer like this one does not wander around looking for a chance victim. He knows that couples come to this park at night but he does not know the territory. He does not know the victims and he begins a process of observation. He must have spent several nights, hidden in the darkness, observing movements, watching the habits of each couple. He must have had a high degree of certainty about the situation on the day he unleashed his aggressive impulse. He knew that the couple was alone, that there would be no witnesses. After completing his hunt successfully, he proceeded to dismember the prey... excuse me for expressing it like this, but it's better to establish parallels. Then he dragged the corpses several hundred metres just like a leopard or puma would. Remember that the corpses of both girls were missing the nipples and that these were not found, which leads us to think that the killer took them with him. Every hunter collects pieces of his prey. The horns of the deer or the nipples of the girls have an identical significance."

"From what we know, in the case of Carolina, there was no trophy," said Gustavo.

"In the last case, perhaps because of the circumstances in which the crime was carried out, the last two phases were missing, I mean the dismemberment and collection of the trophy, but in every other aspect the conduct of the hunter takes place with a surprising clarity. The killer did not act on any day, but on the day of a local fiesta. Think about it, in the midst of a firework display that allowed him to cover up the noise of the gun. He knew exactly which was the girl's room, what the window looked out on and at what time she would arrive home. That must have required many hours of following her, of close observation. He was clear about how to enter and leave the property, and he probably planned to cut the telephone wires. Probably also, although this is a little more hypothetical, he considered the possibility of entering the house to complete the job if the conditions were right. It would not surprise me if the noise that the grandfather heard was made deliberately so that he'd open the door."

"But he did not insist," said Gustavo.

"Correct. That's why I say to you that this is not a killer who takes risks."

"The gringo's contributions are good, interesting, but they have left me more worried than before," Don Jovel said after Pedroso had left. "This Psycho seems less and less real to me. It's as if we were being fed a tale of suspense piece by piece. Don't you get the same sensation?"

"Something similar," said Gustavo, "but I don't know what torments me more, the killer or this detective, he seems so sure of everything he says that sometimes I have difficulty believing it."

The director agreed, but his expression was blank.

"We'll see what comes out of it," he said. "For now, let's try to complete this profile."

9

For 20 minutes she tolerated his rancid breath on the nape of her neck, the noise of his anxious breathing, the chewed fingernails, and the daft comments on every line she wrote. She felt rage, nausea, the urge to vomit and to shriek. She highlighted the text on her screen in black and put her finger over the delete button. Then she swung around on her chair to face Mr Grey.

"If you don't let me finish in peace, I am going to wipe out this article and go home," Maricruz threatened him. "I can't put up with it any longer."

The gringo stepped back astonished and the entire newsroom, packed with journalists rushing to meet their deadlines, became shrouded in a tomb-like silence.

"What's up?" he smiled. "Our star reporter is very tense today. It's okay, okay," he said backing off. "When you've finished, give me the article and I won't change it."

He made a half-turn and set off for his office, which was in the other part of the building. A few seconds later the entire newsroom erupted in spontaneous applause and Maricruz was held up as a heroine.

In recent days, Mr Grey had been obsessed with the Psycho.

Since the government had stopped piling on the pressure over the case, the adventures of the disemboweller had become the news of the year. Mr Grey pursued Maricruz relentlessly, demanding that she find more and more information, asking for more and more interviews, and refusing to accept it if she did not publish any news about the case. He learned about the theory of the Clan spun by the mysterious José Manuel Sandoval; he knew of the existence of documents and tapes and demanded to have them. He wanted Maricruz to get back in contact with the informant and even offered additional resources (a one-off) to find out his whereabouts. The appearance of the twelfth corpse attributed to the Psycho threw him into virtual paroxysms.

"You don't understand," Maricruz had told him. "I don't know how to contact this guy Sandoval, I don't even know if that's his real name, I don't know where he lives. I doubt he is even in the country."

"Good journalists never say 'I can't'. They try and go on trying until they somehow manage it," said the gringo.

"That's fine," said Maricruz, "the only thing that occurs to me is to put an advert in the paper asking him to get in touch. I don't think it'll work, but it's the only chance we have."

"Right, we'll place one. If it doesn't work, we'll try something else. You'll see that we'll manage it in the end," he said enthusiastically.

In recent weeks Mr Grey had lost weight, incipient dark circles had made his gaze sadder, and his mouth had turned down at the edges. All that remained of his fingernails were a few shreds of pink skin, almost bloody, at the edge of his cuticles. He would arrive at 8am to go over the paper with a fine-tooth comb, a task that took an hour and a half and which began to get on his nerves from early on. At 9.30am he held his first meeting with the section editors and heads of design to complain about all the blunders in that day's edition and to plan the new working day.

At 11am he confirmed the advertising schedule. At 12pm he inspected the reports about distribution and responded personally, albeit by telephone, to subscribers' complaints. At 1pm he

locked himself in his office to eat something, which usually consisted of a few chunks of carrot or cucumber, a salad and a slice
of bread and mortadella cheese, or whatever occurred to his
housekeeper to wrap in a piece of tinfoil. At 1.30pm he visited
the administrative and financial section, a territory that for a
long time had been ruled by his wife. He had begun to make
incursions a few months before interfering with editorial – not
without defeating a fiery resistance from the Italian, who was
convinced that someone was putting their hand in the till. He
interrogated the accountants, went over the books and signed
cheques. From this part of his schedule he would emerge more
stressed than from any other, suffering fresh doubts and the verbal swipes that the woman threw at him, but ready for three of
four meetings with reporters whom he had assigned to special
investigations that were generally impossible. Later it was time
to put the newspaper to bed, which was becoming increasingly
complicated because he not only wanted to cast his eye over the
articles but also to choose photographs and decide on the layout
of the pages. He left between 10pm and 11pm, overloaded with
work and his heart heavy with sinister apprehensions.

"I don't know how long I'll do this for," he had said to Juan
José by way of an excuse, "but I swear to you that this is essential if things are to go well without my having to keep on top of
everything."

"What you want is for everyone to do things the way you think
they should be done, but you won't achieve that in a hundred
years," said the editor. "A way to interconnect people's brains
doesn't exist yet."

"We'll see," said the gringo.

Pedro leapt up. "It can't be," he exclaimed. He sat down again,
looked over the notes he had just made, confirmed the dates on
the calendar and let out a loud shout. Maricruz saw him coming
towards her, waving a bundle of papers and exclaiming "Eureka"
with the expression of someone who had surely discovered the
principle of Archimedes.

"It's incredible," he said, holding out sheets of paper covered with strange sketches, linked by arrows in intricate patterns. His eyes sparkled and he made a face that conveyed joy and despair combined.

"What's incredible?" said Maricruz, trying vainly to decipher the doodles.

"I knew it," said Pedro trembling, "or rather I sensed it before I could be sure. Look," he said, taking one of the sheets and pointing to circled dates: 6th April, 14th December, 11th February, 14th June. All the crimes coincide with a full moon, one or two days before or after, if not on the day of the full moon itself. Do you see? Are you actually capable of understanding the importance of this discovery?"

"Which is?" she said.

"Doesn't it seem significant to you that the serial killer only acts when the moon is full? Haven't you heard about the influence exerted by the planets on human beings, the way they determine our consciousness."

"Get serious!" said Maricruz, faking astonishment, before punching the air. "You know nothing about astrology Pedro – you are a bullshitter. Besides, it could just be coincidence."

"Coincidence?" the society editor insisted.

'The three attackers, wearing army fatigues and with their faces covered by balaclavas, entered the petrol station after midnight in a sedan car and fired at the sales staff with heavy-calibre weapons...'

"Don't you realise," Pedro raised his voice and shook the reporter by the shoulders. "These murders could be linked to a satanic cult. Black magic."

Maricruz stopped typing. Her expression was a mixture of disbelief and morbid curiosity.

"That's a little outlandish. Besides, you said that some dates coincide with the full moon and others don't."

"A difference of one or two days."

"I admit that I'm an ignoramus, or rather a novice when it comes to astrology, but there is something I'm absolutely clear about: from the point of view of magic rituals, the important thing is not so much the culmination of the phase, or whether the moon is new or waxing, what really matters are the conjunctions that occur in the areas that are nearby during these phases."

"Make sense or get lost," Maricruz waved her hand.

"If you don't believe me I can arrange for you to meet someone who does know. She's an expert – what's important is that you don't underestimate this opportunity."

Maricruz nodded '...and they demanded that they handed over the money in the till. Álvarez, the security guard in the restaurant next to the petrol station realised what was happening and tried to intervene, but the attackers opened fire.'

She shouted as the society editor moved off with a defeated air: "Get me the interview and if something good comes out of it, I'll buy you a beer."

Two days later, Pedro and Maricruz were standing outside an old wooden house opposite a church in the Los Angeles district. It had a porch with some rickety beams that had started to collapse on one side. The paint had lost its original green and was now an ambiguous colour, rotten in parts and scorched by decades of sun and tropical winters. A narrow window, covered by red cloth curtains, must have let in little light. A glass spyhole in the door served to screen visitors.

Pedro pressed the white button on the wall and a musical chime came from within. The door opened and an elderly woman appeared smiling, overdressed and excessively made-up. She had puffed-up hair and a kilo of jewellery and silverware, including necklaces, rings and bracelets.

"Pedrito, my love," she exclaimed. "It's been so long since I've seen you. Where have you been?"

He hugged and kissed her. "May I introduce my friend Maricruz."

"Lovely," the woman determined after one glance.

"Please come in. In this job I am known as Madame Fronvac," she greeted Maricruz with a kiss on the cheek. "But that is just strategic – marketing, as they say. To my friends, I am Irma and any friend of Pedro is a friend of mine."

It was a house of ancient design, although its interior looked better kept and cleaner than the exterior. The first part consisted of a long hallway with mosaics, at the side of which were the closed doors of four rooms. The passage led to a rectangular shaped salon, spacious but dark, furnished with two three-piece suites, an ostentatious sound system and a television with a wide screen. Madame's work room, which her clients had to walk through the entire house to reach, was not large, and resembled those caverns of prophecy and spiritualism that you see in the films: a round table in the centre with its predictable crystal ball, ancient candlesticks, a large chart of the zodiac on the wall and portraits of peculiar men with deep gazes and dressed in multicoloured turbans. Maricruz stared intently at them and Madame noticed her interest.

"They are masters. If one day you'd like to know about them, it would be my pleasure," she said, inviting them to be seated at a round table. "Pedro says you are not here to have your cards read."

"Let's say that it's a technical consultation. I suppose you've heard about the crimes of the Psycho?" Maricruz asked.

"Horrible," Madame exclaimed. "It's incredible for this to be happening in a country like this, so peaceful."

"They have assigned me to cover the case. A couple of days ago Pedro made a discovery which to him seems very important. To be honest, I am not convinced, but we wanted to hear an expert opinion. The point is that all the crimes have been committed during the full moon or on dates close to the full moon."

The woman fluttered her long eyelashes, which looked false to Maricruz, and directed a look of interrogation or perhaps approval towards Pedro.

"I don't think I have heard this before," she commented.

"I don't think that anyone else has realised, apart from your talented disciple," Pedro said, tapping his fingernails on his leather jacket. "There are four murders and all four took place on the night of a full moon or on the eve of a full moon. I don't think it is chance. I have tried to explain to my friend the impact that such a discovery would have, but she says I am making something out of nothing because not all the crimes occurred on the actual date of the full moon."

"Let's see children, show me the dates," Madame Fronvac sat down in front of a circular diagram full of incomprehensible icons.

A moment later Irma Solares traced her long red fingernail over the surface of the paper, looked at them if she was returning from a journey and then relaxed smiling, stretching out her arms in a movement that caused her jewellery to jangle.

"Your instinct was right Pedro," she said. "On the four dates the moon was in a house favourable to the sacrificial rituals, there is no doubt."

"Explain that to me," said Maricruz.

"As we all know, the moon takes 28 days to circle the earth and each day it is located in a determinate position in relation not just to our planet but also to the sun. We call each one of these positions lunar phases, but astrology has long known them as abodes or houses. The first of the moon's 28 abodes is the one that is in perfect alignment with the sun: the star king shines fully over one of the sides and the other side, the one we see, is hidden to us. This is a critical point known as hyleg, the vital point of our world. At this moment there is an intense concentration of energies that can be harnessed for different purposes, but that in general is much feared by those who are aware of its power. From there begins a descending process of 14 days until the full moon. Then begins the ascending 14 days, until the new lunar conjunction, the new hyleg."

Maricruz shrugged her shoulders.

"The fact is," said Madame Fronvac, "that in each house the moon exerts different types of influence."

"I recognise my ignorance," Pedro intervened, "but I thought I heard you say that the houses close to the full moon were favourable to sacrificial rituals. It seems to me that those of a malevolent nature are those of the new moon."

Madame Fronvac pointed her fingernail at her friend's chest. "The full moon is the point opposite the hyleg, it is light versus obscurity, white versus black. The full moon is the moment when the evil forces are weakest. That's why the rites of black magic are aimed at calling the arrival of the black moon, or rather the entrance of malignant power in the moon. It is an ancient idea. The Egyptians considered the new moon as the moment when Osiris, the god of death, entered to rule the world."

"A little complicated, dear."

"This passage of the lunar phases is significant in almost all cultures."

"All this sounds very interesting, but I still don't see the link," said Maricruz. "How does this confirm that the Psycho has deliberately chosen the days of the full moon to commit his crimes?"

"I'm not saying any such thing," said Madame Fronvac, "but it's important that you know – so that you can draw your own conclusions. Even today numerous sects exist that are based on the cosmogonies of ancient civilisations, worship their gods and follow their rites. Sometimes these rituals get mixed up and confused with other kinds of practices, for example with satanism, and they produce things that are truly strange."

"Which means," Pedro cut in visibly excited, "that the crimes might be the work not of an individual but of a sect."

"Possibly," Madame conceded.

"Or it might also be that killer acts alone but that at some stage he had contact with occultist practices," Maricruz surprised herself with her enthusiasm for the idea, thinking for the first time that there was something coherent in all this theorising.

There was a brief silence – a tacit truce which the three took advantage of to formulate new questions, until Maricruz spoke: "And how would this fit in with the idea of human sacrifice?"

"Generally, societies that practised sacrifice had religious or practical motives to do so. The sacrifice was meant to please some specific god and to prevent misfortune, normally of a natural origin, such as floods, droughts, earthquakes... The leaders of the cult would drain the blood from the sacrificial victim, then open them through the stomach and remove their organs. This, supposedly, would satisfy the sadism of a particular god."

"The Psycho disembowels his victims," Pedro recalled. "He takes out their sexual organs. Couldn't this be a ritual practice?"

"Well," Madame conceded, "if we link the fact that the crimes occur in the same lunar phase with this other aspect of mutilation, I think the thesis makes a lot of sense. Besides..."

Madame Fronvac or Irma Solares (Maricruz could not always distinguish which woman was revealing herself at a particular moment) paused as if she were looking for a loose end, the thread that would provide continuity to the fabric of her next thought.

"What's up?" Pedro asked.

"I was thinking that perhaps I could put you in touch with some people who know the subject more directly. I mean – who are involved with sects. I have a contact who... But, please give me a chance. I would have to consult him first," she said and changed the subject. "Have you thought why the killer only treats women brutally? Doesn't it seem strange to you?"

"The police theory," the journalist answered, "is that this is a man who hates and deeply fears a woman, probably his mother, and that through killing he is destroying this other female figure."

"It's very likely to be that," Madame agreed. "A complex psychological mechanism that provokes him to eradicate – in the symbolic object – the object that he hates. But this psychological theory is not enough to explain everything. This criminal needs an ethical justification to do what he is doing, or the guilt would end up destroying him – and only religions or political philosophies provide these type of grounds."

10

Lidia is married. Someone told me today and I couldn't believe it. Her, married? Not even the takeover of the news department by the gringo has caused such a deep depression. Lidia, the impeccable, the divine, belongs to another, she goes to bed each night and wakes up each morning next to another. Another who shares her most intimate memories, her sweetest dreams. Another who they say is solvent and in a position to put the world at her feet. Since I couldn't believe it, I asked her myself, I approached on whatever pretext and started a casual conversation.

Married or single?

I let the question loose among others, trying to feign disinterest, putting a hint of curiosity in the words, but she tried to read something beyond the tone of my voice, beyond my gestures, and she searched for my eyes. There was a sparkle in her clear pupils. Questions, replies, confessions. I don't know. They were signs of a strange language, codes of an impenetrable heart. On the other hand, those little mirrors of the soul must have betrayed me. They must have revealed my tribulations, which must have seemed many to her, because a sad smile was etched on her lips.

"Married," she said in a weak voice, almost a whisper... as if that would lessen the bitterness of the news, as if saying it lightly could really make it lighter. She jumped straight to another subject.

"Could you cast an eye over my articles, if it's not too much trouble?"

I agreed, charmed, although I had to confess that I'm completely ignorant of this stuff. I can't distinguish a Picasso from a Dali, I confuse Schubert with Delibes – when it comes to modern art, painting looks like a load of dirty marks and dance is an acrobatic spectacle. She took it as a joke. She granted me one of those smiles that lights up her whole face and everything within a radius of a few metres, before returning to my desk.

I've thought a lot about inviting her to lunch. It wouldn't look, at first, in any way suspicious. Just a chance meeting in the corridor, around midday, a nonchalant 'Hi' (How are you? Do you have the time? Yes, it's nearly 12 o' clock, 10 to 12. How quickly time passes, doesn't it? It's almost lunchtime. By the way, do you have any plans? Would you allow me to invite you to lunch? Yes, I would be delighted.) It would be so simple and yet it's so difficult. The idea of rejection causes genuine terror, I am paralysed by the thought of being ridiculed. On the other hand, what would I gain with this approach? What chance do I have with a woman like her? What can a man who has nothing, offer a woman who has everything? She has physical beauty, talent, love, luck? To attempt it would be absurd although no one has ever said that logic or good sense apply in affairs of the heart. Normally it is our dreams that rule us and direct our behaviour, not the other way round. How can I stop her image from pursuing me? How can I stop her voice resounding constantly in my dreams? Feel the air is impregnated with her scent? But neither is it possible that I'm in love. It's a long time since I stopped believing in love, in the Easter Bunny and the headless horseman. It must be caused by tiredness or lack of sex.

Except for one detail, they hadn't found anything extraordinary or striking, reported officer Aurelio Morales, a corpulent man and with crude features, whom people always described by alluding to his considerable height and abundant moustache.

"The girl worked in a blood bank for the Red Cross. Her friends say she was a normal person, friendly, kind, co-operative," he read the notes in his notebook in the order that he had written them down. "All the stuff they say when someone is cold meat although when they were alive they didn't like them one bit," the official said and a dog-like chuckle shook his stomach. "The important thing is that they noticed no unusual behaviour – nor did they hear that she had any problems with anyone. She didn't usually go out with them at night," he went on, "but it seems that this was for religious reasons because she was involved in a Protestant sect. We visited the church and talked to the people closest to her. The same thing: a pleasant girl who had no vices, very into God, according to her brothers. They call each other brothers, you know, even though they are not even third cousins. No one remembers her being nervous or anything. The neighbours: the same."

"Did she have a boyfriend?"

"Let's see, it seems there was someone prowling around her... nothing very formal. One Isidoro – what a name," he let out another noiseless chuckle, "but he doesn't know anything. He says he saw her from time to time, a couple of times a week. They went to church together or to eat Chinese, outings like that. He says that on the night of the crime he was at the sect and then he went straight home. Various neighbours who attend the same church confirm his alibi."

"And the detail you mentioned?" Gustavo asked.

"We made a list of the victim's friends and acquaintances and found something interesting. She was a friend of one of the suspects in the case of La Cruz de Alajuelita, the one they call Three Hairs. It turns out that she visited him a few times at La Reforma jail."

"And you consider that a detail of no importance?"

"I didn't say that it was of no importance boss, but neither do we have a way to link it to the crime. The girl visited him in jail, that's all."

"What kind of visit?"

"Not conjugal, if that's what you're thinking. However, one informer recalls that the man was courting her, and that the girl didn't pay much attention because of the age difference, or something like that."

"Yet she went to visit him in jail."

"Well, yes, but people from these religious groups usually do that. They visit prisoners, old people, they go to see sick people in hospital. Relatives say she did it out of Christian charity."

"In any case, it sounds pretty strange," said the homicide chief. "Give me a written report, but keep investigating this matter, it might be a lead."

The agent left the office almost at the same time as the intercom buzzed and the cracked voice of the boss summoned Gustavo to his office, on a matter of extreme urgency, it told him.

The homicide chief went unwillingly because he had promised to meet Maricruz to go jogging then have lunch together. He had just 20 minutes if he wanted to arrive for their date on time. If Don Jovel dragged his feet, he would have to call her and cancel the meeting or ask her to wait who knows how long, to which she – with absolute certainty and rightly – would respond by telling him to go to hell.

He responded to the call, but with a very firm resolve: he would not permit anything, no matter how urgent, to destroy his newly acquired goal of being happy.

"It's possible that we've got the guy," said Don Jovel, straining his voice to complete the sentence.

"The guy?" asked Gustavo, not understanding to whom the term referred.

"The Psycho," specified the director of the Judicial Police, holding up a sheet of paper in his trembling hands. "A few weeks ago this anonymous letter arrived, but there have been so many that at first I thought nothing of it. However, when Pedroso said yesterday that we should look for a hunter, I saw the light. At first I thought I had made a mistake, but I spent the entire morning searching everywhere until I found it," he waved towards a tower of paper that seemed about to give way under its weight: three months of letters, memos, communiqués and other documents of improbable usefulness.

The anonymous person suggested that they investigate a man called Guerra, a nurse by profession, a hunting fan, a former Sandinista guerrilla on the southern front of Nicaragua who had been observed behaving strangely. The subject, the note said, would go out for night-time walks in the mountains and practised shooting at his property in the hills in the south of Desamparados with, the informer believed but was not absolutely sure, an M-3 machine-gun. During the past year, or year and a half, the informer added, his character had changed progressively, becoming hostile and reclusive, a fact that was recognised both by relatives and friends from whom Guerra had radically distanced himself.

Gustavo made no comment but gave Don Jovel a strange look that might have signified anything from absolute indifference to paralysing astonishment. For a few seconds, the boss waited for a clearer reaction but did not get one, so he decided to continue revealing information.

"I asked for a report in the archive and you'll see how interesting it is," he went over the document with his index finger. "Ten years ago this person was investigated for a crime of medical malpractice at a hospital in San José. A woman died because of an error in administering medicine, an injection which instead of helping her, induced a cardiac arrest. According to the investigations, the mistake might have resulted from some confusion about the names of the products. But the problem was that it was impossible to determine, beyond all reasonable doubt, who had administered the injection, even though all the signs point to this young man."

"What else?" Gustavo asked, glancing impatiently at his watch.

"I'm going to ask you the same question in 24 hours – so let's get to work."

"After lunch," said Gustavo, getting to his feet prematurely.

Don Jovel could not hide his surprise at seeing the most compulsive man he knew postponing a matter of such importance until after lunch.

"What's going on?" he asked intrigued.

"I have a date."

"Is it with a journalist?" Don Jovel pressed him, his mouth betraying a hint of malice.

"Yes, with a journalist. Is there some problem?" Gustavo answered, disgusted.

"Not really, no – but everyone knows that you are going out with that news reporter. What's her name?"

"Her name is Maricruz Miranda. She is a good friend – nothing more."

"I'm not interested in what you do in your private life but I urge you to be careful. People are saying that you are the one who is leaking information and I have the impression that this is not doing your reputation any favours."

"We are close friends, we go out often and the situation could develop," the homicide chief confessed. "But we have an agreement not to mix personal with professional matters," he lied. "Each to his own."

"I believe you, of course," Don Jovel assured him, although an ironic smile undermined his words. "The problem is those colleagues of yours who talk behind your back. They are more venomous than cobras, you know them."

Gustavo nodded. For a few seconds he was lost in thought, his arms resting on the back of the chair and his head resting on his chest. Then, he lifted his face and glanced out of the window at the view of western San José, where he could see the social security building, the domes of the national theatre and the metropolitan cathedral. A couple of kilometres further, in the same direction, was the park of La Sabana and his immediate destination.

"Do you know what, I don't give a damn about them," he said finally and left the office without seeing the astonished look of Don Jovel.

The vision dazzled him. She was wearing grey lycra shorts, very tight-fitting. The little that remained hidden could be seen through the material and the rest, those perfect legs from the ankle to the buttocks, looked so tempting he felt he was suffocating. Her top half was uncovered apart from the stripe of her sports top, and she wore running shoes with no socks.

They ran around the track 15 times, six kilometres exactly, in an oppressive heat and under black clouds that threatened an afternoon rain. They finished soaked in sweat, their muscles deliciously tired, and in a good mood, bolstered by a cold shower and a light lunch – green salad and curried chicken breasts – on the terrace of the Tapia bar. There, anointed by the fumes of lead, sulphur and carbon monoxide from the heavy traffic; splashed by the first drops of an enormous downpour that would later flood half a dozen neighourhoods and districts of the capital, Maricruz made the announcement that destroyed the life of Gustavo Cortés.

"Last night I received an unexpected proposal," she said, "from Jorge Luis."

"Jorge Luis?"

"Yes, the friend I mentioned to you once – the systems engineer."

"What type of proposal?"

"Marriage."

"And how did you respond?"

"It was very difficult for me to decide, but I accepted."

She could see how his happy expression crumbled all at once, as if a demolition charge had exploded inside. He said nothing. He lifted to his mouth the piece of food that he had just sliced and chewed slowly, with a wandering, ruminating look.

"I thought you weren't so interested in him," he said after chewing the meat carefully, with the grinding power of the despair that was gnawing at him. "In fact, I thought you weren't seeing him any more."

"He is not the kind of man who would make me ecstatically happy, of course, but you have to be realistic. The more intense the emotion, the more fleeting is the effect. We've been going out together for years, first as friends and then as boyfriend and girlfriend. Jorge Luis wants me and he is offering me a nice house, a nice car, a peaceful life, with no nasty surprises or economic difficulties. He is prepared to devote more time to our relationship, to be a faithful and loving husband. He would like to have two or three children, which is exactly my idea of a good-sized family. We agree on these and other things. Looking at it positively, what more can a woman ask for in a world dominated by machos, selfish, inconsiderate, and even violent men?"

"You told me that he seemed more interested in the software than anything else, you included."

"Really? I said that. I must have been annoyed by something, but it's not true. I feel that I'm important to him."

"That intimate relations had been a disaster because you weren't in love."

"The sexual thing can be conquered, it's a question of training and all that stuff about being in love or not, is not important. In any case, they say that being in love passes after the first year of marriage and never returns. Isn't it like that?"

Gustavo took a serviette and folded it several times, taking care on the corners, on the folds, until he had formed a dunce's hat, which he then undid just as carefully. He was incapable of thinking coherently, of saying one more word, of looking her in the eye. His emotions were a whirlwind and he was shocked by the idea that the girl might realise the extent of his confusion, and of his pain. He would have loved to have words – more than words, good points, resources, solid and abundant arguments to dissuade her. But he didn't.

"You are about to commit suicide, marriage without love is suicide, a decision like that has to take time" he wanted to say, but he couldn't. He wasn't the person to say it. He would have loved to tell her that he loved her, assure her that he could have made her happy, but such a declaration would have seemed untimely if not ridiculous. The most appropriate thing to do was to ask for the bill, kiss her on the cheek and wish her, with the ready smile of a practical man with no soul, all the happiness in the world. All the best. Sayonara. Adios. Au revoir. Arrivederci. It was the most upright thing to do in the circumstances but his body would not even respond enough for him to pull himself together.

"I also have news for you," he said at last. "It seems that for the first time we have a firm candidate."

A firm candidate? Maricruz wondered. "What are you talking about?"

"A suspect. It's possible that we're close to catching the Psycho."

The announcement was magnificent. It made her want to have a notebook to hand and start filling it before flying off to the newsroom to write the chronicle of the century, but she could not imagine a less opportune moment. She had just thrown a dart at the heart of a man whom she imagined would fall to his knees, imploring and tremulous, and he was delivering a cold commentary on a work matter. Was this perhaps a cover-up of wounded dignity? A tantrum of feigned indifference? Or had she erred in her strategy? Didn't they say that a woman's heart was infallible, that the feminine soul is a pure instinct of love?

"What do you think?" Gustavo asked his silent companion. "The news has made an impression on you, hasn't it?"

"Absolutely," she smiled with intimate sarcasm. "I am stunned."

"At this point I can't give you any details because we don't have more than a description of a guy, but I promise you that in one or two days you will have all the information. I'm going to work on this right now."

"I'll wait. Thanks."

Gustavo was not surprised that Maricruz went quiet, that she did not try to press him, with subtle arts, for the last detail. Seldom had he seen her so gloomy, in spite of the fact that a few minutes ago she had seemed the radiant, cherished fiancée on the threshold of marriage. Or, was it that he saw in her the reflection of his own sombre mood? Her gaze had got lost somewhere in the direction of the park, wandering over the high trees in a kind of mimetic evasiveness.

"Have you set a date?" he asked at last, just to break the silence.

"In six months," she said without looking at him. Gustavo bit his lip. A brief but hectic internal battle began between the impassive nobleman and the moody and feverish self that took alternate control of his life.

"It's a mistake," he said.

"Why?"

"Happiness is not a state of permanent ecstasy, that's true, but neither is it the make believe of a bolero. It exists and it's possible to find it."

"Yes, really? And how is...happiness? Have you ever found it?"

"Well, I admit that I haven't been very successful in this area. But you also learn from your disasters. I've been thinking a lot lately and I believe I've found the answer. People go along looking for happiness as if it were an eternal spring. But happiness comes from small moments in life."

"And the rest of the time?"

"That was what memory was created for? The happiness of each day is nourished by the memory of what we experienced yesterday, the week before, last year, and by the effort of repeating similar moments."

Maricruz mocked him. "What use is all this to you if you have never made an effort to be happy? With which memories are you going to nourish happiness when everything that preceded it has been a disaster?"

"I wasn't thinking of myself nor of my memories," he said, almost ashamed and ready to return to the only possible reality for him: his work.

11

Mr Grey was shocked by the idea of publishing an article devoted to the lunar manias of the killer. An occurrence, he pronounced, that was very in keeping with the tropical, Afro-Latin talent that produces under-development: everything that can't be explained rapidly and easily according to the rules of logic, is translated into a voodoo code.

He was an atheist, he declared, with deep philosophical convictions and he was not going to expose himself to ridicule by allowing his newspaper to publish half-boiled rubbish about satanic rites, ancient cults that had been revived, lunar influences, sacrifices to the gods. Where the hell did these kids get the time to go off on esoteric tangents? That told him that the workload was insufficient.

"The full moon, satanic rituals! The only thing we're missing is letters to Santa Claus," he roared.

"Excuse my frankness, but your criteria are in no way journalistic, this is excellent work," said Juan José, lifting the printed sheet that the gringo practically threw in his face, "completely professional. That devils are a religious invention does not detract from the fact that many people believe in their existence. And the article reflects this: the possibility that a fantasy of this kind is guiding the behaviour of the killer. Besides, it is only talking about a possibility, it is not saying that this is fact. It collates opinions from people who know something about the subject, it has logical coherence."

"No sir," thundered the gringo. "I don't want it to be published. It offends my intelligence. Why has Maricruz, instead of going after this rubbish, not thrown herself into searching for Manuel Sandoval? There you have an interesting lead."

"We have now published the announcement for eight consecutive days. There is no sign of life. Either he is not in the country or he does not wish to contact us. What do you want us to do? We're not detectives."

"But you are journalists – one presumes. I want you to meet him and get out of him everything he knows. I don't care how you do it. That's all," he ordered in a resolute tone.

Since he had intervened with a heavy hand in editorial affairs, the gringo had not only become more involved with the journalistic staff but increasingly inflexible and disdainful. He treated Juan José with no more deference than Amalia, the woman who put the coffee on his table each morning and whose name he did not even know. The era of great verbal battles with the editor had passed. Now he transmitted precise instructions, when he was not taking an Olympic leap over his authority, and communicated directly with the journalists. Juan José was dumbfounded. He spent half the time cobbling together options, plotting impossible ways to escape, and the other half regretting his bad luck.

The price of dignity is 150,000 *pesos* a month, he said to Maricruz that afternoon.

He no longer looked at her lasciviously: he no longer offered her his languid wandering hands or his nicotine stained lips; he no longer blackmailed her in jest in the hope that she would actually allow herself to be bribed. On the one hand, to feel that increasing loss of authority was battering his temperament. On the other, the presence of Lidia, the memory of Lidia, the dreams of Lidia meant that all his sexual vigour evaporated into purely platonic affection.

113

"One hundred and fifty thousand *pesos* which are indispensable to me, impossible to give up," he went on, "but in my precarious condition, I'm ready to play roulette with them."

"What are you thinking of?" Maricruz was alarmed. "Are you going to resign?"

"No way," he said. "I'm going to rebel. I'm going to publish this article against the wishes of Bill. And if I have to go because of this, I have to go but, beforehand, I'll make one hell of a scandal. I still have friends in other parts of the press."

"And afterwards?"

"Whatever God wants. Neither he nor my friends will let me starve to death – I hope."

"I don't want you to do it for me," Maricruz drew closer and took his hand. A few weeks before, such contact would have caused Juan José shivers of excitement but now it merely left him with a pleasing sensation of emotional closeness. "It doesn't matter to me that the work is wasted. I thought it could be an interesting angle, I even thought that the boss would like it – but neither is it worth such a sacrifice."

"That's very sweet of you," he smiled. "But I'm not doing it for you, but for myself. I want to have this trial of strength with the gringo."

"It might be the last."

"I know, but I've thought about it a lot and I've reached the conclusion that there are some risks that you have to run. Perhaps I'll lose the only thing I have in my life, which is this shit job, but I will have recovered a bit of my dignity. Lately I have realised that I value this much more than I had imagined."

Maricruz let go of Juan José's hand and wished him luck. There was something new between them, something more than a momentary empathy, the kind of solidarity in disgrace or complicity in hatred which unites the most diverse and divergent individuals. In fact, almost all the reporters now regarded their editor in a new light, with a kind of compassion, as if the affront Juan José was suffering affected each one of them. Besides, he had lost the habit of shouting and hurling threats every few steps he took, he scarcely gave out general directions (when the gringo didn't do it for him) so that his image of untamed beast had given way to one of a poor caged animal.

The unusual fact that Mr Grey retired early that afternoon worked in favour of Operation Dignity (as Juan José christened it). A business meeting, he announced, obliged him to leave the newspaper by 7pm, which is why he spent a large part of the day distributing detailed edicts to each department, fearful that his brief absence would result in catastrophe. As the hour of departure approached, his nervousness increased to the extent that he attacked, with ferocious nibbles, a tiny reappearance of a nail on his right index finger, provoking a haemorrhage that nothing could stop. He had to leave, not at 7pm, but at 6pm, to get some treatment and to find a discreet dressing.

The report was published the following day across eight columns, taking up almost the entire news section and a footnote of the main story. It pointed out the surprising discovery that the crimes of the Psycho had been committed in the phase of the full moon or during the days before and reproduced the opinion of several experts in esoteric themes, such as the well-known astrologer Madame Fronvac, that this could be linked to some kind of magic ritual, possibly practised by an ancient religion. The astrologer José Mercurio, whose fame rocketed after he predicted (four months in advance) that the President of the Republic would be awarded the Nobel Peace prize, considered that the crimes might be the work of a satanic brotherhood, or failing that, someone who had, or had had in the past, a link with this kind of sect. A militant feminist psychologist stated, on the other hand, that the murders and disembowellings constituted a typical aberration of a patriarchal society in which women are reduced to objects, in which men grow up thinking that the female was extracted from their ribs to alleviate their boredom and so they have a licence to play with her life and body like any other toy: the moon has been associated with femininity since time immemorial and to kill women at the moment when the moon is most present indicates just how much the killer abhors womankind. Another analyst thought, simply, that the full moon seriously altered the killer's state of mind and that probably not even he had realised the link between the lunar phase and his criminal impulses.

That morning, after a night of little sleep, Juan José invented an attack of colitis, announced that he was sick, disconnected the telephone, swallowed 20mg of diazepam and slept uninterrupted until 5pm. He knew he was fired but he wanted to gather strength for the confrontation that was approaching: at least a day of transition between the whirlwind of a daily newspaper and the agonising peace of his dismissal.

The decision was fortunate because, had he presented himself at work at the usual hour, he would have suffered the humiliation of being detained at the door by the security guard, who had been ordered not to let him pass, not even to collect his belongings. Gripped by an indescribable rage and in a virtual paroxysm, the gringo did not consider dismissal to be a sufficient punishment for the temerity of Juan José, so he plotted a way of dismissing him that would involve the greatest possible humiliation that he was capable of. He had asked to be informed as soon as the editor arrived, so that he could enjoy the scene from the window of a nearby office in a strategic spot. His first reaction – he predicted – would be of annoyance and arrogance, an attempt to impose the extent of his authority (and his body) on the insignificant doorman, who would have no alternative than to follow the owner's orders. "Don't let him in, even if you have to use your weapon to stop him," the gringo had told him. He felt sure that the second reaction would be to demand that Mr Grey appeared to give him an explanation, for which the guard had been briefed. "Mr Grey is very busy and cannot see you," he had to say. The third reaction would be to plead to be let past so he could collect his belongings. Then one of his trusted employees would carry the two cardboard boxes in which he had ordered Juan José's things to be placed, and would put them outside without further ado. A masterpiece of revenge, he told himself, and just the idea of carrying it out alleviated his rage.

At exactly 9am, the hour at which the editor usually arrived, the telephone rang and Mr Grey lifted it almost with excitement, convinced that the moment had arrived. But the call was not as he was expecting, but was from the president of the chamber of commerce, Luis Armando Costas, with whom he had been friendly ever since he had made a significant investment in the newspaper in exchange for a campaign against the tax duties which the government had committed itself to imposing on international financial institutions.

"One hundred points, old man," the businessman said. "That's how it's done."

"How what is done?"

"I am talking about strengthening the newspaper – giving it its own personality."

"Thanks," the gringo affected a genteel smile, as if his caller could see him. "But what in particular are you referring to?"

"The article about the Pyscho. It's most interesting."

"Do you think so?" he asked, astonished, disconcerted.

"Of course. People are tired of economics, politics, traffic accidents... Always the same old thing. This puts us above the competition. What the readers are looking for is something else, a bit of excitement, a hint of well-managed morbidity."

"Yes, of course," the gringo said, arranging his scant hair. "That was the idea, exactly. Do you think we should stick with it?"

"Of course," said Costas. "It would be excellent if we could continue a series about the subject. Don't you think?"

Within an hour he had received six more calls from soulmates, all praising the journalist's highly original focus.

"What's her name?"

"Maricruz Miranda."

"The girl is very talented, you should promote her."

"Yes, of course. She is the best on staff. I am thinking of proposing her name for the national journalism prize... She deserves it."

Three hours later Mr Grey had still not yet decided to reverse the instructions he had given first thing that morning. He was resisting doing that, but then the chief of distribution came into his office announcing that the edition had sold out in record time and asking his permission to print an additional 20,000 copies, and then came his wife, smiling, with a copy of the blasted article in her hand.

"Bravissimo!" the Italian said. "What fantastic work, don't you think?"

The following day, Juan José found his office a little untidier than usual but he did not think this had any special significance. It must have been Amalia, he thought, who provoked huge whirlwinds of paper each time she cleaned. In any case, he said to himself, it would not be a question of hours but of minutes to pack his things and sing farewell. Throughout the entire morning Mr Grey had not meandered around the perimeter of the newsroom, as he had done lately, he had not summoned a single journalist to his office or ordered anyone to distribute a memo. He had vanished and as the hours passed, so the editor's anxiety grew. In all the years he had worked for him he had come to fear his silences more than his outbursts and he began to wonder whether the boss might be working on something more drastic than sacking him. At 4pm, in the most formal tone, the secretary informed him that the director general wanted to meet him and the journalist Maricruz Miranda. The idea of being fired almost filled him with relief, but Maricruz? Was he thinking of firing her as well? Would that be his revenge? To make him feel responsible for the fate of the girl?

"I will defend you to the last," he promised her as he guided her to the gringo's office.

"I don't think you are in a position to defend anyone," she said in a tone that was half pitying, half ironic, "but don't worry, he will do me a favour if he fires me – it's time I got a decent job."

Mr Grey was on the telephone. From his desk he regaled Juan José with a smile that seemed to indicate the death sentence and gestured with his hand for them to sit down next to the meeting table and to wait a few moments until he had finished. Meanwhile, Amalia came in with coffee and pastries for three, a detail which left them completely puzzled.

"He's making me nervous," said Maricruz in a low voice.

"It looks bad," agreed Juan José. "I think he plans to poison us."

But the gringo looked cordial and friendly as he sat between them and took a sip of coffee.

"Well," he asked. "How have you been?"

"Fine," Maricruz answered for both of them. "I think."

"I'm pleased," said Mr Grey taking another sip of coffee and looking towards the board. "I want to show you something interesting."

He sketched a pair of co-ordinates and two lines at the centre.

He is mad, thought the chief of news, he has been consumed by schizophrenia. Or he may want to delay the agony.

"This space here, at the right hand of the intersection," pointed Mr Grey, "marks the gap between increasing resources and constant resources. And it also measures decreasing performance."

He let out that long throaty sigh he used when talking about circumstances he considered complex or disastrous.

"You'll be asking yourselves why I'm talking about all of this," he continued. "Well, simply because something like this is happening in this company. So what can we do?"

He paused briefly and gazed at them with the look of a high school teacher measuring his students' speed of thought.

"Mysticism!" he exclaimed. "That's what. Imagination! Talent! What this girl has showed in the last couple of days." He pointed at Maricruz with the full length of his left arm. He put the pen aside and went to sit next to the two astonished journalists.

Juan José was holding his prominent chin in the palm of his hand, his elbow on the table.

"Where is this going?"

"Towards success," the gringo proclaimed in a theatrical tone, without understanding or wanting to understand the meaning of the question.

"I mean," said the editor, "what is this meeting about?"

"I need us to make an extra effort," the gringo said at last. "To deepen this theme of the Psycho. I want a big series of reports that exploits all the possible angles. I want us to find Manuel Sandoval. If you do, I promise you a salary increase and a week's paid vacation in a hotel at the coast."

Maricruz suppressed a laugh. A foolish expression spread over Juan José's face. And then there was a long, uneasy silence in the office while they adjusted their state of mind. The best thing would have been, perhaps, to pretend – as the gringo was doing – that nothing abnormal or strange had happened and that this was simply a routine meeting. But the editor felt that to carry on like that would have been more tortuous than to know the truth. He was not going to wrestle with this intolerable doubt for several days and give fresh impetus to his problem of insomnia.

"I don't understand," he shook his head. "A few hours ago Maricruz's article seemed to you a pile of rubbish. You didn't want to publish it. What changed your mind?"

"I never said that," Mr Grey proclaimed. "You will not believe what I said – right? Maricruz? I had a few small doubts about the focus, but then I was convinced that it was a great idea... In any case, what's the problem now that everything has been clarified? Let's go," he stood up. "Let's lift the mood and get to work."

Perhaps it was this small victory over the gringo that boosted me. Or some small gesture from Lidia. Or was it an aggravation of my madness? The fact is that in the end I did it. Not as I had planned, feigning spontaneity in an occasional encounter, with an innocuous smile and look, but in the most obvious and ostentatious way. At 11.50am, with the desperation of someone who is going to eat alone yet again (to eat for the simple purpose of calming the stomach acids), I put out my hand, lifted the telephone receiver and dialled her extension.

"Would you accept an invitation to lunch?" I asked that pleading question straight off, with no twists or turns or concessions to fear. If she rejected the invitation it would be the last one. I would know that I was making myself look ridiculous and I would back off.

I asked the question and immediately I asked myself if it was the right one. It's been some 10, 12 (I no longer know how many) years since I approached a woman with amorous intentions. I approach all of them with a certain brutality, with the intention – I have to admit – that they take it as a joke and reject me with friendly animosity. Faced with their ironic responses, I fake reactions of humiliation and pain – but this is a game that is more or less transparent. Each person has their own madness and mine is this attachment to solitude (or fear of disaster, as that psychologist told me – the one who I went out with for two weeks and sent packing when she made the first attempt at psychoanalysis). In truth, I don't know if Lidia took a long time to reply or if I was capable of thinking so many things in a few seconds. Both situations seem unlikely to me, but the fact is that a whole raft of ideas went through my mind before she answered.

"Why not?" she said finally. Clearly it was a response more for herself than for me. As the semiologists say – something that annoyed me so much in my university days – the visible meaning of the words is just the tip of the iceberg.

How many things would Lidia have thought during this lapse, how many negatives had opened and closed successively, how many risks were weighed up before her mouth uttered that brief and nebulous response.

"Just give me 10 minutes to finish this paragraph."

I sank into the chair and breathed out, anxiously, all the air that had collected in my lungs.

And now what? Noodles, seafood, meat? Junk food, my staple diet, was out of the question. I could not imagine lips such as Lidia's shining with the thick animal fat of a Sicilian pizza or a fried chicken, corrupted by synthetic hormones and monosodium glutamate. A hamburger overflowing with mustard and ketchup upon the immaculate whiteness of her hands seemed to me a profanity. For her, food would have to be the transparent green of her eyes, the softness and paleness of her skin, the floral aroma which she exuded in the mornings. Salads of tender lettuce, asparagus and hearts of *palmito*, grilled salmon, prawns in garlic, slices of duck resting in the discreet beige of a mushroom sauce… I imagined while I was waiting for her. Once I had decided the basic characteristics of the meal, the question was where. It's surprising how difficult it is to decide where to eat, even in a city like San José which is buzzing with restaurants. The quality of the food was crucial, and a priority, of course – but the atmosphere also mattered. I thought about a peaceful, warm place that, nonetheless, would not have a romantic air. An elegant place that was not ostentatious (moderation seemed to be the main organising principle of her beauty?) and, besides, it should be fairly close to the newspaper. To summarise, this choice taxed me greatly since I am not what you call a man of vast gastronomic culture, and what I frequent most of all – when I do decide to abandon the voluntary seclusion of my apartment – are cantinas that smell of piss and fry-ups.

The figure of Lidia, smiling from the door, with her youthful clothes and her handbag, surprised me as I drifted in anxious indecision.

"Shall we go?"

I got up in one go – put on my jacket and as I went out, collided with a leg of the desk. I almost fell head over heels but I was saved by the narrowness of my cubicle in which there is always a wall at arm's length. How true, I have to admit, is the phrase that every misfortune hides at least one advantage.

"What do you fancy eating?" I improvised a question to rescue me.

She shrugged her shoulders and looked serious, perhaps because of the responsibility I had suddenly thrust upon her.

"I don't know," she said, but a moment later her face lit up. "For days I've fancied eating some Mexican tacos. What do you think?"

"Great," I said, relieved. "I know a couple of places."

And then, outside the building, came something absolutely predictable. She turned naturally towards the prehistoric cart, which she called 'your car'. "We are going in your car, aren't we?" And what was I going to say? Let's go in your Bee-Em-Double U automatic, with electric windows, central locking, air-conditioning, a car that her husband probably gave her on some birthday and which was the only pompous thing about her? I opened the door twisting the key that neither opened nor closed anything because the keyhole had rusted away seven years ago. I put the pile of books and old newspapers with which I usually travel at my side for lack of better company, and with huge and badly disguised shame, on the back seat. However, she seemed to be happy, or she faked it with exquisite skill, in that ancient artefact.

"I was curious to go in your car," she commented when the motor started. "They say that cars reflect a lot about the personality of their owner."

"Really? This is a bad-tempered car," I said with genuine astonishment.

"Not at all," Lidia smiled. "I would say that it is a spontaneous car," – she underlined the word 'spontaneous' by searching for my eyes – "and very welcoming. The only thing missing is that somebody needs to organise it a little."

The sweetness of her words were on the point of killing me. Curiously, after first causing a pleasant sensation, they had the effect of a punch. My soul hurt, which I presume must be located near the bone at the base of the sternum, where your school chums thump you to wind you.

We arrived at the last place in the city that would have occurred to me: a café selling Mexican snacks, smelling of pork fat and some spicy sauces, which offered 20 minutes of a *mariachi* serenade to diners while they ate lunch.

When the *charros* were not bursting our eardrums with their trumpets we talked about what colleagues talk about when they are not in the office: work. Although I confess I found it enormously difficult to concentrate while I was looking at her and trying not to imagine how it would be to caress that red hair, or to take those impeccable white hands between my own, or to kiss those defiant lips, tinted with a warm animal fat. I admit that, seen from a rational and objective point of view, the incidents in the restaurant do not justify my mad illusion, which has me on the point of reaching for a glass of vodka, dancing a bolero, writing poetry or throwing myself out of the window of this damned apartment into the wild bohemian night. If I have to be honest, I have to admit that – apart from my lascivious thoughts – everything was correct and appropriate, perhaps a little rigid on my part since I have lost fluidity in my dealings with women. And yet there is something about her that nurtures my hope, enigmatic fluids that connect us beyond words and gestures, beyond skin and eyes. Am I dreaming?

12

Maricruz held out her hand and her fingers brushed the telephone. She only had to press six keys (a combination of figures that she couldn't get out of her head) and her problems would be solved. It was enough to adopt a neutral tone, ask for a date with a strictly professional purpose and ask Gustavo for the information he had offered her a few days before, when it had occurred to her (at that time it seemed like fun, less so now) to invent the story of her imminent marriage. She had tried it several times that morning and, on each occasion, an uncontrollable fear had made her step back.

Once again, Pedro was her shoulder to cry on. At mid-morning she took him to a nearby park, far from the indiscreet ears of her colleagues, and she poured out the whole story of her botched manoeuvre.

"I don't know what's going on. I must be going mad," she concluded. "I thought that the idiot would throw himself to the ground like a worm."

"Humiliate himself? Is that your idea of love?"

"Of course," she opened her arms in a cross as if to express that obvious truth. "Love is a vocation and service always requires a little bit of humiliation – to modulate the vanity."

"What you want is that the man lowers his defences so that you can dictate the rules of the game. Love, sweetheart, is still all about power," sighed Pedro. "Okay, so now what are you thinking of doing?"

"Not me, you, my dear friend Pedro, who has never let me down. Call your cousin and ask him for the promised information, which will give Gustavo a good excuse to come looking for me?"

"Absolutely not," said Pedro, jumping up. "The time has come for you to humilate yourself. Pick up the telephone, call your Romeo and tell him that this story of the marriage was a lie, a wicked strategy to ensnare him. And by the way, ask him for the information for your story."

"You are crazy," Maricruz was astonished.

However, she would have drunk from that bitter cup, in line with Pedro's recommendation, had it not been for a combination of things that fate (if fate exists) concocted. When she had summoned sufficient courage to call Gustavo, his secretary told her that he was out of the office and that he would not be back until after midday. She didn't leave a message. She thought about trying to leave one, but soon afterwards she received an unexpected call from the mysterious José Manuel Sandoval. He was calling, he said, from somewhere in Colombia, where he had heard about her interest in another meeting with him, which coincided with his interest in passing on some new and interesting clues to her. The difficulty was that it was not a matter to be discussed over the telephone, but if he went home he would be in grave danger. It was to be supposed, besides (supposed right, thought Maricruz) that the newspaper would not be prepared to cover the expenses of her trip to Bogotá. So he proposed to meet in a few days in the Panamanian capital, where they could talk for as long as needed. He would call again in the afternoon, he said, to pin down details.

Again she faced a serious dilemma. To travel to Panama to interview a guy who, from any way you looked at it, was sinister and unpredictable and, by her rules, extremely dangerous. On the other hand, considering how he had insisted on her obtaining another interview, Mr Grey would pay, uncomplainingly, the expenses of her trip to Panama, but he would not consider paying for a companion. He would probably ask her to risk her life for the future of the business and in the name of some mysterious professional principle.

"Certainly," Juan José agreed, "a big risk is involved. You risk your neck and the company gives you no protection, won't even buy you a life insurance policy. What's more, if they kill you, I don't think they'll say a mass for you in gratitude, the old atheist would think that a waste of money. If you don't want to go, the gringo will never hear about this phone call, as if it never existed."

Maricruz nodded. After all, she thought, it was more comfortable and safer. Why play Russian roulette if, in any case, the firm would never value her gesture? Nor did she think that Sandoval would come up with evidence. If he had not done so in the beginning, why should she imagine he would do so now? She was about to thank the editor and accept his silence, but finally she told herself that no reasoning could dampen her appetite for answers. However much she thought about it and however great the risks, she would end up deciding to go.

"I can't refuse," she confessed. "I would go mad thinking that perhaps I had lost a golden opportunity to get to the bottom of the matter."

"I knew that would be your answer," said Juan José. "You're like a dog who scoffs eggs without even burning his nose. What we'll do is try to get the gringo to pay for someone to go with you. What's more. I volunteer."

"Really?" Maricruz was happy. "You would go with me?"

"To the ends of the world," said the editor, removing with elegant reverence an imaginary Cordobés hat.

It was not as difficult as they thought. In a matter of hours, Mr Grey had done a deal with an airline in exchange for some publicity and obtained trips to the Panamanian capital for them.

Two days later they descended at the Omar Torrijos international airport to an irascible city peppered with popular protests which the soldiers of General Manuel Antonio Noriega were trying to suppress with sticks and tear gas. Public employees, to whom the military government was trying to deny part of their salaries, were in the streets demanding full pay immediately. The unemployed were seeking new jobs or new subsidies. The political opposition was demanding electoral guarantees.

The situation seemed perfect to kill two birds with one stone. Juan José took advantage of the trip to compile information, undertake interviews and take photographs to be used in two big reports about the Panamanian crisis. However, the meeting with Sandoval was so problematic that they had to prolong their stay by four days. They had agreed that the informant would call Maricruz at the Hotel Costa Rica on Thursday morning, the day of their expected arrival in Panama, but the flight was delayed by three hours and the first attempt at making contact failed. Sandoval did not call again until Friday. They agreed to meet in a restaurant in the shopping centre, but on the same day, a few hours before they were to meet, a bloody clash broke out between university students and riot police from the defence forces. In the midst of the desperate confusion, once again the meeting did not take place.

They met finally on Saturday at a café near the American zone, although in a tense atmosphere because the presence of Juan José, of which Sandoval had not been informed earlier, made him nervous. The man seemed anxious, he had lost weight and had dark rings (Maricruz did not recall seeing them at the first interview) under his eyes, which added a shadowy aspect to his sterile glare. As soon as he realised that Juan José was there, Sandoval took Maricruz to one side and reproached her for not having warned him in advance that she would be accompanied by a bodyguard.

"He's not a bodyguard," Maricruz protested boldly. "Juan José Montero is the editor of my newspaper. Whether you like it or not, it is he who will decide whether what we have here will be published. So you either accept us as a package or we will all have wasted our valuable time."

"He does not inspire trust in me," Sandoval resisted. "And you know well what I have risked."

"You can trust him as much as me. Juan José is an experienced and serious professional."

The man hesitated for a few seconds, observed from a distance the portly journalist with knitted eyebrows, and smiled with a trace of malice.

"Are you afraid of me?" he asked.

"Your air of mystery does not impress me, Mr Sandoval. I am a young journalist but I have spent several years reporting on news and I have met many rough and dangerous types. You don't seem so threatening."

"Are you sure?"

"I said you don't seem it, but neither do I know who you are, where you come from or what you are up to. Was there a particular reason why I should have come alone?"

Maricruz fired off the question with the conscious intention of finding out just how cynical he was. She put her hands in the pockets of her jeans, stood with her feet slightly apart and waited for his answer while she stared confidently at Sandoval.

The mocking look on his face disappeared suddenly. He looked at Juan José again, quickly scrutinised the place and shrugged his shoulders. "It's okay," he gave in without answering her question. "We all made an effort to get here, let's not go backwards now."

Maricruz nodded triumphantly and pointed to the table where, chain-smoking, serene but alert, Juan José followed the scene out of the corner of his eye, ready to intervene if necessary.

"I'll be honest with you," said the editor after the ritual of introductions, "the owner of the newspaper has the idea that you have some very useful information, information that is vital to clear up the massacre at La Cruz and its links with the Psycho. However, I am sceptical. I've come to the conclusion that this is about manipulating us for some reason that I don't know, and in fact you know nothing about this matter."

"So, why have you come to meet me?" he said, and his thin lips elongated in a sign of irritation.

"We are paid a wage, we follow orders."

"What Mr Montero is trying to say," Maricruz tried to soften her companion's tone, "is that we need clearer elements to arm a story. Everything you gave us the other time might seem coherent, more or less, but we don't have a single bit of proof to back it up. Do you understand? In journalism we cannot simply go on what is said by someone whom we cannot even identify publicly, much less when it's about a delicate matter such as this."

"I gave you documents, cassettes. What more do you want?"

"We don't know how genuine they are."

"To prove the authenticity of this evidence is your job, not mine," Sandoval shrugged his shoulders. Then, he made a gesture that Juan José interpreted as an unconscious show of arrogance. "I have run risks to give you important clues... I have spent money that I don't have to come here to collaborate with your newspaper and all I hear are absurd reproaches."

"We are not reproaching you for anything," said Maricruz. "On the contrary, we appreciate that you have put yourself out so much. We're only trying to make you understand what our limitations are in using the information."

"Why are you talking in the plural? What you are saying now is not what your friend has said," Sandoval looked angrily at the expressionless face of Montero.

"I said that I'm sceptical and I am, but I have nothing personal against you," Juan José tried to rectify what he had said. His words were a conscious provocation, aimed at testing the man's temperament, and in just a few moments he was able to form a picture of just how potentially aggressive he could be.

"Alright," said Sandoval. "Ultimately, I don't care what I do with the information. I'm going to share with you my latest findings, and that will be all. Don't keep looking for me, don't pressure me, because I have no need nor wish to pursue this game."

The man had discovered, through means he did not want to reveal, that the crimes of the supposed Psycho were also the work of the Clan, just like the murder of a former security minister and a wave of armed attacks on bank agencies, petrol stations and other commercial establishments. It was all part of a campaign of terror – he explained – an attempt to push people into extreme panic, to demonstrate the incompetence of democracy and sow a widespread discontentment with institutions and established powers. There would be more murders of women – he predicted – and the authorities would not be able to prevent them because they were lashing out wildly, looking for the killer among common criminals. By the time the Clan starts claiming responsibility for its attacks, not against innocent civilians but against clearly identified political objectives, the bourgeois power would be so weakened that the people would hail them as heroes, thousands of people would come together and the revolution would finally be inevitable.

Juan José suppressed a smile.

"That," he said, "sounds ridiculous, if you'll pardon me."

"Yes," Sandoval replied, "all political strategy sounds ridiculous as long as it has not triumphed. It might be no more than a couple of dilettantes, but they are convinced they're going to win."

"Terrorism hasn't triumphed in any part of the world," Juan José assured him.

"That's usually what people think. What happens, in reality, is that terrorist tactics stop being useful from a position of power, or in any case, they give them other names. Generally, they are called exemplary justice. What is the death penalty if not a form of terrorism? What does the judge do when he orders capital punishment if not claim revenge or intimidate society, to warn others of the horrifying punishments that are applied for certain crimes. The point is that there is a terrorism justified by power and another justified from the perspective of rebellion, but essentially they are the same."

"You might be right," said Juan José, "however, we are not interested in a theoretical discussion. What we need is proof this movement is responsible for the crimes."

"I can't give you the proof you want."

"But you said you had..." Maricruz interrupted with a trace of anxiety in her voice.

She had put all her hope on this interview. She had believed it could transform the course of the journalistic investigation and, at the very least, make the police think about a new hypothesis.

Now came this idiot with the story that he had no proof of anything, which was equal to saying that the journey was a waste of time and money. It meant that they would have to put up with tirades from Mr Grey and several weeks of intolerable pressure.

"I said that I had clues," said Sandoval, "very important clues. If you want proof, you will have to look for this on your own."

"What clues?" asked Juan José, no less disappointed than Maricruz.

Sandoval searched in his jacket pocket, took out a photograph and showed it to her. In it appeared a man and a woman. She was young and attractive, with lively eyes, wavy chestnut brown hair and a perfect smile. He looked a little older, he was thin, of average height and with a thick beard with a few white hairs. Both were posing for the camera and embraced as friends do when they appear in photographs.

"This," he explained, "was Lucía, who I told you about. The man at her side is the new chief of the organisation. His *nom de guerre* is Braulio, but his true identity would surprise you."

"Surprise us," said Maricruz.

"He is called Adrián Gómez. He is the eldest son of Hipólito Gómez, a man who is heavily involved in the security bodies and who in the 1950s occupied some very important positions in the public forces. Adrián looks inoffensive, but he has no scruples and he can be terribly violent."

"What kind of clue is that?" Juan José groaned. "There must be violent or potentially violent guys in the country by their millions."

"That is not the clue, that is an introduction," said Sandoval. "The clue is this: according to the police, the victims as much from the crime of La Cruz as from the supposed Psycho were killed by an automatic machine-gun M-3. If you don't know, this type of weapon was brought to the country by the government during the 1950s. It is an antiquated gun, which the United States used in the Korean war and got rid of afterwards by selling it to third world countries, such as Costa Rica. All these weapons should be in the arsenal of the Ministry of Public Security, but what is certain is that some of their officials took them home. Some are registered, others not. But it would not be difficult to follow the trail. Hipólito is one of those officials who kept an M-3 at home, and I'm told that Adrián has it in his possession."

"The police say the weapon used to kill the women at the Cruz de Alajuelita had been stolen from the house of a former minister by the men who were accused of the crime."

"No, no – it seems one M-3 of several that are in the hands of individuals was stolen from the house of this man," Sandoval corrected, "but no one can confirm that it is the same one used to kill the women. What's more, I believe the police have based their investigation on this false trail to mount their hypothesis. How do you explain that two of the supposed killers at La Cruz are dead and the other two are in prison and that they have carried on killing women with the same weapon?"

"They say there was a fifth man involved," said Maricruz, "and that he is still free. The authorities suppose that this person, whom they have been unable to identitfy, is the Psycho."

"If that was true, the police would have identified him by pressuring the others. Do you believe that the police have no way of making a criminal talk, however reluctant he might be? The way to solve this case is to find the murder weapon."

"And where is the weapon?" asked Juan José.

"Investigate this Mr Gómez, follow his steps carefully and he will take you to the weapon. I'm sure of it."

"We are not the police," Maricruz objected. "Following someone is not the kind of work that we do."

"Well...perhaps you have connections in the police. They can do it," he suggested.

That was it. Sandoval repeated part of what he had said in the first interview and insisted it would be the last time he helped the journalistic investigation, that he would return to Colombia on the first plane leaving that day, and that neither they nor anyone else would hear from him for a very long time.

13

For the first time in several months, Juan José felt optimistic, light, as if he was undergoing a kind of internal rebirth. He whistled the tune of a merengue in the newsroom, lobbed a couple of jokes at the news reporters and gave a sweet pastry to the culture editor, which she accepted politely while blushing.

After a black coffee and a cake for breakfast, he went unhurriedly to the office of Mr Grey. He carried in his hand a portfolio with the final product of two months' intense work by himself, Maricruz and two other journalists. A jewel – he thought – a work of art of investigative journalism. For a moment he managed to believe that those six pages would have the power to turn back the clock and put things in their proper place. For a moment he imagined Bill Grey concentrating on the financial matters of the newspaper and keeping his hands out of the editorial operation.

The six pages contained the first of several reports about a political-military brotherhood that called itself the Clan that was apparently responsible for the last wave of attacks on petrol stations, supermarkets and bank branches throughout the country. It drew attention to coincidences in the modus operandi in each one of these attacks; put into relief the surprising ease with which their authors had managed to escape once they had committed their crimes; transcribed declarations from some authorities who confessed their confusion about the skills of the criminals; identified their boss as the son of a former high-ranking security official, without revealing his name, and indicated the presence of several leftwing militants in its rank and file, among other discoveries. Finally, it promised for the next day's edition an astonishing revelation about the massacre at La Cruz and the killings attributed to the Psycho.

Mr Grey looked like a sad puppy as he listened to the whole story, detail by detail, about how they had been able to weave this impressive fabric from Sandoval's clues.

"Now," said Juan José jokingly, "at what beach are we going to spend our paid vacation?"

"I always keep my word and you will have your vacation," replied the gringo, "but this does not interest me."

"What do mean?" the editor moved away from the arms of the sofa, scared of slumping on to it.

"This is pure fiction," groaned Mr Grey, "and now I have more urgent matters for you to investigate. For example, I want you to investigate this construction firm," he indicated a pile of correspondence, "and to find out everything bad you can, unfinished contracts, tax offences, private adventures of the owners... Even better if we can pile on them sodomy or paedophilia. I am going to destroy this bastard or my name is not William H. Grey."

Juan José stood up, put the palm of his hand on the desk and edged his face as close as possible to the haggard features of Mr Grey.

"I want to understand: are you telling me that you don't want the report for which you made us travel to Panama, for which you were ruining our lives and for which you made us work like galley slaves for weeks? Do you want me to throw it in the trash can, to tell the reporters that it's a piece of shit and they know where they can stick it? Is that what you are ordering me to do?"

"Don't use that tone with me," said Mr Grey, who got up halfway but could not hold the position and fell back heavily on to his chair. "The only thing I want is for you to investigate this firm for me and that we turn it to dust."

"I'm going mad," Juan José gripped his hair with genuine desperation, without deliberately trying to be theatrical, but with the therapeutic intention of refraining from a fist fight.

"This idiot took away all his advertising. He wants to ruin us and it's your fault," Mr Grey shouted.

Juan exclaimed with a choleric laugh that distorted his features: "It's my fault?"

"Yes, sir," the gringo assured him. "You allowed us to publish that article about the housing developments and we became enemies of the Montoya brothers, one of the most powerful companies in the construction industry, in case you didn't know. A pile of shit, a real pile of shit Mr Montero. All the journalists in this country are damned Bolsheviks, they hate businessmen and attack them without motive, and make me bankrupt into the bargain."

Juan José sat down again. Or rather, so big and heavy was he that he slumped into the chair, and then he smiled. All the anger and feeling of impotence drained out of him and were sucked towards the far reaches of his soul, in the same way the shit vanishes into the abyss of the lavatory when we flush the chain. He looked at Mr Grey and his smile became a thick, suffocating laugh.

"Don't laugh," said Mr Grey, looking at him popeyed.

"Now we are not making sense," said Juan José, using the plural with the intention, perhaps unconscious, of his words being not a direct allusion to the director's mental health but collective self-criticism. "A few months ago, you removed me from my responsibilities, you yourself censor the articles, you revise what is allowed to go through and now you want to blame me for your mistakes. There's more, the day that this article was published, I was in Panama, working on this bloody thing."

The director and president of the newspaper was going through one of the worst periods of his life. To his self-imposed routine, which including leading the daily meeting of the editors and heads of design, the revision of advertising, distribution issues, administrative problems and the closure of the national news edition, a new element had been added: the personal inspection of the printing processes.

Everything began with a misprint in a page of advertising, which led to a protest from the client. With the aim of placating the customer, Mr Grey offered to publish the advert again for free and decided to remain that night to revise the proofs to ensure that this time it would go out without mistakes. After an hour and a half in the printroom, while he was waiting for the proofs, he was able to make an alarming diagnosis about the lassitude and inexperience that dominated that part of production, a part – he said to himself – that was essential for the success of the whole firm. On the following day he summoned the staff concerned and made a sensible analysis about the importance of reaching the highest level of quality, of maintaining the machines in tip-top condition and observing any technical indications with particular care. To guarantee such results, he told them, he would make the sacrifice of personally supporting the printing process, bringing his vast experience in the field of graphic arts. It would be a matter of a few days, he excused himself to the head of the print room, until he managed to get things on track.

He had spent a month leaving the newspaper between two and three in the morning. He would arrive home with his ulcer in flames, on the verge of tears because of his sciatica and with his mind blank. He would drink a glass of milk and fall into a restless and desperate sleep that lasted two or three hours before starting his work day with the conviction that life is no more than the infinite repetition of a single day, each one identical to the last.

He grew thinner, his eyes became more bulging and his jaw sharper, his ears gave him a Dracula-like look that was frightening at a distance. Little by little, he lost his concentration. Despite boasting that he had the memory of an elephant, he mixed up the names of his employees and mistook the day and time of appointments, which obliged Majorie to make a superhuman effort to deal simultaneously with his mail, his memorandums and make the telephone calls he had ordered and to interrupt him every half an hour to remind him of the next item on his agenda. At times, he could be seen wandering around the corridors for no apparent reason, his scant hair unruly, and looking bewildered. Halfway through a telephone conversation he might confuse the identity of his interlocutor or abruptly change the subject.

It was the era in which the newspaper changed its editorial line 17 times in one month. One day he ordered all the journalists to focus on financial angles: politics and finance, finance and sport, public finance, private finance, pure finance. Two days later he was ranting on about how the sections of news, election politics and society had been neglected. One week he was demanding that they dig deeper into health and education problems and the next he was declaring that all that was a waste of time and resources and they had to focus on the world of theatre. And when the newspaper was boiling with hot news, he became obsessed with exposing corruption scandals. The journalists tried to adjust to the changes as fast as they could, but some felt so confused that they always remained two or three steps behind. That increased the gringo's nervousness, aggravated his bad mood and made him more prone to nonsense.

"What?"

"That I was in Panama when that article was published so the only person who is directly responsible is you," Juan José repeated with a triumphant smile.

"Is it possible?" Mr Grey asked indifferently. "I am under so much pressure that I no longer know what day it is."

He stood up and paced around the office, pausing to contemplate the wall with Monet's *Nymphs*, which excercised a kind of hypnotic attraction over him, and he remembered a day in Moscow. The high towers of the Kremlin and a long line of workers wearing thick jackets and Cossack hats and each with a piece of dried fish under their arm, waiting in line to acquire their small luxury, a jug of German beer. If it had not been for that afternoon, he thought, and for that gallery of prints next to the bar, which he had only entered to warm up a bit, he would not have known Camila, the woman who stopped at his side as he observed Monet's *Nymphs*, nor would he have collided with his journalistic vocation, nor would he have discovered his business skills. He would still be a world traveller, a stinking North American hippie smoking marijuana in whatever corner of whatever European city, washing plates or weeding gardens to be able to eat and smoke.

"Which article did you want to publish?" The gringo stopped, his gaze wandering, still full of that wintery Moscow landscape, on to the undaunted face of the editor.

"The investigation of the Clan, the matter is linked to the Psycho. Do you remember?"

"Okay, publish it tomorrow."

"It's in two instalments."

"Tomorrow and the day after then."

"Aren't you going to go over the article?"

"Why? If I revise it, I will certainly not agree with it, I will ask you to write it again and you will get in a bad mood. Isn't that right? Rather leave it as God would have it."

"Okay," Juan José shrugged his shoulders and left the room as quickly as possible.

"As God would have it is merely an expression, because you will know that I am an atheist from philosophical conviction," said Mr Grey without realising that Juan José was no longer in the room.

But the worst of all was that he had discovered that Camila was cheating on him. With his own eyes he had observed the sweet Camila of his sorrows, naked, sweaty and carried away in the arms of Mr Nobody. Camila, speaking deliriously in an obscene and febrile Italian that she never used with him. Camila, prisoner of a bestial orgasmic tension, which had so often made him both happy and unhappy in a similar trance, the kingdom of an ecstasy which he had thought exclusively his. How he regretted returning home that day without warning, how he regretted his stealth, his incontrollable curiosity, his masochism. If he had at least been able to tell her that he had witnessed it all, if he had been capable of reproaching her, of abandoning her forever or killing her in the act...but he scarcely managed to feel a slight wave of nausea. A sense of physical ill-health...and, afterwards, nothing, or almost nothing. He did not remember if that was how jealousy was for her or other women in his life but everything he felt inside seemed more like fear. Yes, he was afraid of losing her, that one day she would go away and his whole world would collapse like a fairytale. Camila had the keys to the kingdom of his fantasy and a single gesture of her hand could erase the present and cancel the future.

"A fiendish mess, that's what he said, in those words. And you're the one to blame for spreading rumours to encourage that journalist's fantasies of being a detective."

The officer observed his boss with his sad rabbit's eyes.

"It seems that the boss is pretty pissed off with you."

Gustavo shrugged his shoulders. "It's been weeks since I've seen Maricruz. I haven't even talked to her on the phone. The truth is that if Don Jovel knew her he would realise that there's no need to spread any rumours at all to her."

"The fact is the story is not easy to believe," García admitted. "The chick must be a bit soft in the head, don't you think?"

"No insults, she's my friend."

"That's what they're saying around here," the officer gave him a mocking smile, which Gustavo chose to ignore.

"Besides, I have a hunch, I believe that although the version is essentially false, it might contain some key which could help to clarify this 'fiendish mess', to use Don Jovel's words."

"But how, boss? We already have a suspect."

"We have a suspect, sure, but we haven't solved the case. Besides, think about this: the attacks are fact, we also think they have been committed by a well-organised group, with resources and access to certain information. We have no proof that there is a political motive but neither do we have reasons to discount it. The only thing that doesn't square with the newspaper is that there is a link between these facts and the Psycho's attacks, but at least half or a third of this could be along the right lines. For now, let's make a list of all the people who fit the characteristics of this guy that the newspaper says is head of the Clan."

"She must know. Why don't you ask her?" García suggested mischievously.

"Getting information out of a reporter is not as easy as you might think."

The first difficulty, Gustavo imagined, lay in re-establishing the relationship after the unfortunate last date. Maricruz would probably not be interested in talking to him, but more than this he was worried whether he himself would be capable – confronted by her olive-green eyes, her cruel smile – of appearing spontaneous and of concealing the deep resentment that he felt. What should he talk to her about? He would be obliged to stick to subjects that were strictly to do with work, and his conversation would have a tone so unnatural that it would end up making his feelings clear. Otherwise, in a fit of spite, he would direct at her all the reproaches eating up his soul like worms but that he had kept to himself because of pride.

To marry for convenience, for comfort, to someone you don't love at all because he had not been capable of telling her he loved her at the precise moment that she had wanted him to. He was sure that this was the true reason. The truth is that women never stop being capricious girls, capable of ruining their own lives and those of others when they're in the grip of an illusion of passing rage. Moreover, he wanted to forget it, pretend to have forgotten it, to let his defences down. Yes, he was hurt and confused, he recognised that, and it was a good decision to stay away from the little snake – but work must come first, and personal issues had to be subordinated to professional duty, as had always been the case before Maricruz. To work against such a principle was to continue being enslaved to emotional blackmail. So he picked up the telephone, dialled the number of the newspaper, and asked for Miss Miranda.

At the other end of the line, she had a dizzy turn on hearing his voice, although she had been totally convinced that such a call would take place, since Gustavo would not be able to resist the challenges she had thrown out, obliquely, with those reports.

"You can imagine the reason for my call," Gustavo adopted a tone which he imagined would sound neutral and professional. "I am referring to the articles. Can we talk about them?"

"Of course, when?"

"As soon as possible, if possible today. What time?"

"At seven o'clock at your house," Maricruz suggested.

"At my house? It could be somewhere else, if you like...we could meet at..."

"At your apartment," she insisted. "If it's not there, there won't be any meeting."

He agreed, nervous and confused.

It was a long, strange day. He reached the conclusion that the girl just wanted to amuse herself, to put him in an uncomfortably intimate situation to see how he would react to her charms. She wanted to see him suffer, perhaps with the unconscious need to nurture her ego, to feel loved, desired and at the same time forbidden, the vanity game from time immemorial which some women are able to practise until it aches.

The day became even stranger with the meeting with Aurelia Carranza, whom he had not seen for several weeks. They met in the lift but Gustavo found it hard to recognise her. She was not wearing her thick spectacles, she looked thinner and less formal. She had cut and dyed her hair in soft brown tones which harmonised with her marvellous, mellifluous eyes.

"What a transformation!" He exclaimed on meeting her.

She smiled, conscious – and probably satisfied with the effect – of her change.

"It's good to bump into you. I was going to call you because I have something very interesting to tell you. Can you come to my office?"

"Right now?"

"I think it would be best right away."

Gustavo was going to lunch but he agreed to follow her. Once in the office, Aurelia seemed indecisive. She seemed nervous and she talked around some casual topics, as if avoiding the issue, as if regretting at the last minute.

"Is something wrong?" he asked, noting her strange behaviour.

"Promise me total discretion. The truth is that I'm frightened. It's about the case at the Cruz," Aurelia rubbed her hands. "Yesterday I interrogated a witness, someone very close to the suspects. We talked for more than two hours and it seemed to me that the guy softened a bit and took me into his confidence and made a confession that he probably would not have made in other circumstances. He told me that not four but five men took part in the crime."

Gustavo paused for a few moments to consider that revelation, a fact that fitted splendidly with the theory of Aníbal Pedroso.

"It could be the information that we are waiting for to solve the case. Did he tell you who it is?"

"No way. When I asked him to reveal the identity of this person, he went crazy. He flew into a panic and started shouting that he could not, that why had he opened his mouth, that he would prefer to be in jail than to be the target of revenge from a guy like this. The only thing I could get out of him was that it was a guy with a lot of power – to judge by his reaction."

"We would have to interrogate him," Gustavo thought in a loud voice.

"Don't even think of it," Aurelia Carranza jumped out of her chair. "If the man suspects that I gave you this information, I don't know what could happen to me. Gustavo, it's a very dangerous situation."

"I'm not thinking about doing anything that could put you in danger. I assure you, but somehow we have to get that information."

"There's something else, something that seemed even stranger to me," the judge said with an uncertainty in her voice, telling herself perhaps that now there was not much to lose.

Gustavo looked at her with incredulity, pondering how everything about this case was strange, confused and elusive. What else could happen that would confuse it even more?

"He says that at the scene there was a sixth person, a woman who was not one of the victims. He would not identify her, but at least he confirmed to me that she was a close friend of one of the suspects, a kind of girlfriend, lover... I don't know."

"He said a woman?"

"When he referred to her he called her the Kid, from which I deduce she was quite young."

"It's strange alright. It's the strangest thing I've heard about this case so far, stranger even that the reports in *El Matutino*. Have you read them?"

"Yes. They seem absurd. By their account everything bad that happens in the country is a political conspiracy. Not even common crime exists."

Gustavo nodded, although he did not agree with everything the judge said. In the journalistic version there was a dark element, a detail that resisted analysis, but whose importance he could sense. It was not a conviction, just a sensation that at times grew stronger. He had read the articles over and over again, underlining phrases, extracting them from their context to place alongside each other, interchanging them in a game of association that he often engaged in and that sometimes enabled him to read between the lines. Yet nothing clear had emerged and his intuition continued to nag at him. That was why he had undertaken, slightly embarrassed, to meet up with Maricruz again. Perhaps, without knowing it, she would have the answer.

"It's difficult to imagine a woman being involved in a crime like this," said Aurelia, "that's why I doubt whether it's true."

"Are you one of those people who think that evil is only a masculine attribute?"

"Of course not. But I do feel that the perversity of men and women finds distinct forms of expression. Perhaps it's because of our weaker constitution, but we tend more to cause psychological harm; men, by contrast, have a greater propensity to physical brutality."

"If it's true what this individual says, the woman could have participated solely as an observer."

"Perhaps under pressure," suggested the judge. "Remember that before the victims turned up, the group had been drinking and taking drugs. If we add to this the supposition that we are dealing with a young girl, you must expect that she did not have the character or willpower to object, first to the rapes and then to the killings. What's important is that if we manage to identify her she could be a key witness, no?"

"It's a good analysis, except for the last bit, the bit about her giving testimony," said Gustavo.

"Why?"

"Because she's dead," he asserted.

Aurelia was astounded. The sharpness of thought and the unforeseeable way in which the homicide chief reached certain conclusions had forged his reputation throughout the Judicial Police. It was said that he possessed a kind of premonitory ability, that he was even clairvoyant. She recognised his skill at affecting an air of mystery to make himself interesting, but this was too much. How could he reach such a conclusion when they weren't even sure the person existed?

"It's intuition," he tried to explain, "but reasonable at that. I'm thinking that everything the person you interrogated told you, about the fifth man and the presence of the woman, is true."

Aurelia challenged him: "Who, then, is the fifth man?"

"If I knew, I would have the case of the Psycho wrapped up," said Gustavo, "but for that I need to discover a way for your man to give us the information without compromising you."

He did not know why exactly, but at the end of that improvised discussion, when he was just about to leave the office, Gustavo turned to her and asked her the question that perhaps he should have asked long before or perhaps he should never have asked at all: "Have you decided where to have lunch?" Aurelia shook her head. Then he invited her to have coffee nearby in order to continue the discussion. She looked at him, smiling.

"You're a married man," she said. "You're not trying to seduce me are you?"

He was lost, his tongue tied, hearbeat raised.

"Divorced, and for many years," he managed to say just in time to avoid revealing his timidity, although the same bashfulness stopped him from referring to his real intentions, leaving doubt hanging in the air. Minutes later, when they left the station, the judge broke the silence that had taken hold.

"The truth," she said, "is that I'm not hungry and have very little time. So let's get straight to the point, Gustavo, let's just do what what we are going to end up doing anyway."

He did not have time to decide just how much in agreement he actually was. He had never considered Aurelia Carranza his type, although once he had surprised himself thinking about her white skin, her long neck dotted with freckles, her large breasts. He genuinely liked her, but he had always considered her part of a distant world to which he had not been invited. For this reason, the proposition caused terrible confusion and left him at a loss for words, and all he could do was drive the car to the appropriate place. But, having her there naked in that bed in the motel, sweet and almost timid in her intense whiteness; her eyes gleaming, lips cold and chilled; him falling into her embrace, resting upon the copious flesh of her breasts; he soon felt that he was returning to a warm and longed-for home, to a lost refuge that he never wanted to abandon. He kissed her softly, violently, with nostalgia for all those past and future kisses. He caressed her body centimetre by centimetre, squeezed it, licked it and sucked every crevice with the hunger and thirst of the shipwrecked man. And on penetrating her and hearing the triumphal groan that came from her throat, his whole body exploded with joy in a firework display of sensations that made him extraordinarily happy.

It is absurd, Gustavo said to himself over and over again, absolutely ridiculous. He owed Maricruz nothing, had not tied her down with any type of commitment, no duty of gratitude. On the contrary, it was he who had motive to be annoyed, even to detest her, yet every time he thought about her he was tormented by guilt. A repulsive complex of the unfaithful man churned over in his guts, the disgust of the traitor. Absurd, he said to himself, absolutely ridiculous, but as night approached the sensation of guilt grew stronger and there was no way of exorcising it. It was not that he regretted what he had done. If there was anything good that had happened to him in the last few months (perhaps years) it had been the judge's unexpected gift.

Although out of the ordinary, he thought, that hour and a half in bed had redeemed him. It had made him feel like a man again. A mixture of virile vanity and unexpected tenderness gripped his soul. A magnificent experience that on his part he had no doubt he would prolong, although he was totally ignorant of Aurelia's intentions. They had not talked much before saying goodbye, merely a "thanks a lot, that was nice"... a pair of stock phrases, more like courtesies than the confession of lovers. It could well be, of course, that for her it had been a relief, the mere satisfaction of a whim, and that tomorrow she would send him packing. However, he saw no other obstacle to keep deepening the relationship with Aurelia, if she wanted to.

But in the irrational side of his conscience the guilt persisted. It was as if he had been split in two: a free man, ready for novelty, and a stupid one, faithful to a mirage. The latter, the imbecile, lived through hours of dread thinking that Maricruz – the betrothed, the imminent bride of another – would stumble upon his adventure, that she would read it in the shine in his eyes or in the smell of fresh hormones upon his skin. Who knows what level of incongruence the day would have reached had it not been for that call, one that moved all his emotional energy in another direction, that obliged both to cancel the meeting.

Two dead bodies had been discovered on land next to the highway between San Vicente and Tres Ríos. The man had been shot in the right temple and the woman had been mutilated and finished off with a shot in the left temple. This time, the killer did not have time to play hide-and-seek with the bodies and showed signs of having been surprised. A man passing by heard noises that he thought were suspicious, took a few steps into the thickets and saw the macabre scene illuminated under the light of the full moon. In his statement to the duty officer, he said he had had the fleeting, nearly phantasmagorical vision of a beast dodging between the mallow, leaving behind a sickening wake.

The news also shook the newsroom of *El Matutino*. Mr Grey not only agreed to publish the story but showed particular interest in giving it the best display. However, he was of the opinion that this time they had to put more emphasis on being critical.

"Let's shake up the director of the Judicial Police and the public security minister," he told the head of the newsroom. "Let's make it clear that there is a problem here of ineptitude, make people ask how it is possible that a crude lady killer mocks the state's entire investigative apparatus so easily."

"So the government adverts don't matter to you any more?" responded Juan José.

The gringo sighed.

"If from time to time you had taken the trouble to ascertain how this newspaper is managed, you would have found out that the government withdrew its ads two months ago. But sure, the pure journalist doesn't dirty his mind with matters of money, right?"

"Now I understand," smiled Juan José.

"That's the way it is," the gringo hunched his shoulders, "for better or worse."

Mr Grey was going through a phase of scrutinising how the state functioned. Investigative journalism and biting criticism, he proclaimed like a mantra, which was causing great confusion because just two weeks before he had been obsessed with financial themes. Suddenly, inexplicably, as often happened, something diverted his attention towards matters of public administration. Now it's clear, thought Juan José as the gringo specified some of the epithets that should be applied to the incompetent police officers: the change occurred because he did not manage to convince the government to continue conceding him official advertising. And the newspaper's punishment, he deduced, must be related to its reports about building projects, which had angered the construction group of the Montoya brothers, partners and favoured friends of the transport minister, second cousins of the deputy housing minister, among other close connections.

That reflection illuminated a chain of other thoughts: Mr Grey's abrupt mood changes were, it seemed, related to commercial affairs and not always, or not in a simple and straightforward way, to his mental fluctuations. Perhaps, if he managed to penetrate a little further the winding trail of the finances, he could anticipate certain reactions to newsroom activities that otherwise would continue to appear enigmatic and unpredictable. The problem resided in the fact that that was the exclusive fiefdom of the evil Italian, who openly hated him, although for unknown reasons. Simple racism, he supposed. She never spoke to him unless it was to complain in an authoritarian tone about the excessive telephone bill, to haggle about the staff's days off, arguing that the company operated its own labour regulations, insisting this was legally possible because the lawyer had said so, that the Labour Code only applied to construction and other manual workers. She would keep her distance when addressing him, with a sickened look on her face, and vomit out those and other absurdities in good Spanish although with an Italian accent, then turn her back and return to her remote office refusing to listen to any replies or any type of argument. How could he get close to such a firebrand?

"Okay," said Juan José. "We'll do as you say."

"Can I trust you?" the gringo asked, pointing at him with his long index finger without a nail.

"No, I don't think you can trust me," the head of news said, "but we will do as you ask."

It was quite difficult to convince Maricruz, who considered the journalistic blackmail they wanted to involve her in as immoral.

"You yourself have said that this is inadmissible, that reality cannot accommodate commercial interests," she argued.

"I still think so," said Juan José, "but what is happening this time is that, commercial interests aside, the gringo is right. There are 15 bodies and the police are still wandering about in the dark, they haven't even wanted to comment on our reports. They neither deny nor confirm them, nor do they say anything about anything."

"Tonight I was going to meet Gustavo Cortés," the reporter said.

"Really? Why?"

"I don't know, it was his idea, but I think it was precisely because he wanted to comment on our reports. But then the new victims turned up and we had to cancel the meeting."

"You sound a bit frustrated," the head of news said with irony. "Does attacking your prince in blue worry you? If so, I can assign it to someone else..."

"I'll kill you," Maricruz shouted from her desk. "I've been in this from the start and I'm not going to let anyone take it off me."

"Okay, it's yours... but let's do what the gringo wants. All you have to do is whack those in charge up above, good and hard."

Juan José was convinced that the authorities deserved strong criticism and there was no shortage of experts, analysts and observers ready to share their criticisms at the slightest invitation. All she had to do was formulate the right question and ask the right person and the pages would fill up with censures, reproaches and ridicule, he told the reporter. But, at root, the idea of experimenting with a new strategy was maturing in his mind. Not a strategy of power, because he had begun to doubt that that would be beneficial, or even satisfactory, in that madhouse. What was developing, as a last and desperate resort, was a strategy of survival.

14

Aracelly was a girl. She was just over 15 but already refining her plans to marry Víctor Julio, who was 18. They would marry in a year, if he managed to settle into his new job. They would live with the girl's family for some time while they built a house on the small plot her father had offered Víctor as an early inheritance. A year's savings would pay for the wedding: a bridal gown with a long train, a lively party in a local hall, a studio photograph for posterity and a honeymoon on some Pacific beach. Aracelly particularly liked Samara. The rest would sort itself out on the way. At their age, and under the influence of a Mexican soap opera, one imagines that everything that is not love, desire and pleasure in physical intimacy, is just a trivial extra. Besides, many young people like them were plunging into the nuptial adventure. To be specific, that night they were returning from a wedding of some friends and were walking towards Aracelly's house in the hope of coming across an empty taxi. The road, which was usually dark and solitary, was shining in a moonlight that made it almost seemed like day. In that area houses were scarce, with just one or two dwellings every quarter of a kilometre, small islands in the midst of dense maize and coffee plantations.

"The murderer must have spied on them through the vegetation and emerged as the pair passed," Gustavo said.

"Or waited for them in a car or on a motorbike," Morales added.

"No, I don't believe that," said the homicide chief. "The man who discovered the bodies is sure that he heard the killer flee the scene into the mountain. If it was as you say, the vehicle would have remained in the street."

"That's perfectly logical," said Don Jovel.

"Besides, the killer is far too smart to go around in a vehicle which could be identified at any moment. I am sure he is an assiduous pedestrian, at least when it comes to committing his murders," said Gustavo.

"Any sign of resistance from the victims?" asked Don Jovel.

"Nothing, and the only footprints are those of the girl. The beast seems to fly, he leaves no trace," said Morales.

"Do the forensic studies show that the killer is the same as before?" the director asked.

"There's no doubt," Doctor Meneses drummed his fingers, "there can't be two individuals with this skill and this kind of obsession. Everything fits."

"In that case, we are fucked," said Gustavo. "We don't have a suspect."

The director of police scratched his head with four fingers of his right hand. He seemed tired and impatient.

"Might there be some kind of mistake that in some way has undermined our surveillance?"

"No, sir," Morales assured him. "As there was a full moon, we decided to mount a special operation. All that day we kept a close watch on the subject. He left his house at 7.30pm, we followed his car to the Limón bar and he was there with a woman until 11.30pm. A police officer stayed at the bar the whole time and did not take his eyes off him. Afterwards, he dropped the woman off at her home in the La Cruz district and returned to his place at 12.15pm. By that time the bodies had already been found."

"It's impossible, therefore, for it to have been him..."

"Exactly," said Morales assuredly, "we're back to square one."

What the director most regretted was that Guerra had seemed the perfect candidate: a man with military training, linked to a medical discipline, a keen hunter. The investigation revealed that he had had problems with his mother, although it was not clear whether he had been the victim of abuse or maltreatment during his childhood.

"There may be another lead," said Gustavo.

"Really?" Don Jovel looked at him with astonishment. "You didn't say anything…"

"It's more of a supposition, but it's all we've got right now. It has to do with the articles published by *El Matutino*. But I have to clear up some doubts and when I have something more solid, I'll let you know."

"If I were you, I wouldn't waste my time," said Aníbal Pedroso. "According to my criteria the theory of a collective serial killer cannot be sustained, much less one with political motives."

"To be honest, I don't believe in this theory," the homicide chief stressed. "It's more that it's about some evidence. As I told you, it's just a hunch. Let's see…'

"I hope that this evidence is not the invention of your beloved journalist," said Don Jovel, annoyed. "I've had that up to here…"

He was restless, nervous, almost paranoid. The newspaper reports that morning, with ferocious attacks on the Judicial Police, had caused him more problems in a few hours than the Psycho had in two years. The president of the Supreme Court had phoned him to express his concern at the turn which events were taking; the security minister had also called him to reproach him, in a much less cordial tone, that the bad image (so he did dare to say something quite nasty: 'bad image') of the Judicial Police was sticking to him. Even his wife had taken the liberty of reproaching him for helping out the killer. She reminded him that he had adolescent daughters and told him to put his hand on his heart and think about whether, realistically, he had done everything possible. He didn't even reply, so as not to spoil his breakfast. "All because of this arrogant upstart who you've been flirting with," he unleashed his rage on Gustavo.

"I already told you that this case would bring hassle. Do you remember?"

Instead of reproaching Don Jovel (it did not seem like the right time) he proposed calling a meeting with everyone involved in the case, including Pedroso, in the hope that a free exchange of ideas would shed some light. The boss accepted because nothing better – or worse – occurred to him.

Gustavo gave in to the pressure from his boss. "Someone has sold *El Matutino* the idea of a political conspiracy, it's very elaborate with many details, some of which concur with reliable information that we have. That does not mean that the version has been verified, only that we have verifiable details. A modicum of reality... Do I make myself clear?"

"What's the point?" Don Jovel said with growing impatience.

"The point is that someone is trying to divert our attention. And this someone knows that there is nothing more effective, to convert a fiction into reality, than to spread it through the press. When the media imposes a lie, there is no way back, it doesn't matter how much you try to validate the reality. Who wants to throw us off the trail? I don't know, but I think that if we could identify the newspaper's informant, we might be on a new trail."

"It sounds very interesting," Aníbal Pedroso commented. "There are serial killers, not all but some, who really enjoy getting involved in the investigation, mixing up real clues with false ones, demonstrating their own intelligence."

Maricruz spent three hours looking through the photographic archive of the Judicial Police and an hour and a half looking at the immigration records, but it was useless: the face and the name of José Manuel Sandoval never appeared. He had, for example, no prison record; he had never been investigated seriously for his activities and political links; he had left the country through legal means and the most probable thing was, Gustavo concluded, that the secret informer of *El Matutino* had presented himself to the reporter under a false name. Such results strengthened the suspicion that his story was nothing more than a deliberate attempt to divert attention.

"Would you agree to collaborate in an identity sketch?" Gustavo asked.

After much struggle, the homicide chief had finally managed to take the reporter to the arena of his choice: not an intimate one where they could blend professional interests with the whims of the soul, but the cold police building, packed with people and hustle and bustle. To do that, he had to threaten her with a formal summons.

"There are two ways to do this," he had told her in response to her initial refusal. "Either you come voluntarily, like a good citizen, or I ask the judge to bring you by force."

"You wouldn't do such a thing," she mocked him. "You wouldn't want problems with the press, would you?"

"I have already had enough problems with the press and I am going to have a lot more if we don't manage to unravel this case. I assure you it's the last thing I want to do, but I am prepared to, if it's necessary."

Deep down, what Maricruz had wanted was this meeting, although the scenario was not ideal. Gustavo's insistence meant that her articles had achieved one of their goals, which was to provoke exactly what was now happening without having to resort to the necessity of being humiliated. For that reason, she had given in after putting up stubborn resistance.

The sketch pleased Maricruz as it faithfully reproduced Sandoval's basic features, according to the image in her memory, and it managed to capture the inner shadow that she had detected in his look. The drawing passed through the hands of 40 agents and dozens of police officials, but the face was not recognisable to anyone, except for a secretary for whom it revived a memory that was so distant and imprecise as to be useless.

"Thank you," he addressed himself to the reporter, "for your willing help."

Maricruz got as close to the homicide chief as she could. "Don't treat me like this," she said. "I need to talk to you in private."

Gustavo tried to ignore her. The previous night he had had supper with Aurelia at a pleasant restaurant, and both had managed to dispel their earlier doubts. There existed, they recognised, a mutual attraction before their first sexual encounter but no one imagined that what had happened would be possible. Aurelia was the victim of a prolonged matrimonial catastrophe: six years in which she had made all manner of well-intentioned and futile effort to set things right, until realising and becoming convinced that love either exists between two people or not at all. In practice, she and her spouse merely inhabited the same house – she explained – she was separated and only maintained the façade of a relationship for the emotional stability of their two children. However, during that time she had never been with another man and it was impossible to explain from where the brazenness and cheek had come from with which she had invited Gustavo to her bed that evening. "It was something of the moment," she said. "I felt as though I was drunk." The spark for her reaction, without doubt, was having confirmed that her husband visited a lover, a suspicion she had had for a while with an increasing degree of certainty. It wasn't a surprise, she told him that night – to a certain extent she liked having a solid motive for demanding the divorce she had so often dreamed of.

"You were an escape. In some way I used you and I am truly sorry...but at the same time I swear I have never felt so good about sex and I have never wanted so much to repeat the experience."

"It doesn't matter," he said. "It's rare that relationships begin at zero, generally they begin where others end. A new love comes and turns your life around as the other is leaving."

"How pretty that sounds. You are something of a poet, aren't you?"

"We're all poets in some small way. What's often missing is the muse."

She smiled and stroked his cheeks.

"Who is your muse?" she asked.

He would have liked to have replied it was her, but he could not. As soon as he had uttered the word "muse" his mind had strayed to the olive-coloured eyes, the luscious mouth, the golden skin of Maricruz, her cruel smile. And from something he had read, a memory came to his rescue.

"Melpomene," he answered. "The muse of tragedy."

He tried to ignore her, but here was his Melpomene ready to cause a scandal in front of all the staff of the Judicial Police, gradually raising her voice, saying: "Don't treat me like this, I don't deserve it, I want us to talk," and – because there is nothing that threatened Gustavo Cortés as much as being made to look ridiculous in the work arena – he gave in.

Even in the office of the homicide chief, Maricruz was a bundle of nerves. She fidgeted nervously and her elusive eyes were the murky and confused green of a jungle. She was there, where she had asked to be, but she did not speak. He stood waiting, his arms folded over his chest, in a challenging pose, although his heart was beating.

"It was a lie," she said at last. "The marriage...all that. I made it up that I was going to get married, that I was in a relationship with Jorge Luis. It was a game."

Gustavo's mind went blank. Then it spun: questions, responses, deductions, conjectures, were springing up all over the place, provoking the sensation of a series of brief explosions. A game? How could an adult toy with their own emotions and those of someone else? Isn't a game something that girls play? How could he be so confused about the whole thing? And how could he have fallen in love with a child? Either his rational mechanisms had failed completely or Maricruz was a clinical case of multiple personalities.

"What kind of game is this?" he asked.

"A stupid game," she responded. "I hoped to make you jealous."

That unexpected confession turned everything on its head. A few hours before, for the first time in an eternity, he had had the feeling that his personal life was beginning to fall into place. Aurelia was the mature woman whom reason advised: she had suffered the disenchantment of marriage; she seemed disposed to a broad relationship, to try out a love without conditions or demands. She was not without bitterness but she was imbued with an inexorable practical sense. He told himself that Maricruz had rightly chosen a man of her own age, capable of offering her the attention that her youth and beauty demanded. This time Destiny, Providence, Life or whatever you call the invisible hand that controls everything, had resolved things for everyone in a merciful way. He ignored the fact that the perfect order is an ephemeral state, a casual station in the chaotic movement of the universe.

"I just wanted you to know," she sighed and offered him a wavering hand, "I am afraid of losing you."

Camila Noceti was listening open-mouthed to the editor. He was standing and she sat in front of a pile of bills, her forehead furrowed, with the sour mouth with which she usually greeted the staff. She would have preferred them to address her in Italian or in English, but she understood perfectly the Spanish in which Juan José Montero made his inconceivable revelation.

"What are you saying? Are you completely sure?"

"As I said," Juan José said. "They take out a roll of paper every three days, in the first distribution truck of the morning. They have perfected a system to do it quickly and discreetly. To camouflage the roll that is missing, they accumulate a part of the wasted newspapers to give the impression that there was a huge loss, which is explained by the deterioration of the machinery. Do you understand?"

"And how did you find out about this?"

"Ramiro, the boy who started recently as a newspaper assistant, has become quite friendly with me. He told me that he has nothing to do with these shenanigans but I'm afraid that they will involve him. On the other hand, he didn't want to make the complaint because he didn't want to make enemies in the print room. He considers them dangerous people. The employees that I told you about are the ones involved, including the night guard and the truck driver."

"I understand," said Camila and looked at Juan José in a new way. "We're going to investigate. And you must be discreet. Not a word to anyone."

He nodded. "I would prefer that you didn't associate me with this matter. And as far as Ramiro goes..."

"Don't worry," she interrupted. "If someone has nothing to do with it, someone has nothing to fear."

The information had landed like a ring on her finger. Initially he was in doubt as to whether to report the thieves but he reasoned that all the disgust and resentment he felt towards the gringo were insufficient reason to turn a blind eye. Their differences of opinion were many and deep-seated, but they had nothing to do with the vandalism against the firm that fed him. So he would do it in any case. So, why not get some advantage out of this to benefit his new strategy? Because it's disgusting, he told himself, because it implies acting and a gesture of servitude. There were other ways to let the owners know. Finally, after many long and difficult internal battles, he decided to swallow his scruples stoically, and for once in his life, submit his simple and vulgar opportunist interest to the virtuous conduct which so much stagnation and so much poverty had provided him with.

Two days later the scoundrels came out in handcuffs amid a blizzard of policemen, reporters from the competition, television cameras recording live and direct, curious onlookers who happened to be passing by and others who were there less coincidentally.

"It was exactly as you told me," the Italian told him later. "Bill and I would like to thank you..."

Juan José held out his hand to stop her in her tracks. He was not going to allow his gesture to be interpreted as a favour that could be repaid with money or something like that, as she surely intended to do. The debt would not be settled with a dinner at a luxury hotel or a silver-plated pen engraved with his initials. His gesture, he wanted to make clear, had no material value.

"Please, Camila," he used her first name for the first time. "Don't thank me. I am an employee of this firm and I have a duty to defend it."

"Well, in any case, Bill told me that he owes some paid holidays to you and Maricruz. Take a few days off," she said and she handed him a ticket with his name that entitled him to four days, with everything paid for, at a hotel in front of the intensely blue and calm sea of Ballena Bay.

This morning my head hurts and my mouth tastes like a bird's nest, but it was worth it. The party at Pedro's house was brilliant: beer and whisky in abundance, sandwiches, salsa and merengue until we dropped; solemn drunks, memorable fools. There was something for everyone, including me.

Next, I will relate some facts worth noting:

One. After the ninth or tenth drink, Diana had a great idea. She revealed right there, to everyone's surprise, that being a striptease dancer had always been one of her oldest and most secret dreams. Emboldened by alcohol and the malicious coaxing of some of her friends, she decided to enact her fantasy there at that very moment. To the rhythm of *Gran Vals Brillante*, chosen by the dancer herself who wanted to feel, she said, as if she was in a classic cabaret, she began taking off small items of clothing (her headscarf, her belt, her shoes and stockings) and little by little, dared herself to take off larger items such as her jacket and blouse, until, at the shout of "More!", she removed her jeans. Then she lifted them from the floor and held them in front of Gabriel's face, her shameful and ashamed boyfriend, who made an effort to smile. The joke might have been limited to the innocent display of her legs (long, firm and attractive, to tell the truth), but notes of various denominations began to fall on the carpet and the lights were lowered to create a shadowy atmosphere. Her body made contortions worthy of the Cirque de Soleil, she liberated her bra (or better said, its lean contents) and finished the number by stripping off her panties without bending down, without lifting a leg, via a sleight of hand that left us dumbfounded. Then she left, moving backwards with a frenetic wiggle of her shoulders and bathed in applause, until she reached the bathroom. Just like that – the way she came into the world, is how we, the journalists of *El Matutino*, now know her.

Two. Gabriel who usually boasts about being very liberal in relationships, was visibly peeved, although he was pretending that he had enjoyed himself greatly. I noticed how he avoided Diana and began to drink uncontrollably. He glugged down his drinks angrily, one after the other, until he lost his smile and his wish to communicate, which in him was stronger than his instinct for survival. Soon after, with his gaze drifting and in a muffled voice, he announced that he do would do his 'streep tease', which he then began to perform with clumsy movements of his legs, but he found it hard to remain standing as he reached to take off his shoes. The public barely laughed at that moment and from then on they ignored him like any other drunken idiot. Then, submissive but brooding, he settled in the armchair and went to sleep. Half an hour later he awoke and rose like brewer's yeast and began to have a heated discussion with Diana, accusing her of being perverted and inviting her to make her living from sex, to which the young economics reporter responded with roars of laughter. Finally, our Othello decided to leave and did so shoeless because someone had hidden his shoes and there was no way to find them. He left with a slam of the door.

Three. Pedro also drank too much and developed an exaggerated affection for Kevin, one of the editorial assistants, a journalism student with the features of an Arab boy, who was shy and a little affected and had recently joined the team. From the beginning, he devoted painstaking attention to him, which then became insistence, pestering, a state of siege until at approximately 1am – the walls caved in and he surrendered. Our host and the boy disappeared without anyone noticing the evasive manoeuvre at the time. It was, without doubt, the best dish of the night because however many rumours there had been about the sexual tastes of the society editor, based on what were until then simple presumptions, that was the moment of truth. Pedro came out of the closet officially.

Four. Given the remote possibility that the party would lavish new emotions on us, I decided to leave. I had barely begun to say goodbye when I noticed that Lidia was doing the same. We met in the doorway. We went out together into the cold of the night. In the street just one lamp was still lit but there was a cloudless sky with a full moon the size of a football stadium. That night I had arrived without my old banger, stuck in the garage because of I-don't-know-what problem, and I was ready to go home on foot when the girl stopped me: "I'll give you a lift," she said. The rest is a confused story. I remember that I got into her BMW with a certain discomfort (luxury intimidates me), we went a couple of kilometres chatting lightly about the events of the night, then we started for some unknown reason to talk about more intimate subjects, we confessed our mutual wish to share something more than work. I don't remember the exact words, I don't know at what moment I told her that I loved her, I don't know if she confessed the same, I only remember that I took her hand, her soft, cold hand and I held it for a long time between mine. I don't know if I asked her to park the car or she did it on her own initiative, but the fact is she stopped it and we kissed; we shared a long and moist kiss in which not only our mouths were involved but all the bodily organs together, all the plains of consciousness and the future of our lives. Well, that's what I felt. I don't know about her.

I recognise that in the past I have laughed at these romantic novels that line the shelves in bookshops, backed by the names of millionaire publishing houses. I know that I loathe this romantic kitsch and I have always defended my thesis that love is a deceitful and cruel business in which there is always – at least – one certain loser. However, I admit that this morning I ordered a bouquet of roses for her, in the purest pink I could find. I was aware that she will never be mine, that her kiss was no more than an act of charity towards a poor, lonely man, but I had no words to thank her for her gesture, the good intentions with which she had complicated what remained of my life.

15

Pedroso was in the city for more than a month and the whole time he remained silent. He would come two or three times a week and would sit down to read dossiers for whole afternoons or mornings, making notes. He would wander through the corridors or sit next to the windows to contemplate, in an abstract way, the view of the city. Then he collected his things and left as silently as he had arrived without asking any questions or making any comments, without saying more than was strictly necessary. One day he turned up at the director's office and handed him a file that contained, according to him, the complete profile of the killer.

"My presence is no longer necessary," he said. "I have completed the description of the killer as precisely as the facts permit. So I am leaving this very afternoon. However," he looked at his watch, "I still have a few minutes to clear up any doubts you might have."

The report described the Psycho as a man of around 30, who was white and thick-set. He probably hailed from the upper class, with links – his own or through his family – to big business or politics. He had undertaken medical studies (very possibly unfinished) and was a keen hunter or mountain climber. His home must be outside of the triangle formed by the districts of Desamparados, Curridabat and the Unión, the area in which the murders had occurred. At some point in his life, the report added, he must have been linked to a leftwing or rightwing paramilitary group. They should look for a man who was mentally unstable, prone to episodes of euphoria and uncontrollable rage, the son of a woman who was extremely dominant or aggressive with her children but who had strict moral criteria. "The idea of the mother as a prostitute, which was initially suggested, does not fit in with the socio-economic level," the report noted. It considered it unlikely that the killer was a smoker or used hallucinogenic drugs and, in normal conditions, it was to be expected that he was sexually impotent.

Gustavo read the entire report without suspicions or resistance. He knew that each affirmation corresponded to a reasoning which, whether verifiable or not, must be rigorous and tied to an implacable logic.

"It's a shame that you have to go, I would have liked to work longer with you," said Don Jovel. "But, finally..." he scratched his head in that simian way. "I know it's a stupid question, but what do you suppose we should do with this?"

"The idea of this kind of study is to narrow the universe of suspects, restrict the investigation to one type of individual, in one geographical area, but it does not take the place of ordinary police work. My advice is that you use this as an aid and carry on."

The director glanced over the document quickly and paused when he came to one sentence.

"Why do you think the killer comes from the upper class?"

"I have already put forward the reasons why I believe that the Psycho was present at the massacre of the women at La Cruz, so we can proceed from that as a given," said Pedroso. "If we take into account the confession of one of the accused to the judge in the sense that in this scenario there was a fifth man, our suspicion acquires a degree of certainty. Why don't they inform on him? Why should a witness say that he would prefer to die than create problems with this mysterious individual? Simply because they recognise that his power is unique."

"This does not necessarily mean that he is upper class. It could be that he has a lot of power in the underworld," Don Jovel objected.

"It's unlikely," said Pedroso. "We're not talking about the head of the mafia, nor the chief of a gang of drug traffickers, we're talking about a deranged guy whose vital energy has been focused for years on his obsession with killing women, which he did not dare to do until recently, which indicates that his natural environment is not one of a common criminal. Besides, it is indisputable that the subject has advanced knowledge of anatomy, which leads us to suppose that he is a professional in the area of medicine and I don't think that the underworld is overflowing with people who can give their children the luxury of university studies. If criminals like these fear him so much, it must be because the source of his power is beyond their domain. Besides, remember that two of the four accused died in strange circumstances. One in a brawl at his own home and the other while playing Russian roulette. We don't know if these deaths were unrelated or if someone paid for them, but there are two witnesses fewer. Very convenient, don't you think?"

"Three," Gustavo interrupted, "because I am sure that Carolina, the girl who was murdered by a shot through her bedroom window, was with the others at La Cruz and according to the judge's informer, witnessed the killing. As you know, apart from a fifth man, it is very likely that a woman whom they nicknamed the Kid, a girl who was a friend of Three Hairs, was at the scene of the crime. We have not been able to obtain a statement or a definite proof that Carolina and the Kid are the same person, but we know for certain that Carolina had a relationship – a close one, let's say – with this person and that she visited him several times in prison. Months after the massacre, the girl joined a religious sect. It was a strange decision because there had been nothing of this kind before. We think that the experience of witnessing the crime pushed her to seek spiritual help. Possibly to deal with some feeling of guilt, although we believe that she was no more than an involuntary spectator."

"That would help to explain why this crime does not fit into the scheme of the other three, after the massacre at Alajuelita," said Don Jovel.

"So it was not the perverse passion of the killer but the necessity of eliminating another witness," Pedroso deduced. "We have to ask why, of the five witnesses, two survive. Is it because they are in jail, perhaps?"

Gustavo considered the possibility for a few seconds, then discounted it.

"I don't believe so," he said. "In the days when Galleta and Viruta were killed, they were all free. In being planned by someone, both murders followed a selection criteria. Perhaps those who were considered weaker, more likely to talk were the ones who were killed."

"Perhaps there are death sentences which have not been carried out," Pedroso said approvingly.

Don Jovel changed the subject: "The area where the Psycho lives. How did you reach that conclusion?"

"Statistics," said the agent. "It's proven that an organised serial killer establishes his radius of action as far as he can from the area where he lives. The distance varies, in vast countries like the United States they can travel from one city to another, or from one state to another, to commit their crimes. It might just as well happen that the killer is a neighbour of one of his victims, but there is a one in ten chance that he lives in a different geographical area. Security is the number one element. The wider the area of search, the less chance of success for the police."

Don Jovel scratched his head, he sighed. The more he got to know about the case, the clearer it was how little he knew.

"Why do you suppose that he is not a smoker?"

"Because the way he handles his victims, in fairly dark places, is only possible for someone who has excellent vision, and a cigarette habit harms someone's faculty to a significant degree. On the other hand, a drinker or someone who uses hallucinogenic drugs would not have sufficient mental control to manage the scene of the crime in the way the Psycho does. In this case, sobriety does seem to be a very important ingredient."

"Amazing," exclaimed Don Jovel. "With ten men like you we

would clean this country of criminals. Explain the stuff about why the guy is impotent."

"What I mean is that – in normal conditions, and I underline normal – it's to be expected that he is sexually impotent. This means that he would not manage to achieve a normal erection in a normal meeting with a woman although it's possible that he reaches orgasm by killing and mutilating his victims. His fear and his hatred towards the opposite sex are so great that perhaps only in this way can he achieve satisfaction. That," the agent stammered for a moment, "that has a grave consequence: it means that he is not going to stop of his own accord, he is going to carry on until he is caught."

"But where to start?" asked Gustavo. The profile by Pedroso completely broke the guidelines of the previous investigation, and, far from narrowing the universe of the suspects, it widened it to dramatic dimensions. Previously, among other suppositions, they had focused on delving into the criminal records and approaching their informers in the underworld to come up with a guiding hypothesis. In future, they would be looking for the killer among the rich kids of an extensive zone of the city, scrutinising the private lives of people addicted to their privacy. In other words, the investigation was going uphill.

And yet, Don Jovel argued, the earlier efforts had proven useless. The killings continued, panic was gripping the people and pressure from all sides was increasing. There had to be another approach, because a perfect crime does not exist, but what there is in abundance is incompetent police, he declared.

The problem, both recognised, lay not just in halting the course of the investigation and turning it around by 180 degrees but in finding the suitable person to manoeuvre around the environment in which the killer must operate. The homicide detectives had their contacts in the districts in the south among under-age drug traffickers, counterfeiters, swindlers and other such specimens, criminal diehards. How could you send them out to investigate wealthy people or those with political influence, as the FBI agent was proposing? The result could be disastrous.

Something serious must be going on, thought Juan José when he saw Mr Grey's emaciated face, three-day stubble and vacant look. He had the serene and horrendously unhappy expression of someone who has lost hope and does not intend to regain it.

"Sit down," he said without taking his eyes off the wall, or rather not from Monet's *Nymphs* that brought him back to those distant times when he was happy.

"Do you know what I'm most afraid of?" he asked after two minutes that, to the journalist's mind, seemed unending and spectral.

Wary, Juan José indicated that he did not by making a guttural sound. At that moment, the effects of an inopportune word were impossible to predict.

"Disaster," said Mr Grey, still not turning to look at him, "that's what I fear the most. And to think that I dedicated 20 years to this, a third of my life travelling the world, being nothing or nobody, gripped by the incomparable sensation of total irresponsibility. Have you ever felt that? I can tell you that it was the best period of my life."

The editor looked at him impassively. He had heard innumerable tales from the gringo, but never an intimate confession, never a word about himself.

"But you get tired of everything, you know. One day I got tired of poverty, of washing plates in restaurants in Paris or scrubbing the floors of some house in Dublin for a couple of Irish pounds, of eating one day and not the next. When your spirit is very free, the slavery of the body, always so concrete, can be intolerable."

Now he looked terrifying. His eyes betrayed the intense night he had spent before, the scarce flesh on his face shook involuntarily, small lines of blood criss-crossed the skin of his fingers without nails.

"So, I opted for success. At 40 years of age I vowed that I would never let myself be humiliated by any man or woman in the world. And I managed it until now. I always managed what I wanted, big or small. But, what do you think? As time goes by, I start to realise that success also wears you down, I am worn out, Juan José, bloody success is killing me. Worst of all is that however suffocated I feel, I would not be able to leave all this, the idea of going back to poverty terrifies me."

Alarm bells had started to ring for Juan José Montero. Such words, he said to himself, could not be coming out of the mouth of William H. Grey, encompassing as they did concepts that were incompatible with his basic instinct, contradicting the very reason for his existence, which was limitless profit.

"And do you know to whom I owe my success? Nobody knows, not even I knew it until recently. I owe all this to Camila. She discovered what was in me, she showed me the way to success, pushed me forward when I was on the point of losing heart. Deep down, I am nothing more than her work. She is the true and only Bill Grey."

The gringo let himself fall heavily into the chair, although at that moment his destiny felt as light as an autumnal leaf.

He moistened his dry lips with the tip of his tongue and smiled sadly.

The expression on his face softened. "How was your holiday?"

"Wonderful, it's a century since I spent such peaceful vacation. It's more than...It's a century since I had a vacation.'

Mr Grey nodded, but in a vacant way. He contemplated his wretched fingers and then looked at the head of the newsroom.

"Camila is very impressed with you. Your denouncement of the theft seemed to her a great proof of your loyalty. Besides, she told me that recently you have worked with her on some great ideas to get adverts."

Suddenly, it seemed to Juan José that there was not a lot of enthusiasm in his voice. Instead, he detected a note of reproach. "I know what you're up to, you don't fool me," his rigid mouth seemed to say.

"I'm pleased to hear that, that she understands my position better. I have explained to her that my differences with the administrative section are strictly journalistic ones, that I have always understood that the newspaper's destiny is mine too."

"She has asked me to give you the chance to carry on in charge of editorial."

Juan José's face lit up. His pleasure was suddenly spilling

over, as if an internal flame had been relit.

"But I'm not so easy to convince," the gringo's smile spread over his face and took on a touch of sadism. "I am going to do what she wants, but only partly."

The editor would continue to co-ordinate the work of his journalists, but on the condition that each morning he appeared in the office of the director-president, notebook and pen in hand, to receive precise instructions for the day ahead. Besides, Juan José had to commit himself to supervising the photographic work and design of the pages, making himself personally responsible for mistakes. In this way, Mr Grey argued, he returned part of the lost independence to the editorial staff, he made his wife happy and freed himself from a couple of his many obligations, which were causing him much stress. Additionally, he wanted him to get rid of some regular contributors in the opinion section and to take charge of the editorial section, which would – he said – "result in an important saving for the firm... whose financial success matters so much to you," he added in a tone so apparently natural that it seemed almost free from irony.

A truly one-sided business, Juan José said to himself. In the midst of his madness, the gringo retained a crucial reserve of lucidity to take the advantage at any juncture. Nevertheless, it was impossible to be in a worse situation than before and any change had to mean some kind of improvement. On the other hand, he thought, the gringo was not asking him for his opinion but informing him of a decision that had been taken. He imagined he had won, or at least had drawn, in a battle that had been almost given up for lost.

Blanca Morales met for supper with her great childhood friend Dolores, talked to her for 30 minutes and they arranged to talk more about past times the next day. However, her mind stayed drifting in the archipelago of faded memories: evenings of hopscotch on the pavement outside the block of flats; Saturdays of dancing at Federico's (two *pesos* to get in and the right to a coconut christened with cacique liquor or gin); furtive dating;

school and the lost opportunities... so many things! It was in that inventory of nostalgia that the face appeared, and then came the link between the portrait that was lying on her desk and the puny and timid neighbourhood boy who never stopped looking at her but did not greet or ever say a word to her, even until she lost contact with him. The man in the portrait was stouter, of course, his childhood features had lengthened and hardened, but he had something unmistakable about him. Returning to her office, she studied the drawing for a long time, as they had taught her on those technical courses, and then in parts: the hair, the nose, the forehead, the eyes... of course, she thought, it was his eyes, that look more dead than shocked, of a fish who stares at us from their liquid world as though we are nightmare beings. But, what was his name? Alvaro, Juan, Ernesto, Francisco? It was a common name, she thought, she recalled, but so much time had passed that names piled up, one on top of the other, in the shelves of her memory. Blanca looked in her bag for the business card of her friend Dolores and called her home number.

"There's something on my mind that won't let me sleep," she explained. "Do you remember that skinny guy in the neighbourhood, the one always looking at us like a zombie."

"Of course," said her friend. "But let me correct you, he was always looking at you, he followed you, he would die for you, the idiot. And he never spoke to you, did he?"

"No, never," said Blanca. "Do you remember what his name was?"

"Of course, he ended up marrying my friend Silvia. Don't you remember? She was with us at school and she lived on the other side of the street. We see each other now and then, she comes to my house or we have a coffee at Giacomin. Guess what, the bloke turned out to be a real son-of-a-bitch, he even hit her."

Blanca interrupted to stop the chat, which was of no consequence to her. "Who would believe it? With the face of someone who wouldn't hurt a fly! But, tell me, what's his name?"

"Manuel."

"And the surname?"

"It's a bit unusual. I have it on the tip of my tongue. If you want, I'll ask Silvia, but what's this about?"

"I'm making an inventory of boyfriends, lovers and admirers, from the platonic ones of my early days to the hairy gorilla who I threw myself at last week out of pure lust."

Dolores was laughing. "You're kidding me, aren't you?"

The next day Blanca went to the homicide chief and told him who the portrait reminded her of.

"Perhaps it's not important," she shrugged her shoulders, "but he looks like someone I knew many years ago. Here's his name," she handed him a scrap of paper.

"Manuel Funes Sandoval," Gustavo read and a shiver ran from head to toe. He did not know why, maybe because he was impressed by the simplicity with which the guy had concealed himself behind his own name, or because he thought the discovery might open a door towards the truth. But the homicide chief put his entire department on the case and after two days, he had a complete, exhaustive and surprising history of the mysterious character.

It's too late, he wanted to say. I cast you aside the moment that you killed my dreams. Now I have another love, and I regret that all this has been the result of a stupid game. We'll see each other around some time but, in the meantime, girl, grow up.

He would have said it. He wanted to say these exact words... out of shame, self-love, common sense. But those eyes were fixed on his, as inescapable as quetzals, as alluring as sibylline stones.

"I'm afraid of losing you," came from her lips with a slight quiver, but her body was an open book to any reader. That's how he understood it... he only had to take the hand she offered to enter into a world of limitless possibilities: all her skin, her taut and perfumed flesh, her inexhaustible breasts, her contagious laugh and her intense gaze. All his: her sweat, her youth and the transparency of her emotions. No secret, no intimacy to which he was not invited – now and forever.

16

"I am going to explain it to you because you are my friend," he said, "although I hope that you don't take it as an apology. Let's say that in essence I am bisexual, I love women but not only women. I am not a promiscuous type. When it comes to sex, I am closer to ascetisicm than in any other practice. I have spent almost two years without a sexual relationship with anyone."

"That doesn't change anything."

"Look, the newspaper is full of sluts, queens and lesbians. Sexual commerce goes on there like on a Greek beach and you complain to me, and I'm more circumspect than most."

"You can do with your arse whatever you like," said Maricruz, without abandoning the tone of reproach. "The point is that I thought our confidence was reciprocal, I have always told you my stuff."

"Double M, your life is a crystal cabinet, transparency costs you nothing," Pedro answered. "My life has always been a disaster."

Maricruz escaped by gazing out of the window towards the half-light of the city, towards the dense and persistent rain and the heavy evening traffic. There, distant and silent, she remained until their car crossed in front of the Pacífico park. Two drenched drunks were fighting over the last drop in a bottle of methylated spirits and the branches of a dozen laurel trees, bent over by the weight of the rain, brushed the grass.

"It must be around here," she said.

Pedro nodded, followed instructions and reduced speed. Halfway along the block, they found the house, exactly as Madame Fronvac had described it: the façade was sea blue, the portico had an old wooden bench and an almost imperceptible sign over the entrance with gothic letters that spelled 'Esoteric Society'.

Maricruz felt a surge of adrenalin. A week before Madame Fronvac had called them to tell them about a strange group linked to certain lunar rituals. She had discovered their existence while making enquiries with friends in the trade, one of whom had put her in touch with someone who she supposed was the cult's officiator, an irreproachable citizen, she explained, who looked like an English gentleman. Her information indicated that he was the administrator of a pharmacy, a serious and honourable man, with a large family, whom no one would have suspected of being disposed to any extravagance, least of all to practices of doubtful concomitancy with the precepts of the Catholic faith, Roman and apostolic, which he actively and publicly professed. She didn't know, Fronvac said, about the group's specific activities, nor how many members it had, but it was clear that the 'Esoteric Society' was just a name for appearance's sake and that its real interest was witchcraft. The ritual included a cult devoted to the moon and some form of blood offering, although there was no reason to suspect that they were practising human sacrifice, she concluded.

From the first moment, Maricruz's mission was to infiltrate the group. She was not motivated, in truth, by an immediate journalistic interest because it was evident that Mr Grey would not permit even a casual reference to the subject, much less a report (and now was not the time for new attempts at audacity, such as the one he had permitted Juan José a few months earlier). It reflected, rather, her incontrollable curiosity. Madame

Fronvac tried to dissuade her by pointing out the dangers of the adventure, but such warnings did nothing but stoke her fascination.

"I won't be able to sleep five hours in a row ever again if I don't manage to confirm something about this secret cult," Maricruz told her after many days of requests and many others of refusals, until the astrologer gave in on the condition that Maricruz kept her word that the case would not be written about in the newspaper.

"I am risking my neck for you, don't let me down," she pleaded.

Don Vico (as the president of the pagan cult called himself) seemed wary, argued Irma Solares, and she had to sell him a coherent story with no loose ends. For sure, he liked the idea of bringing two new disciples into the cult, especially if they were young, middle-class, educated and intelligent, but they still had to explain the source of their interest in a way that was absolutely credible. The sect would probably ask for concrete information and would try, before inviting them, to confirm at least such details as their telephone numbers, occupations and addresses. They both had to invent a presumed identity and, above all, avoid mentioning anything that could link them to journalism.

"The truth," said Pedro as they stood slightly wet in front of the door, "is that I don't know why we are doing this if it's not even going to be used in an article. Is there nothing that you're afraid of?"

"I'm afraid of almost everything, Pedrito," Maricruz admitted, suddenly recovering her affectionate tone towards him. "Earthquakes freak me out, getting in an aeroplane makes me want to shit myself, falling in love terrifies me. But that is precisely the problem, that danger attracts me, it hypnotises me."

"We are fucked," was all Pedro said as the door opened.

The woman who opened it looked rigid, with severe lips and eyes. There were no signs of her chronological age in her face, but certain deep lines of the kind that usually indicate disappointment, perhaps a life of many failures, Maricruz thought later, recalling the events of the adventure. She neither greeted them nor asked them anything, she simply looked them in the eye and expected them, the new arrivals, to speak.

"We are looking for Don Vico, we are Ana and Rubén, on behalf of Madame Fronvac," Pedro announced in the exact words he had been instructed to use.

The woman did not introduce herself, just let them pass. With a gesture, she invited them to sit down in a small, badly lit waiting area and disappeared through an even darker hallway without saying a word. Pedro nudged Maricruz to call her attention to a photograph which hung on the wall in front of them, from which a man in a grey turban and with a sapphire as a 'third eye' in his forehead stared out in a terrifying way.

It was not long before Don Vico appeared. He was of medium-height, with black hair that was, frankly, decadent, and long, clean hands that he extended first to Maricruz then to Pedro, with a very gentlemanly air, just as Madame had said.

"It's a pleasure to have you with us," he said. "You're a little early, aren't you?"

"We are nervous," said Maricruz.

"All the better," he said. "That way we can talk a bit before the ceremony begins."

He led them through a narrow passage to a small, simple room, neat and perfectly neutral, with no element that would suggest the nature of the group.

"I understand that you're a philology student," he addressed Pedro, who nodded.

"And you're a history student," he asked Maricruz.

"That's right, a graduate."

"I imagine that a philologer and a historian make a very complementary couple... in academic terms, I mean."

"We have a lot in common," she said.

"Such as an interest in lunar rites," noted Don Vico. "'May I ask where this comes from?"

"Well, I've been a fan of esoteric literature for some time," Pedro cut in according to the guidelines that they had agreed. "I have read books and I am a subscriber to several magazines on the subject, but it was Ana, while working on her thesis about religions and the Asian mode of production, who discovered that the cult of ancient gods is still alive in some parts of the world. We began to investigate. We read a lot of reports, we sought the opinion of a mountain of experts and all agree that these ancient gods are the source of great power, that they can listen to our requests and influence our lives. What we never imagined is that we had a brotherhood here, so near to us."

Don Vico smiled. It was difficult to decipher the exact meaning of his gesture, but it contained more satisfaction than malice and both took it as a sign of his approval.

"That's the crux of all this," he said. "I would say that you are pretty much on the right track. In reality, we believe in a cosmic power that is the source of all powers, a power that you might call God or Destiny but one that is sole and universal. The ancient peoples were on the right path when they sought this authority in nature, above all in the stars, because the strength of the universe resides in the universe itself, not outside of it. However, the big institutionalised religions, in the service of politics, deviated and brought people towards visions that were increasingly more abstract than divine. In this way, mystical knowledge has been converted into a monopoly of priests and others who have been corrupted, who act as intermediaries between the spirit of the gods and the people."

"To manipulate people," said Maricruz.

"You've put your finger on it: that's how the idle and privileged castes come to the fore. That is how they justify the domination by a few men over the rest of their kind."

"But, the ancient gods, Weren't they also abstractions, in their way?" Maricruz dared to interrupt Don Vico.

"Not at all... and you, as a student of the subject, should know this. Isis, Diana, Hecate, Parvati, they are just names by which the people in ancient times referred to the moon in its different phases. The moon was the supreme deity, which acquired diverse names because it was capable of being incarnated in feminine beings who populated the earth and ruled human destiny."

"And the masculine gods?" Pedro interrupted.

"They were simply consorts. The image of the all-powerful

Zeus, which we have, is a manipulation perpetrated by the media, an image adapted to our patriarchal culture. For the early Greeks, real power resided in Hera. In the more ancient Hindu tradition, authority rested in Parvati and not in Shiva. But all these gods were emanations of the planet, an entity that was feminine, unique and trinitarian."

"A trinity, what do you mean?" asked Maricruz not managing to hide the note of astonishment in her voice.

"There is much to learn," he said with an indulgent gesture, "but let me tell you that this mystery is not the exclusive legacy of Christianity. The concept of the trinity was contained in the selfsame phases of the moon: the full, the new, the waxing-waning, which at the same time are the vital moments and personalities of the goddess Diana, the sacred maidservant; Isis, the matron, giver of life; Artemis the wise old woman whose image coincides with that of a witch. The virgin-mother-wise woman. You only have to substitute the names for more appropriate ones and you obtain identical combinations."

"Is it certain that the cult of the moon is effective?" said Pedro, affecting the expression of an innocent child.

Don Vico smiled and placed a paternal hand on his shoulder.

"The moon exercises an extraordinary influence on us because it is the planet that is nearest, from the moon cosmic power emanates in abundance and we only have to do the right thing to use this force to our benefit."

"The ritual," said Maricruz.

'The ritual," Don Vico broke off the discussion, "which I must certainly prepare. If you want to take part in the ceremony, you may do so but you must first put on these." He handed garments to both of them. "When you are ready, you can go through to the salon," he indicated. These were long white capes with conical hoods in the style of the Ku Klux Klan, Pedro observed. On the chest was a drawing of a black circle containing strange zoomorphic designs.

In the salon, about 20 people, all hidden by the ceremonial outfits, formed a wide, silent circle around Don Vico, the only one whose face was visible, who held in his hands a small broom.

When Pedro and Maricruz entered, he asked them to join the circle, then he put on his hood and remained for a couple of minutes in silence, his head bowed as though in meditation.

The meeting took place in a spacious room with no furniture other than a small square table covered with a white linen cloth upon which were resting half a dozen lighted candles and a collection of diverse objects such as bottles, wooden sticks and string. Don Vico began to move around within the circle formed by the participants, in concentric movements, from the centre towards the circumference, sweeping the air with his broom.

"With this tool of our will, I cast out the forces of evil and disorder. Outside, outside... do not interrupt our ritual tonight. Do not disturb our ceremony," he said, making furious sweeps with his broom.

The believers began to repeat his words in co-ordinated and monotonous voices that together acquired a sinister resonance, an acoustic surge that startled Maricruz. Suddenly, everything was profoundly silent again. Then, Don Vico went to the altar, took water from a bottle and some salt from another and mixed them in an earthenware bowl. He stirred fastidiously while uttering new invocations. He put his hand in the bowl and began to sprinkle the salt water around the room.

Don Vico went silent again and stepped back. Then, he announced that the time had come to close the circle. Maricruz felt an anonymous hand take hold of hers. Her other hand sought that of Pedro and with it she completed the human chain through which a strange energy began to flow (she could feel it with absolute certainty). Something produced in her a mixture of fear and sensual pleasure, the temptation to flee and another, each time more powerful, to abandon herself to the experience.

The master raised his arms and announced:

"The circle has closed, now we enter in the neutral zone of all worlds in a time that is not time, in an indeterminate place, fitting for the encounter of gods and men."

A mist began to cover the floor of the room, the air became inflused with an intense smell of sandalwood and the voice of

Don Vico sounded deeper, as if it were coming from some distant caves.

"Oh, lady of the night, we invoke you, accompany us today in our ceremony, goddess of goddesses, queen of many names. I summon you, virgin of the woods, huntress of the winter plains."

Once more the group followed their master. The invocations must have lasted several minutes, their intensity growing, and Pedro had the sensation that the temperature in the room was rising many degrees above normal. He began to sweat copiously beneath his hood. Suddenly, Don Vico stood up, now the prisoner of violent shakes, and his words acquired a distant resonance. It could not be his voice that shouted, full of pain: "*Ayay, ayay, ayaya, ayo, ayo, ayay.*" The arms that waved in the air could not be his, nor could it be his legs that pushed him from one side to the other in a movement that seemed aerial, while the rest of the brotherhood intoned: "Earth, air, fire, water, return."

Some time later, Don Vico recovered control of his body and returned to the centre of the circle, taking a tray with small wooden sticks and distributing them to those present with the good news that the goddess had descended and was present to listen to their wishes and to receive offerings.

At that moment the woman who had opened the door to Maricruz and Pedro entered. She wore neither the gown nor the hood, like the others, but a kind of black tunic, crossed at chest height with two silver strips in the form of an X. With one of her hands she held aloft a live chicken by its head and with the other she controlled its body as it struggled frenetically. Don Vico took a dagger, showed it to the participants and with a precise, almost elegant movement, beheaded the bird with one stroke. A shower of blood splattered the walls, the altar and the white tunics, while the participants celebrated euphorically, with a growing pleasure and in some cases ecstasy.

How long could the ceremony have lasted? Pedro and Maricruz wondered afterwards, while they tried to reconstruct the events and explain their sensory (and extrasensory) experiences. Watch in hand, they calculated that they had been in the house for 2 hours and 40 minutes, but real time did not fit with their subjective experience of it. For Maricruz, it might have gone on for an entire night while Pedro assured her that he had felt (an inexplicable perception) the precise moment at which time stopped dead and everything began to occur out of time and space.

However, it was not these unusual perceptions that most impressed the reporters, but what happened once the ceremony was finished, when Don Vico stood between them and asked the brothers to greet and welcome the new members.

One by one, in an orderly line, the members filed past, always wearing hoods: they held up the palms of their hands and wished peace and beatitudes on the new recruits. A strange protocol, Maricruz was thinking as a pair of chilling eyes fixed on hers and an unmistakable voice affected her so violently that it left her about to faint.

It's curious: I have listened to the Concert at Aranjuez countless times and I place it as one of the classics I enjoy most, together with the waltzes of Chopin, Mozart's *21st Piano Concerto* or Vivaldi's *Four Seasons*. However, on Sunday I listened to it again while I was thinking about Lidia and the notes took on a new meaning. Joaquín Rodrigo, I imagine, must have been dreaming about a woman to conceive such a beautiful score. A woman like Lidia, someone capable of suggesting this strange alloy of gentleness and strength that Lidia has within, with a physical appearance that combines simplicity with Renaissance-like splendour. Yesterday I gave her the record. She asked me the reason for the present, and I told her that I loved her and that, if I were the composer, only inspired by her would I be able to create such beauty. I think she blushed, and she said something about feeling overwhelmed. I didn't want to overwhelm her with my adoration but at times I can't control it.

Since the night of the party, we've maintained a discreet but constant relationship. We see each other out of the newspaper two or three times a week, we eat together and talk at length with an open list of topics that avoids, scrupulously, any allusion to her relationship. One day I tried to broach the subject of her marriage and she cut me off: "We can talk about anything but this," she decreed. I respect her decision, of course. I tell myself that I have no right to interfere in her life and that I should be satisfied with the little that she gives me, that the fact of having a place in her heart, however small that might be, should be enough to keep me happy. However, to be excluded so radically from one part of her life makes me anxious. Is it possible, I ask myself, to love someone whom one doesn't know or whom one only knows a part of? How many unknown Lidias are behind the Lidia that I know? The woman absorbed in the intimacy and routine of her home. Is she the same one as in the newsroom? I tell myself 'No'. There must be an inifinity of gestures, reactions and feelings that only break out in the warm atmosphere of home, that place where two or more people take refuge from the world, to be more themselves and less what others demand. Because a home, a place that is so foreign to me, must be something more than some walls and a roof under which to spend the night.

Yesterday, after I gave her the record, she took an envelope out of her bag with some passport photographs of herself. "I didn't come out very well," she said, disappointed. She gave one to me and this detail swept me through a vortex of nostalgia back to my adolescence, How long has it been since a girl gave me her photo? I couldn't say. In my adolescent days the gesture amounted to a gift of the soul, but it might be that she just wanted to give me a photograph of herself, to reciprocate in some way my gesture of giving her a record. I don't know. Lidia almost always seems indecipherable to me. Later, I was struck by a premonition that, when all was said and done, all that would remain for me of her would be this fleeting moment caught on camera, some green eyes dazzled by the flash, and a neutral smile. For several hours, the initial happiness gave way to a terrible desolation.

17

"I am afraid of losing you," those words had a powerful effect on the mood of Gustavo Cortés. He would have liked to respond that it was too late, that he had already erased the illusion of her love and that now he had something real, the love of a mature, sincere woman: all the arguments that his mind had organised into an implacable discourse while he fantasised about his hypothetical revenge. That was what his basic instinct advised, that is what he had decided to do, if the occasion presented itself, with absolute certainty. But he could not. He accepted the hand that she offered him with resigned silence, with no hesitation so as not to break the spell, and he let himself be led where she wanted to take him, to a world of uncertainty and anxiety, which he feared so much.

For the first time in ages Gustavo acted on impulse, he did not think about his work or about the tacit agreement he had reached with Aurelia. He thought only of the persuasive power of those six words. Maricruz had not said "I am sorry." She had not resorted to expressions such as 'I love you', or 'I need you.' Spontaneously, she had said "I am afraid of losing you" and this declaration, he thought, contained involuntary confessions, born of the unconscious and therefore sincere, stripped of poses or manipulative games. He did not stop to consider on what such a theory was based, he merely let himself be swept along by the power of her two imponderable olive-coloured eyes.

That's how things were with Maricruz. They had not been formally together for two weeks and he already felt as if he was in a situation that was irrefutable, as if the old world, that came before her, had been nothing more than a meticulous preparation for a real and definitive life, which began and ended with her. A few days had passed since the afternoon on which she had decided to pronounce those six words and begun to take control of his life. His apartment was being transformed by small but continual changes. A piece of furniture that moved position, a vase that appeared on the corner table in place of a clay flowerpot, new touches in the kitchen, in the wardrobes, in the bookshelf. His diary, normally empty so that he could accommodate any pressing work matter, was full of unusual reminders: Monday 13:30 lunch with MM, Tuesday 18:00 cinema Magaly, collect MM at newspaper, Wednesday 18:00 gastronomic kamikaze in Chinese restaurant with MM.

Even the more distant future was being swallowed up by this enormous and involuntary consumer of his will. "When we are old, I want us to buy a boat and go and live on the beach so that we can watch sunsets over the sea, sitting at the dock with a glass of beer in our hands," he would say.

"Papa is furious," she said while she rested her head on his chest. "He is threatening to disown me as his daughter. I don't believe he is suffering because of my absence, what he can't stand is to lose a single atom of authority."

"And your mother?"

"Resigned. She is suffering because I left, I think."

"You don't regret it?"

Maricruz paused a few moments to consider the question and wanted to give a sincere answer. "It's strange," she said. "At first I imagined that the change would make me feel strange, I was afraid that I would feel depressed and would want to return. But no, the truth is that each day I feel better. I feel as if this is the place I had to come to and at last I arrived."

"This is your home, but you're not going to confuse me with your mother," said Gustavo. "In the first place, I am your contact in the Judicial Police."

"By the way," said Maricruz, "I have been thinking of returning to the cult, to confirm my suspicion."

"I don't want you to go back there, it's dangerous."

"I swear it was him," she insisted. "I have to confirm it."

"Didn't you say they were all wearing hoods?"

"But his eyes are impossible to mistake. Besides, the voice was the same. And the boots, Gustavo, those Texan boots with steel toecaps that emerged from under the gown were the same."

"They make those boots on an industrial scale, they're fashionable. Besides, even if we were right, nothing guarantees that Manuel Sandoval, or whatever he is called, is the killer. It's true that aspects of the profile fit him, but others don't."

"Let's see what we have," said Maricruz, counting on her fingers. "A mother who was an aggressive prostitute."

"Not exactly," Gustavo corrected her. "A mother who was not there very much."

"According to your own report, the woman was working as a waitress at night and received customers for sex during the day. She gave the son no affection or attention of any kind. In this respect he fits the profile perfectly."

"Let's say that he does."

"Now we know that he was involved with the Guatemalan rebels. That means, he knows how to use weapons, that he learned to get around in mountainous terrain without leaving tracks, and that he ably managed the techniques of conspiracy."

"But he is not from the upper class; we know that he does not have medical knowledge..."

"The age fits: 34. He seems not to be addicted to drugs or alcohol," said Maricruz, "he's probably impotent since he has no children despite being married, but the most important thing is that he forwarded false information in a deliberate way, he tried to divert attention towards another objective."

"I admit he's suspicious, but that does not mean you have to put yourself at risk."

"In that case, I renounce my collaboration with the police, I will co-ordinate the whole thing with my editor."

"You're as stubborn as a mule," said Gustavo.

The police investigation had revealed abundant details about the life of Manuel Funes Sandoval, but far from leading to a certainty, it introduced new and profuse doubts into the case. The immigration registers could not confirm that he had left the country in the past two years, except for a three-day journey to Panama, at the time of his last interview with Maricruz and Juan José. Similarly discredited were the threats he claimed to be facing, as was his presumed self-exile in Colombia. Consequently, the rest of his story – the leftwing militant group which he said he had belonged to, the campaign of terror and its link with the crimes against the women – the entire smokescreen vanished. All that remained was the mystery of the man himself, his past, his environment, his motivation. Everything about him was obscure. From his early years, the neglect he had experienced was clear. He was looked after for a while by an old grandmother or by neighbours who sympathised with his loneliness and took him to eat or to sleep at their homes. The few testimonies that the police were able to get from that era described him as a sad and silent boy, with strong tendencies to solitude. His adolescence had not been markedly different. He had no girlfriends, no adventures or true friends. At one point he spent three years studying, but this amounted to nothing. He had graduated with a weird combination of courses from the University of Costa Rica, the majority of which he had had to retake. They say that he passed his time contemplating the multi-coloured exterior of the School of Sciences and Letters from a window of the Guevara Bar, an eternal cup of tea shaking in his right hand and a book about yoga (which no one knew if he read) open on the table. Neither were there any consistent explanations about his means of survival during this time, since it was unlikely that he received help from his family. Later he worked selling encyclopaedias and dictionaries, briefly worked as a lawyer's assistant, tried to become a security guard, and

became a writer. They say he still has the drafts of two unfinished novels. One day, unexpectedly, no one knows under what
influences, he ended up among the Guatemalan rebels, fighting
alongside commandante Rodrigo Asturias, known by his *nom de
guerre* Gaspar Ilóm. Two years later he reappeared in San José,
attached for equally inexplicable motives to one of the personalities of the capital's jet-set, the bombastic and boastful Bruno
Robledo. Since then he had had no occupation other than to
accompany the rich boy everywhere, acting as a driver and security guard, procurer or messenger. Shortly after he had returned
to Costa Rica, he had established a relationship with a humble
girl who worked for a business, whom he married after a brief
engagement. No children, said the report in its summing-up.

"You're as stubborn as a mule," said Gustavo. "Do whatever you
like."

She laughed. The hilarity did not hide the harshness of the
sentence. Maricruz felt that she was in love, had decided to
share her life with Gustavo, was even prepared to sacrifice a
part of her independence, but her choice was not entirely irrational. Before attempting her reconciliation, she had made a list
of the aspects of her life that were not open to discussion and
those that would be the subject of negotiation. Among the former
was her profession. That implied having the freedom to continue
her work, the right to establish the relationships she considered
opportune, and to run the risks to which she herself was disposed. Without being obliged to explain herself after the fact.
She knew, besides, that love is a risky adventure. Gustavo did
not seem to fit with the prototype of possessive macho, but she
was conscious that the sensation of belonging could grow over
time. How would he behave then, when he felt that she belonged
to him physically and emotionally? Would he try to impose his
will, would he demand special prerogatives? Anything was possible. People can change according to their context, she told herself, and living together would be a very different context.

On one side of the scale were these and other imminent dangers, but on the other were her intelligence and strength of

character. She would not try, she told herself, to discuss the subject with Gustavo because the fact of starting a debate itself implied a certain relinquishing of rights. The most effective thing would be to impose the rules by living them. At Gustavo's first attempt to take control, she would respond with absolute vigour, in such a way that the principle of her independence remained firm, like a natural law.

"And how are you going to get the guy to take off his hood? Because clearly he wears it to protect his identity."

"Perhaps I will propose a little oral sex so that he would take it off without me having to ask."

"You're crazy," he exploded and Maricruz collapsed in laughter again. "I thought the hood was above all an element of the ritual and that, outside the ceremony, the members of the sect could know each other's faces."

"The precautions must be above all with new people."

"Well, the bastard might also recognise you and then they will all know that there is a journalist who has infiltrated their group."

"I have already thought about that. My plan is that Pedro and I arrive very early and observe through binoculars from a distance all those who go in. They can't put their hoods on until they go in, can they?"

"We could do that with a couple of officers without you having to expose yourself."

"Of course, but my idea is to be able to talk with him once we are inside and win his confidence, and ask him why he attends the cult."

"He could just as well lie, invent any old story. I don't see what there is to be gained from this business, only risks."

"Well, I'll run them anyway," said Maricruz thinking that perhaps Gustavo was not wrong, but that this was the first important test of her independence and she wanted to show how much she was boss of her own decisions. A decisive moment for the future of the relationship had arrived and she could not back down in the face of a good argument.

The opportunity presented itself the following Tuesday. They arrived an hour early and parked a block away. They had got hold of a car with tinted windows, allowing them to watch with binoculars without arousing suspicion. For an hour and a half they saw passers-by of all shapes and sizes but none tried to enter the house.

"Have we got the day wrong?" asked Pedro.

"No," said Maricruz. "I am sure. The meetings take place in every lunar phase and now we have the waning quarter. There could only have been some change at the last minute."

They got out of the car and walked towards the house. They knocked on the door and no one answered. Then they noticed that there were no longer curtains in the windows and discovered, in spite of the half light, that the rooms were empty. The small plaque that read 'Esoteric Society' had gone.

A woman came out of the house next door, observed them suspiciously and hurled the answer before they could ask the question.

"They've gone. They left the house two days ago... thank God," she said making the sign of the cross.

What the devil am I doing here? I wonder as the woman lets her skirt fall from her waist and reveals her long white legs, with the texture of pineapple. How did I get here? I ask myself, without lifting my gaze from those steppe-like breasts, vestiges of a distant opulence. I look at her not knowing what to do, as startled as a little boy, as if I was initiated just recently in the mysteries of the flesh. I am startled by the woman, her nostalgic breasts and her huge thighs. I am intimidated by the scale of this room in half-light, its badly made bed, its peculiar smell of a musty monastery.

How can I stoop so low? I don't know, I have no answers for that. Nor can I claim that I was tricked, that I am victim of an ambush, because I had abundant indications of what might happen, I could abort the situation through an opportune manoeuvre but I let it happen. Idleness, complacency, complicity? I don't know that either. It's difficult to ponder the deep motives for both my omissions and my actions. I mixed work interests with personal ones. I accepted those prolonged chats in her office. I agreed to accompany her to her business meetings. Then came a couple of dinners, the confidences about my past life and about hers, sorrows and dreams. In my desperate attempt to understand Bill Grey, I wanted to be an ally and she told me some key secrets about his behaviour. Suddenly, Camila started to have a defined human condition as far as I was concerned and I imagine that I started looking less like a stinking native to her. Everything, until this point went according to my own strategy but now I feel that I'll lose both control and probably the opportunity I've been working for to recover a part of my independence. Now it is too late to rectify it: Camila is here, virtually naked in the middle of the room, hinting at me with a gaze that looks implacable, beckoning me with gestures that don't belong to her. She offers her body imagining perhaps that is is an undeserved gift, excessive generosity for a man like me. And I almost tremble because I don't know, although my arms and legs are moving, if the rest of my organism will respond to this call. I don't know if I will be able to stand the texture of her skin, the smell of her armpits, her tense voice forcing on my ear words in an unknown language.

She has left on a thong of red material, a timid triangle like a wavering door to the dark nothing. She begins to move towards me with slow, insinuating steps. Her hair loose, her smile ecstatic. They are not hers, those sensual movements, but they want to be. Her legs are close together and one rubs against the other, provoking a slight tremble in the inner thigh, where the muscle is more flaccid. She is definitely not a sensual woman but, on the other hand, she is explicit.

The moment has arrived, I think. I must advance as well, undress and offer her my arms, but I don't react. Now she is coming as close as she can, as if she wanted to touch my chest with her index finger with which she is indicating that I am a coward. She does not do it. For the first time she really smiles... ironically. Then she goes over to the armchair and sinks into it with a graceful turn. I think this is amusing and this gives me weak and unexpected hope. I'm not saying passion, nor desire but a hope, a vague expectation.

"I know what's going on," she says, "you are frightened of me."

Yes, I am afraid. I could have said 'panicking' and it would have been more correct, but to admit that would not be virile. I try to smile.

"No, it's not that," I lie, "it's that I feel weird. I thought we hated each other."

Camila loses her composure. She opens her legs and lets out a laugh. I didn't know that she was capable of such a human expression as a laugh.

"Don't be stupid," she exclaimed. "I'm not doing this out of love, but neither do I hate you. Why do you hate me?"

In reality, I don't believe I do hate her. I should, but I realise that I only despise her a little, even less than I despise myself.

"You are a slave driver, you humiliate people and you mistreat the workers."

I didn't want to say that. I said it because suddenly I was gripped by a crushing desire for revenge. Fear has confused me with some sudden and unstoppable wish to insult her, to take her by the hair and flog her decrepit buttocks. A strange violent sensation is growing in me that awakens my libido.

"It's true," she says ironically, "I am a witch." Now she laughs between her teeth, mockingly, she seems to enjoy her own game. "Take off your clothes and I'll show you how bad I can be."

She is twisting like a snake, gyrating, licking her lips. She lifts a breast with her right hand and offers it to me. "Suck it!" her half-open lips seem to say, although she says nothing, she just offers the large, dark breast, whose formidable hardness is a last glory amid so much ruin. My shaking ceases with the taste of that almond beneath my lips. I say nothing, I do nothing more. I just let myself be carried away by the surprising skill of her hands.

Now, reliving those strange moments, some of the strangest in my life, I realise that sex can be a fairly mechanical operation. I don't know if the same thing would occur to women. For us men it's enough to have the caress of some tender fingers, the suction of some moist lips, to enable the reproductive machine to get into gear. The internal or external beauty of our companion may sometimes enrich the experience, sow nuances, intensities, forms and textures, but once the moment has arrived, the burden of the job runs through the hormones, which are blind. All intellectualisation of sex comes before or after that.

Another thing is the residual effect of intercourse, what remains in the soul after orgasm, and which might be one, among many other combinations, of peace and happiness (desirable result): the need for more (positive and promising dissatisfaction), the urge to escape the scene of the crime (complete dissatisfaction), disgust, emotional collapse, suicidal depression.

Final note: the thing with Camila has left me nothing, a black hole in my memory, a centre of so much gravity that it does not permit memories to escape. However, it has had an important effect on work. This morning the gringo told me that it was not necessary to co-ordinate the news diary because the last few days' work had been impeccable. And he used that word, 'impeccable', with a notable Italian accent, which proves that it was dictated – probably in that same room where we had been so creative.

18

It had gone midnight when the telephone rang. The official on duty apologised for the late hour of the call but said he was following instructions to tell him immediately. It looked as if the Psycho had struck again but, unlike other occasions, the victim, the potential victim, was safe and sound, although very disturbed emotionally. At this moment she was making a statement. Well, they were both making a statement, the man and the woman. Yes, it was a couple. No, they were not injured, just shocked. He would keep them there until he arrived, of course.

Maricruz awoke startled. The silence in the room was so profound that she could hear the entire telephone conversation. When Gustavo hung up, she was doing up her trousers and running around the room looking for her notebook, her tape recorder and other tools of her trade.

"You can't come with me, I'm sorry," he stopped her. "I am going to take care of a work matter and the press is not invited. It's that simple. I will be back as soon as I can."

After a couple of attempts at arguing which she already knew was futile, common sense overwhelmed journalistic hunger, and Maricruz let him go with the promise that when he returned he would tell her everything, whether or not it was publishable.

They looked disoriented when the homicide chief met them, she was warming herself up with a cup of hot chocolate and he was pacing nervously in the corridor. He asked for them to be brought to his office, to which both acceded unwillingly, arguing that they had been very disturbed by their experience.

At first glance, Gustavo made several conjectures about the couple. The woman, who must have been around 30, was tall and dressed soberly and elegantly. She wore jewellery that looked genuine and her gestures indicated a good education and manners. The man seemed a little older and must have also had a comfortable life, judging by the designer clothes he was wearing and the heavy gold watch around his wrist. They could not be husband and wife, he suspected, since there was none of the physical contact frequent between people who have a close relationship, they didn't hold hands or search for closeness with their bodies, but seemed to avoid each other deliberately.

"I'm sorry to waste your time," Gustavo excused himself, "but it's very important that we try to reconstruct events as minutely as possible now that they are fresh in your memories."

"Couldn't we wait until tomorrow?" the man asked.

'The fact is that you are not obliged to stay here. You are not being detained or anything like that, but I have to ask you to make an effort and collaborate. What has happened to you, as far as I understand, was very traumatic and it could be that by tomorrow you have forgotten important details. The mind works like that."

"We understand," the woman intervened and directed a reproachful look at her companion.

She paused and wiped her forehead with a tissue that she took out of her handbag.

"Let me first make an important declaration: my friend and I are married but not to each other. Do you understand? If this comes out, we could both have very serious problems."

"Nothing of this will see the light of day. It doesn't suit us either if this is known publicly, we only want information that helps us identify a dangerous killer. The report will contain information about the facts, but not your personal details."

Her name was Adelia, she was 31 years old and a social worker employed in the prison system. Her friend answered to the name of Joaquín, was 39 years old and a lawyer and employee of the Ministry of Justice. They had conducted a secret relationship for two and a half years, she told him. That night they had been in a restaurant in Tarbaca, and on the way back they had stopped at the side of the road to admire the view of the city lights. It was then that it happened. A man approached the window, pointed his gun at Joaquín's head and ordered them to get out of the car. The night was profoundly dark and silent. There were no other cars parked or driving in the area, nor pedestrians.

The homicide chief interrupted. "I would like you to try to remember: when you went to the restaurant, during the time you were there, did you notice anything strange? A person who was watching you or who was behaving suspiciously? Any situation that didn't seem to fit?"

"No," Joaquín answered. "There were few people in the restaurant. Apart from us, we saw two couples who seemed normal, and a couple of guys drinking beer, they seemed a bit inebriated. Nothing more."

"Were you followed by any car when you were coming or going?"

"As we were driving there, I didn't realise it, but we might have been. Several cars were behind us. That's normal because the road only has one lane and it's fairly narrow. On the way back, we saw no car behind us."

"Where did you stop?"

Adelia answered: "At the side of the road, about two kilometres down from El Burio. We were there for five, at the most 10 minutes, looking at the view and talking."

"You didn't have any physical contact?"

"No, I don't think that we even kissed. We were having an argument, it wasn't that we were fighting exactly but we were not in the mood for romance," she said and they both smiled for the first time.

"I am negotiating a divorce from my wife but Adelia doesn't dare to do something similar with her husband."

"What happened then?"

"The man appeared suddenly," Joaquín explained. "We don't know where he came from. By the time we realised it, he had a gun rammed up against the window and was demanding that we get out of the car."

"What did he say to you? Do you remember his exact words?"

"Get out, get out or I'll blow your brains out."

"We got out and he led us into a coffee plantation at the other side of the road."

"How far did you go?"

"I was so nervous that my legs were shaking, the journey seemed to go on forever. At a particular point he made us stop."

"Where?"

"I don't know, in the coffee plantation. We were going like a threshing machine through the jungle and suddenly he ordered us to stop. He was pushing us. He made us kneel down."

"Did you manage to see him? Could you describe him physically?"

"He was a strapping guy, around one metre eighty, approximately," Joaquín said. "He wore army fatigues and I think his face was painted with dark lines, like military camouflage. However, I couldn't see his features. There was very little light and the guy was very careful that the light that did come into the plantation did not reveal his face."

"Shoes?"

"Boots, like the ones the police wear."

"Did you see the weapon he was carrying?"

"I did nothing else the whole time," he admitted. "I was just waiting for the moment when a bullet blew my brains out."

Gustavo called over the intercom for the guard to ask the weapons depot to bring an M-3 and a Stern to his office.

"Once you were on your knees, what happened?"

"The guy took out a Bible from his jacket pocket. Or at least it was a thick book that looked exactly like a Bible."

"He started to read," said Adelia. "He read the complete chapters one and two of Hosea."

"Didn't you say that the coffee plantation was dark?"

"Yes, but the man read. I don't know how he did it. At least he pretended to read and recited it from memory."

"Might he have made up some phrases, perhaps?" Gustavo suggested.

"No, no," the woman said. "I'm sure it was the biblical text. I studied at Catholic college and the nuns made us read the Bible for at least an hour every day. The Book of Hosea was one of their favourites. I spent 11 years repeating these phrases and I know almost all of them by heart: *'Rebuke your mother, rebuke her, for she is not my wife, and I am not her husband. Let her remove the adulterous look from her face and the unfaithfulness from between her breasts.'* Do you want to hear another? *'Their mother has been unfaithful and has conceived them in disgrace. She said, "I will go after my lovers, who give me my food and my water, my wool and my linen, my oil and my drink".'*"

"He seemed transformed while he read. There was a moment when he got really furious, he was almost shouting and he was moving the gun as if he was shooting us. I thought that our time was up," Joaquín added.

"I remember it perfectly," she said. "It was when he read the part: *'Otherwise I will strip her naked and make her as bare as on the day she was born; I will make her like a desert, turn her into a parched land...'* I thought about the girls he had killed and what they say he did to them, it was terrible."

Her voice broke off in a sob and she started to shake. Her jaw was quivering and her body shook as if she was freezing. Gustavo paused and addressed the man.

"What happened next?"

"After reading the Bible, he devoted himself to yelling at us. He said the world is as it is because of sex, that women have lost their dignity and that someone has to do something to clean it up. Stuff like that, he talked a lot, he said many things, all related to women's virtue. At the end he asked us if we knew who he was but we didn't dare say that he was the Psycho so he insisted: Do you know who I am? And it occurred to me that he was the man who had killed several women, I don't know, I was scared of saying the Psycho – perhaps I thought it would annoy him and make him more aggressive."

"And what did he do then?"

"When I said that he was the one who had killed the women, it seems to me that he smiled. He told us: 'You are lucky, you are lucky because on any other day I would have executed you. Today I can't do it because it's not the right day.' That's what he told us and he ordered us to get out of there running as fast as we could."

"I don't know how I managed to run," said Adelia, drying a tear. "My legs felt like lead, I thought I was going to faint."

"We came out near the car and I don't know how it wasn't stolen since the doors were open and the keys were still in the lock," said Joaquín. "On the way we decided to come and make a statement because at some point we considered remaining silent, but we thought that this was something very serious and the police had to know."

"You did well," said the homicide chief. "Some of the information you have given us is very valuable. Now tell me, would you recognise his voice if you heard it again."

"I am sure. This voice is engraved in my head. I don't think I'll forget it as long as I live."

At that moment an officer entered with a weapon in each arm and, after a signal from the boss, he put them both on the desk.

"Which one looks like the weapon the suspect was carrying," Gustavo asked.

"That one," said Joaquin, indicating the M-3 without hesitation.

"That's the story, more or less," Gustavo took a sip of coffee and chewed the piece of toast. It was dawn and an orange glow was rising over the hills, framed by the window of the dining room.

"I don't have the slightest doubt that it was the Psycho," he added. "The only thing that is strange is that he let them escape with their lives, that doesn't tally with anything."

"Maybe it does," said Maricruz. "We are close to the waning quarter."

"That again," he made a sign of disapproval with his head.

"Isn't it clear enough? The guy has never committed a crime on a date when there is no full moon. I also thought that it was a simple coincidence, but this incident finally convinces me. This couple was saved because it wasn't a full moon."

"Then what was the killer doing in this place at this time?"

"He was preparing his next crime, observing with much anticipation the places frequented by couples. Perhaps he approached this couple out of high-handedness, but killing was not on his programme for the night. Like someone saying, 'I am here, I can show myself, I give myself the luxury of leaving live witnesses, I am so clever that even like this you cannot catch me'."

Gustavo shrugged his shoulders. "And the Bible? That is what disconcerts me. How can such a bloody criminal carry a Bible beneath his arm and sermonise."

Maricruz paused to think and the first of her interviews with Madame Fronvac came to mind.

"Irma Solares told me something that I did not understand at all until now. She told me that something like psychology was not enough to understand the behaviour of a killer, that a man needs a moral base to carry in his conscience such crimes without them destroying him."

"That means that in his disturbed logic, he is doing no more than punish the one who has sinned, especially the woman."

"Not very original," Maricruz commented. "During the Inquisition they burned women who were unfaithful to their husbands and Islamic fundamentalists still condemn them to die through stoning. It's possible that the Psycho considers himself chosen by God to clean up the world."

Gustavo nodded. Suddenly he felt that the killer was planning a new strike. It could be in the days around full moon, as his companion suggested. It was the only thing that was predictable. The place, the victims, continued to be distressing unknowns.

"Step up vigilance on Manuel Sandoval, or Manuel Funes, however he likes to be called," she said.

"We have no other way, I think that I will mount an operation to follow him 24 hours a day."

Maricruz made a gesture of approval. She took the policeman by his hand and led him to the unmade bed that still bore traces of her warmth.

"I have a few minutes before I have to go, would you like to take advantage of them Mr Policeman or have you used up all your energy?"

19

S oaked to the skin, with her unruly monumental fuzz of hair, wearing canvas sandals, a tiny miniskirt in army camouflage and a tight T-shirt, Diana entered the newsroom at around 10am, waving an imaginary banner and loudly singing the Marseillaise. The peculiar entrance provoked an immediate commotion. Her colleagues gathered around her, anxious to hear what, by any reckoning, was fresh news.

"I come to proclaim the end of tyranny," she said. "No more men in my house, no more men in my life. From now on, I promise to throw myself at all those who take my fancy, squeeze them for what they are, immense glands of semen, and then return them to the dustbin, the right place for them. *Vive la liberté!*"

"You got rid of Roberto. At last you managed to throw him out of your house," Maricruz guessed.

"Yes, and I also got rid of that queer," Diana signalled the cubicle in which Gabriel was pretending that he did not understand or care about the racket that was growing under his nose. The statement was unnecessary because the same audience had witnessed, a week before, the scandalous rupture. The public part of the uproar was a loud defence of the essential right of every human person (that's how Diana said it: human person) to

show their arse however many times they liked, in front of whoever they liked, in whatever circumstances, sober or drunk. And
to better emphasise the seriousness of what she had said and to
give her assertion more weight, she had lowered her panties to
show the amused crowd her white and rounded assertion.

"So now I am perfectly and totally free," she said.

There was applause and laughter, some overripe comments,
but the newspaper soon returned to its rhythm of normal activity, although not for long.

The signs of what would happen that Thursday had begun to
manifest themselves on Monday, although no one would have
been capable of anticipating their outcome. That day, Mr Grey
arrived at the newspaper very early, a few minutes before 8am.
He looked disfigured. Between curses, waving his arms and legs
in a ridiculous way that recalled the movements of a marionette,
he managed to inform the head of the print room (to spit in his
face would be a more graphic description) that a printing error
had caused the loss of an advertising contract worth many millions of *pesos*, which would cost not just his head but that of whoever had the slightest responsibility, whether out of negligence,
omission or inexperience. He spent the rest of Monday in an
intolerable mood, complaining about everything that was put in
front of him. The heads of department were the recipients of
degrading 'memos' in which he warned them of massive decapi-
tations (which in his vernacular meant dismissal without compensation). By 3pm he had already 'decapitated' the recently
designated head of the print room and three of his co-workers,
and he personally ordered a police investigation into every section in the hope of finding whoever might be to blame, directly or
indirectly, for the costly blunder. Not even Camila escaped that
catastrophic rage when she had the unfortunate idea of suggesting that he pay legal compensation to those who had been fired,
because it was certain that they would sue.

"We have more than enough experience and we know that
judges always side with the workers and in the end we are going
to have to pay them and the damned lawyer, which is no good for
anything," she said, but her argument only infuriated the

gringo. He shouted her out of his office, saying that if he had to go to court to fight he would and they would see what it means to buy themselves a ruckus with William H. Grey.

Dawn on Tuesday surprised him in the print room, his shirt stained with ink, his face full of stubble, his eyes rolling as he supervised, to the very last detail, the final phase of printing. But, once the task had been completed, he did not go off to rest, as any other person would have advised, but locked himself in his office to set down in black and white the ideas that he had been chewing over the previous day: a diatribe against the paternalist state and its laws to protect the lazy, a furious attack on the vagabond way of life, mother of all poverty and underdevelopment, a death sentence against the minimum wage, the 13th-month bonus, overtime, payments for redundancy, vacations, public holidays and other undeserved rewards for everyday incompetence.

So as not to contradict him, no one reminded him that he had not slept so that, once he had written and revised his article, which he ordered to be published as editorial opinion the next day, he resumed his daily activity just as normal. Although this 'as normal' was only during the first two hours, because the lack of sleep was making him increasingly nervous and irascible. The mental gaps multiplied, to the extent that he forgot the name of his secretary and for a moment confused Juan José with one of his grown-up sons who lived in Argentina and whom he had not seen for two years. The confusion was brief, at the most a couple of seconds, but it was enough to shock him and send him running to take his vitamins, with an extra dose of phosphorus, which he had stopped taking since... he didn't remember when.

At night he installed himself again in the print room, now with the excuse that he had not put anyone in charge of it, but at 1am he sat down to rest on a roll of paper and fell asleep. He woke up suddenly an hour later, when the press started to roll. At 5am on Wednesday morning he went home and slept for two hours, but at 9am exactly he was as fresh as a lettuce, discussing with the head of advertising a strategy to recover the client that had been lost through the printing error. Then strange things began to proliferate. The first to notice it was the secretary whom he asked to "please" bring him a cup of coffee.

"I can't bear that cow," he said, which Majorie interpreted as a reference to Amalia, the cleaner, who usually served him his morning coffee. But suddenly he indicated a photograph of Camila on his desk. "And if she brings me cheques to sign, tell her that I'm not here, that I went to Siberia," he said and smiled in such a vacant way that his face evoked a picture postcard that had arrived from far away.

Later he called Juan José to plan a report about the economic disaster caused by the president Luis Alberto Monge in his rupture with the International Monetary Fund. Noticing that the gringo was experiencing some kind of delirium, he tried to explain tactfully that Monge was no longer president and that it had not been him but his predecessor Rodrigo Carazo, although you could link it with the reduction in aid from the United States because of the Central American peace plan driven by President Arias. "Sounds interesting, let's do it," Mr Grey said, dismissing Juan José in the manner of a Roman emperor. At 3pm he sent out for several bottles of wine and ordered the whole newspaper to cease production to toast the birthday of his mother who had died no less than 13 years previously, or so Camila remembered. This last incident convinced his wife of the necessity to intervene before her husband's nervous crisis led to tragedy. She entered the office and spoke in the authoritarian tone that had worked infallibly during 22 years of marriage.

"Home!" she said. "You have to rest."

Bill Grey did not even lift his eyes from the keyboard. He barely arched an eyebrow and replied with astonishing lucidity.

"Why don't you take one of your sometime lovers? I am busy."

It was the first time that he had reproached his wife for her sexual adventures, which she had supposed he was ignorant of. Disconcerted by his response, Camila set off for her office without saying a word, afflicted by a sudden onset of diarrhoea. That night the director president of the newspaper left early, but he did not go home and no one knew anything more until Thursday morning.

Soon after Diana had announced her emancipation, *El Matutino* was shaken to the core by another spectacle: Mr Grey turned up in a deplorably dishevelled state, his eyes like coal, his face unshaven. He made a silent tour of the building, his face frozen in an inane smile and then, without saying a word, he locked himself in his office. He answered none of the telephone calls that they tried to put through to him and, on several occasions, Majorie put her ear to the door of his office and heard strange nosies: thumps on the wall, murmuring and objects being thrown. Two hours had passed when she heard laughter and muffled sobs from inside the office. After asking him many times to open the door, Camila ordered the security guard to force the lock and confront what had to be confronted, trying not to hurt him.

The sight was painful even for those who hated him, who were not a few. Splayed out on the carpet, with a vacant gaze, Mr Grey was laughing and sobbing intermittently, in the midst of a mess of papers and objects of all kinds scattered all over the floor, including the reproductions of the Impressionist paintings that he admired so much. He offered no resistance, he did not even seem to realise what was happening, when two nurses lifted him up and led him to the ambulance, offering him via a hypodermic syringe a way back to the paradise of lost serenity.

That afternoon, Camila returned, disorientated and taciturn, to the newspaper. Her first impulse was to call Juan José to whom she confessed the details of what had happened.

"I could not repeat the diagnosis in medical terms, but the fact is he is stark raving mad," she said. "It seems he has been using a ton of cocaine. They say that he has the characteristics of a longtime addict and that it's possible he has mixed this with other drugs... amphetamines, anti-depressants, I no longer remember the list."

"He was so strange... the last time that we talked he commented that he felt very tired, that financial success was killing him," Juan José said. "It seemed to me that someone else was speaking through his mouth, but I couldn't understand what was going on until now."

"He told you that? It is odd, my husband is an ambitious man who has always been tireless at work."

"He is a fanatic," Juan José said, "and I don't say that to offend, we are all fanatics in one way or another."

Camila looked at him astonished.

"Aristotle was mistaken when he defined man as a political animal," he tried to explain. "In reality, it would be much more exact to say that man is a fanatical animal. Your husband is a fanatic for money, of the multiplication of his profits."

"That is the rationality of the system," she claimed.

"But a system whose rationality is the maximisation of profits can produce people who are fairly irrational."

"And what is your obsession?"

"Loneliness," he said, "perhaps."

"All I know is that Bill is ill and it's my fault," Camila sobbed shaking her head. "Not only have I been unfaithful, I have also been imprudent. He knew everything and he kept quiet, it depressed him and led him to take drugs. It's possible that he even knows about us..."

For a moment, Juan José was not as moved by the possibility that the gringo knew about his adventures with Camila as by the feelings of guilt of a woman who, until shortly before, he had considered to be a simple contraption of bone and muscle without soul. He had the urge to comfort her, perhaps to wipe away the small tear rolling down her cheek, but the limited trust between them was not enough to justify such an excess of tenderness.

"And why do you do it?"

"What?"

"Screw around?"

Camila seemed surprised by the question. No one, not even she herself, had ever asked it before – so she paused for a while to consider her reply.

"All my life I have been a horny woman," she said at last. "My desires have not diminished with age. Besides, Bill has not been the same for some time. It's not that we no longer have sex, but that it's increasingly less frequent and now he does it reluctantly."

"Do you want to hear something ugly and funny?"

She nodded.

"Before I thought you were insensitive, a cold and evil woman."

"I know," she smiled. "I am the administrator of a difficult company. It's up to me to take cruel decisions and it's normal that people hate me. I am used to that, but what I cannot get used to is hypocrisy, that everyone smiles to my face and insults me and wishes me ill behind my back. That's why I liked you when you said to me the other day: 'I thought we hated each other'," she said, imitating the low deep voice of Juan José.

"I consider myself the loudmouth of the family. In this country, that does not produce many dividends."

"I have realised," said Camila, briefly consulting her watch and changing the subject. "Tomorrow I am travelling to Houston with Bill, I am going to have him admitted to a specialist clinic, to see if they can help him. I will be gone for weeks or a couple of months. During this time you will be completely in charge of the editorial side, but I would ask you not to make important changes, I want the newspaper to maintain the line that he wanted to give it until now. At least in this let's be loyal."

"It will not be easy because his line has not been consistent recently. However, I believe that I'll go along and not only do things that I want to do."

"I see that you've understood, so I'm relaxed about this aspect of things. What worries me now is the financial side. I am going to give instructions to my assistant," she said and vanished with a handshake, polite but a little distant, it seemed to Juan José.

20

In our job strange things often happen, said Officer Marco Aurelio Morales. You investigate a case and by chance discover a crime that no one knew anything about: you follow the lead to one suspect and collide with the true criminal, who had seemed a very upright person. Neither of the two previous cases was exactly that, he clarified, but the discovery that he'd made suggested a new line of investigation. On examining the migration record of Manuel Sandoval he discovered that a couple of years earlier he had been detained by airport officials as he tried to leave the country carrying a weapon, a Makarov with a laser guide. It seems that the weapon was unloaded and that he was carrying no bullets, Morales explained, so the authorities didn't attach too much importance to it. Or rather, it's not that he was thinking of hijacking the aeroplane or something like that because no one is going to hijack a plane with an unloaded weapon, especially if you don't carry the weapon in your hand luggage but camouflage it in a suitcase, as was the case. But the interesting part was not so much this but that Funes was accompanied by Bruno Robledo, the young man who is always appearing on television and in the magazine *Perfile*. And that's where he got the hunch because – he had to say it again – it was nothing more than a hunch, he didn't even know what he was going to find but these strange things often happen in one's job. So he started to look at Robledo's migration documents, a mountain of arrivals and departures. Trips to Miami, Panama, Mexico and Spain, but mostly to Panama and Mexico. At first he had not found anything unusual, there are people who travel a lot, especially people who have a lot of money or whose work obliges them to travel, and according to what they said about Robledo he had plenty of money. And then I almost forgot about this matter, but suddenly a light came on. I started looking at the dates when he came and left, and sensed that there was something in them, but I didn't know what. And I was thinking and thinking about it for days. Until finally, zap, there it was. I saw that the first date co-incided and the second and the third and the fourth. I'll explain. Don't lose faith in me. The discovery, the official explained, was that Bruno Robledo had left the country two or three days after each appearance of the Psycho, stayed away for a while and then returned and soon after his return a new crime occurred.

The homicide chief found the new discovery more than interesting, almost promising, but the director of the Judicial Police showed a lot less enthusiasm.

"It's a bit of a weak lead," he commented after carefully going over the documents that Morales presented. "It's certain that some dates of his departure coincide but there are others that would have nothing to do with it, such as this one," he said, pointing at the list.

"There's a very strange coincidence between those exits from the country and the crimes of the Psycho, I don't think we can discard the possibility, even if it is remote, that there is a connection," said Gustavo.

"What worries me is the time. We've invested a lot of resources in this investigation and there is not a single result that one would say is at least encouraging."

"I want you to investigate Robledo," Gustavo told Morales. "Find out all you can about his activities, his personal history, his family etcetera. But be quick. You have two days to deliver a complete report to me which will enable us to decide whether to keep investigating or dismiss your hunch."

Morales nodded and left. Gustavo remained alone with his boss, who looked at him in a strange way, scratching his balding head as usual, with four fingers of his left hand.

"Are you blaming me because there are no results?"

"You are the homicide chief and for months we've been stabbing in the dark. Now it turns out that the killer even has the luxury of sending us direct messages, leaves witnesses so that we realise how intelligent he is and how stupid we are."

"You know very well Don Jovel, that our work depends on the mistakes made by the criminal. Neither I nor my officers are to blame for the fact that the killer is so astute. Now if you think that this is our incompetence, well..."

"No, it's not about that. It's that... I don't know if I should say it. Promise me you'll be discreet."

Don Jovel confessed that he was working hard on his candidacy to become a member of parliament in upcoming elections. However, the mystery of the Psycho was becoming a stone in his shoe.

"Everyone in the party says more or less the same: very good Jovel, I'm sure that you can play a great part in the Legislative Assembly, shame about the small matter of the Psycho, it would really benefit you if we managed to clear it up before the party convention."

Gustavo shrugged.

"No one would be happier than me to end this. Since you are so interested, let me have more people. I don't guarantee that we are going to resolve the case, but how many more can we have. Ah, and I think it's great that you are standing for parliament, you can count on my vote."

"How many more officers?"

"Ten."

"You're mad," the chief exclaimed. "I can't handicap other departments, I'd be a joke. And neither am I going to ask the court for a *centavo* more. Remember that the president of the court is from the other party and I don't have much influence at that level anyway."

Don Jovel considered his few options. Finally, he came to a decision, but it took him a couple of minutes to get into the right state of mind to propose it to Gustavo.

"Let's make a deal," he said. "I'll give you five men from tomorrow and within a month you will have the killer, or at least a suspect, in preventative custody."

The proposal disconcerted the homicide chief. How could he promise that such a complicated case would be solved within a month? Did the chief think that the lack of firm results was deliberate? Or did he imagine that putting five more investigators on the case was a magic formula?

"The part about the five officers is fine, the other part of the proposal I don't understand," he admitted.

"It's very simple," the director explained. "If we find the Psycho, so much the better. If not, I want a suspect with a lot of circumstantial evidence against him, it doesn't matter if the judge rules out the charges, because by then the party convention will have passed."

Gustavo's first impulse was to throw his papers, the ashtray and any other objects that were at hand at Don Jovel's face. It would have been an eloquent and magnificent response but highly impractical because of its evident consequences. All he had to do, he thought for a moment, was to refuse calmly and firmly, and hold on to his position. During the nine years that he had been with the police, it was the first time someone had proposed such a dishonest act. Although when in the street you heard unjust accusations – the Judicial Police uses torture, fabricates proof, invents convenient scapegoats – such practices had never occurred in his department, not with his consent. And he would not start now after so many years of clean and self-sacrificing service.

"I assure you I will do all that is humanly possible to solve the case, that is all I can promise," Gustavo said. "If I don't manage it in a reasonable time, you can count on my resignation."

"Don't be so self-righteous," Don Jovel responded. "The streets are full of crooks who deserve to be in jail, who have an infinite number of encounters with justice. The only thing you have to do is grab one of them and saddle him with the crimes, afterwards he will be judged innocent of this crime but guilty of the ones he did commit. The important thing is that, at this moment, he will be very useful to us."

"He'd be very useful to you, it would be all the same to me. Frankly."

"Don't be so sure." Don Jovel got up from his seat, went over to the homicide chief and put a hand on his shoulder with all the warmth of a politician in full campaign mode. "If I get elected to the Assembly, I would leave everything arranged so that you would take over my job. I don't think there would be any opposition. It would be a very natural progression because everybody recognises your talent and the quality of your work."

Gustavo didn't know whether to feel flattered or even more offended. The best thing was to put an end to this shameless exchange. He stood up and reiterated to the boss that he would do everything possible to solve the case as quickly as possible.

When she heard it, she almost cried with rage. The news had been right under her nose. She had touched it and smelled it, it had murmured in her ear and yet she had not been capable of detecting it. And now it was too late because a rival newspaper had published the whole story, an exclusive, double-page spread, making her feel ridiculous. Maricruz, incredulous, looked over the text again in search of inconsistencies but all the pieces fitted together with perfect logic.

At least 10 people claimed to have been swindled out of millions and pointed the finger of blame at a chemist who went by the name of Vico. The man, the report said, acted as if he officiated over a moon cult to Isis, to whom the ancient Egyptians attributed infinite powers. One by one, Vico convinced members of the cult – a few more than 20 – that he headed an international committee charged with raising funds to build a magnificent temple on El Caribe island, which was to be the home of the goddess and the meeting place for all her followers in America. He promised to bring from eastern countries great masters in the doctrine so that they could direct the development of the brotherhood and help the spiritual and emotional growth of their members. Some had given him significant sums of money, others handed over loans and mortgages, yet others donated jewellery and valuable titles with the hope of earthly prosperity and salvation after death. Most said they had been recruited by an astrologer named Madame Fronvac who, through various sessions and on the strength of intimating imminent disasters in their lives, had managed to convince them that only devotion to a powerful deity could alter the course of these astral sentences. With much embellishment, she suggested that she could put them in contact with someone she knew who led a select and secretive congregation. Some weeks later, they said, Don Vico announced that some journalists had managed to infiltrate the group pretending to be students interested in esoteric knowledge. He warned that the place they had met in would have to be closed and in less than a week he would call them to arrange a new meeting place. By the time they began to suspect something was up, it was too late – their money had vanished along with Madame Fronvac and the millions they had invested for the good of the cause. It was not known if the suspects had fled the country, but it was a probable hypothesis on which the police were working.

"Do you realise," said Maricruz after gulping down a tequila and relieving her throat with the juice of a slice of lime, "they used us like a pair of idiots?"

"I know it's my fault. I took you there but it was not out of any bad motive," said Pedro. "I only wanted to help. I have known the woman since I was little."

"Gustavo had warned me to be careful of these people. What I don't understand is why they had to involve us in their game."

La Villa was almost empty, perhaps because of the time, barely 5.30pm, and Tilín was drinking a beer reclining on the bar as he listened to Carlos Puebla singing: '*al que asome la cabeza, duro con el, Fidel, Fidel...*' Pedro gestured for another round, a whisky on the rocks and a tequila for Maricruz.

"We put ourselves there," Pedro corrected her. "The old lady Solares did nothing but make a bed for us and we fell into it."

Tilín brought the drinks and moved a chair closer to their table.

"Do you want to buy a bar?" he asked. "I'm selling it as a going concern."

"Again? You're always selling the business," said Pedro.

"This time it's for real," said Tilín. "Perhaps someone else knows how to revive this shit hole. Gorbachev didn't only finish the Soviet Union and socialism, he liquidated this canteen. More and more people are disenchanted with the revolution, some have moved on to social democracy. They don't want to come into a place with pictures of Che Guevara and the music of Silvio Rodríguez."

"You're right," the voice of Maricruz sounded tipsy after her fifth tequila. "I'll buy it off you."

"With what?" Tilín was interested.

"What do you care? Tomorrow I'll come, sane and sober, and we'll talk business, alright?"

"Okay," the owner smiled and went off to serve some customers who were calling for him.

"Don't mess the poor guy around," Pedro said.

"I'm not messing around..." Maricruz said, banging her fist on the table. "I'm going to get the money and dedicate myself to this. Now that it's clear that I'm a disaster as a journalist."

Pedro collapsed laughing.

"I am no good as a reporter, so what do you want me to do? Imagine what they'll be saying about me at the newspaper? I can almost hear the gringo, or what he would have said had he not gone mad: 'I told you Maricruz, that these stories were rubbish, your great source was an old conwoman'."

"It's only a minor cock-up."

"A minor cock-up? It's the most ridiculous thing I have ever done in my life, my report was practically a novel and it was all crap... Crap," the reporter repeated dramatically.

"For God's sake, journalism is nothing but a gigantic factory of fiction. There is nothing that resembles the truth. The only difference between literature and journalism is that the first does not try to pass itself off with a semblance of reality, totally the opposite, and frequently tries to emphasise the fictitious aspect of events that are proven. On the other hand, journalism succumbs if it does not pretend to be exact and trustworthy, a pretension that in itself is a highly amusing fiction."

Maricruz opened her eyes as wide as possible, to try to understand Pedro's arguments.

"If a journalist wants to, he or she can resist pressures and be fairly objective."

"That's a tender illusion, sweetheart, but impossible. Objectivity doesn't exist. There exists not one but many different realities, as many as the eyes and minds that perceive them."

"You're drunk. Booze always gets you worked up about metaphysics."

"I'll give you a simple example: if a drunkard crashes into a lamp post and dies, is that or is that not news?"

"Of course."

"And which aspect of this event is most important?"

"His death, the circumstances of the accident, what he had to drink."

"But there is the deception. Those details are nothing more than external appearance. The 'make-up' of the news. What should really matter is the man, the human transfusion of the man and his real environment. His children. His wife, the lover whom he leaves abandoned, the dreams of his life that he will never fulfil. What drove this man to drink? What went through the victim's mind at the last moment? How much did he contribute to enrich life or how much pain and suffering did he leave in his wake? The value of the lamp post and the car's licence plate are details that should not interest anyone."

"But there is no way of knowing. How are we going to know what went through his mind at the final moment?"

"Correct, the essential is always unattainable, which is why I am telling you that journalism is nothing more than a kind of hypocritical fiction."

"Don't you get it? I have to leave this lousy job as soon as possible. I am going to buy the bar off Tilín and devote myself to decent work."

"And we'll change the name," Pedro picked up the thread, "we could christen it 'Free Enterprise' or 'Bar Neo-Liberalism' to counterract its reputation."

"And what do we do with the wailing wall?"

"Maybe we'll just leave the photo of Che Guevara, which is a symbol of consumer society."

I can't believe it. Lidia told me this afternoon that she is going on holiday. She will spend three entire weeks taking a short tour around Europe. On the arm of her husband. And she's not content just to hit me with this blow, but has to describe the itinerary in full. Paris, to begin with, then Geneva and Lugano, Rome and Venice and finally Madrid and Barcelona. I reminded her that I'll be alone and that I will miss her desperately and she told me off for what she called my 'childish temperament'. It's only three weeks, she said. "You won't have begun to notice my absence and I'll be on my way back." And what can I do? What can I say?

Shouldn't it be the beggar who establishes the extent of the charity?

I spent a few hours consumed by jealousy, but I finally decided that these feelings make no sense. I rationalised it. And her husband, with whom she wakes and goes to bed, with whom she makes love, with whom she eats breakfast and supper. What difference does it make if all that happens in San José or Paris? A little more reflection and the truth illuminates the sad night of my apartment: that Lidia is going to Europe on a trip causes me no more jealously than I normally suffer, but envy, because I know that I will never be able to take this trip with her, nor do any of those daily things that she enjoys. And that means she will never be mine, that I will always be relegated to a small dark corner of her heart.

So, imbued with the philosophy of the inevitable, I bade her farewell with a kiss and asked her to bring me back a little Eiffel Tower, one of those tacky souvenirs that tourists bring when they return from the French capital.

Later, I was thinking about how irrational and how insatiable affection is. They give you a look and you want a kiss, they give you a kiss and you want their whole body, they give you their body and you demand their soul. Dissatisfaction is the constant of love and frequently it is all that endures when there is nothing left to give or to demand.

21

The young woman was beautiful, with the vivacious eyes, distinction and self-assured attitude of rich girls, thought Officer Morales as she invited him into the small apartment, whose luxurious décor exactly suited the haughty bearing and fine manners of its owner. He played hard to get before accepting a Bavaria (although he would have preferred a Scotch on the rocks and she was offering him a bar with all the best brands), because it seemed to him a little delicate, if not outrageous, to allow oneself to be invited for a drink by a woman, however upper class she was. While Lucrecia Robledo was serving him, the officer focused on the details of her home: there was an odd oil painting the size of an entire wall, something with a woman who resembled a stick, that's to say, either a very feminine stick or a lady with very tough skin, above a shelf with some orange-coloured carnations; a rug made of alpaca fleece; and ornaments of porcelain and crystal, and one or two of metal, including a bronze archangel with huge, splayed wings. She must have money to spare, although her taste was a bit weird, he said to himself as Lucrecia handed him his drink.

"You're not having anything?"

"It's a bit early," she smiled and Officer Morales smiled back, conscious that the question was stupid and the answer quite deft because he knew well that a rich young lady does not just share a drink with whichever neighbour's son happens to sit down in her apartment.

He did not need to make an introduction, or deliver a prologue or in-depth explanation because the young woman did this with polite but precise and forceful words.

"Before we talk, I want to explain that I agreed to meet you because I was asked to do so by my good friend, the district attorney Belisario Torres, who promised me that this interview would be completely confidential."

"That was the agreement," the officer said.

"That means they will never summon me to give a statement to anyone, much less a judge or someone like that. Is that right?"

"Absolutely. All we want is for someone close to Mr Robledo to help us with some information, something that guides us in our investigation."

"What do you want to know?" Lucrecia crossed her arms and legs in a gesture that Morales found hard to decipher. Was she ready for a long chat, or was this psychological shutdown?

"Although it might seem strange, we want to know more about Bruno than you read in magazines, something about his family relationships, how he is in his private life, his character, his likes, that kind of thing. I've been told that you know him better than most."

Lucrecia sighed deeply. It seemed an embarrassing request, an oppressive burden.

"Well, yes, I do know him – we are cousins, practically siblings since we grew up together. And I think that your intuition is a good one, the public image of Bruno is one thing and the private man is something very different."

"To what do you refer?" the agent asked.

"To everything," she said. "But tell me, what's he up to this time?"

"To be honest, it's not that he's involved in something. It's a bit difficult to explain but we are just working on a suspicion, it could turn out to be nothing or the clues might lead us to someone else."

"I can't know?" Lucrecia deduced from his ambiguous explanation.

"I assure you that this conversation will be more beneficial if we keep this unknown for now. If you help me, I promise you that at the end I'll tell you what it's about. Agreed?"

Lucrecia grew more animated as she listened. She adored guessing games and she knew that the questions would give her the answer long before the policeman did. So she began to talk without further ado.

"My father and Bruno's father were very close brothers," she said. "By that I mean that my siblings and I spent a lot of time at my uncle's house, we played with our cousins, we ate with them and often we spent the night there, sharing beds and pyjamas. That went on until we were teenagers when we began to grow more distant for different reasons. One of those was Bruno's strange behaviour."

"Strange in what way?"

"From a very young age he was obsessive. I don't know if that is the right expression, but you know what I mean by obsessive. He would always find whatever way to torture us – he hid our toys or broke them. He would attack us without being provoked. Analysing this now as an adult, I would say that he had a particular skill for causing psychological pain. He frequently found a person's weak spot and put his finger in the wound, in deep. How can I explain it? Let's say that, more than a boy, he seemed like a perverse adult, the type of person who has had a bad time and who lives life full of resentment, wanting to take revenge on anything put in front of him."

"Ah," Morales gave a nod of approval.

"These characteristics worsened in adolescence. He became more brutal and his physical attacks on his siblings and cousins became really dangerous. On one occasion he was on the point of killing me."

"What?"

"My uncle's house was on a fairly large estate, with several internal roads. Once I had a heated discussion with Bruno, I don't remember what it was about exactly, but the whole thing was over quickly. With him, you could never discuss anything for long because he would become violent and it was better to shut up or to say that he was right. Half an hour later I was walking along one of these roads when I heard a car coming at full speed. I turned to see my cousin coming full steam at me as though he wanted to run me over. I just had time to throw myself to the side of the road and the car missed me by just a few centimetres."

"Do you really believe that he would have run you over?"

"I'm sure of it. At the speed he was going he wouldn't have been able to swerve or stop. If I had taken a couple of seconds longer to react, you wouldn't be talking to me now."

Morales took a gulp of his beer and swallowed it slowly, allowing the liquid to flow down his dry throat and for the alcohol to awaken his dormant brain cells.

"How old were you then?"

"He is around two years older than me. At that time I was about 15, Bruno must have been 17 or 18, something like that."

"And the other cousins. What were they like? Were they also violent?"

"They were all fairly rough, but none was like him. Marco and Juan Carlos were bossy and brusque when we were playing sometimes. However, they could be affectionate and tender, like any child. Libia, the only girl, is an intelligent and very soft person, even a little shy. We are still good friends."

"Interesting," Morales exclaimed. "And what can you tell me about the family situation? His relationship with his parents?"

"Well, you know that my uncle is a very busy man, always involved in business and politics. He has been a minister, director of institutions, an MP. I would say that for many years, until my cousins were teenagers, their father was a fairly absent figure, although for them he is a kind of hero. My aunt, for her part, spent most of her time making sure that her husband did not leave her, accompanying him on his activities or sitting on women's committees for this and that, charity groups, Catholic women's groups, that type of thing."

"And who looked after the children?"

"Doña Libia, the maternal grandmother, who was like a character straight out of a film."

Morales waited patiently for the girl to explain. As a good investigator, he knew that a tendentious question could alter the meaning of a spontaneous statement.

"She was really a strange woman," said Lucrecia, almost surprised, as if this had just occurred to her. "She had a very rigid moral code, she was super religious, although she always seemed bitter. She subjected the kids to a terrible regime, she made them study the Bible for hours and if they made a mistake when she was there, she punished them terribly. She was one of those old ladies who forced you to stand for half an hour with your face turned to the wall. Today you'd say that such a person is aggressive but at that time people just said that she was a courageous lady and you could see that she kept the children in check."

"How was Bruno's relationship with his grandmother?"

"Because he was the most difficult, he always got the worst of it. She was the only person whom he really feared, sometimes I saw him shaking with the fear of meeting her. However (another strange thing about the family), she also seemed to be the only person whom he really loved. There was between them what I think psychologists call a love-hate relationship."

"Did she punish him physically? I mean, did she beat him?"

"I think that more than beatings it was about instilling terror. Although she would never have touched us, we felt that that woman had an almost supernatural power, that she could do what she wanted with people, crush them with a look or turn them into a pig, like the witches in fairytales."

"Because of the way you talk about this woman, I presume she died. Was it a long time ago?"

"No, four or five years ago."

"One more thing," the officer blinked. "What was Bruno's relationship with his grandmother like when he had grown up? Did it change?"

The girl shrugged her shoulders. She reached out to the coffee table and took a packet of cigarettes. She offered one to the policeman, but he politely refused.

She drew deeply on the cigarette and blew out the smoke calmly, in the manner of a long-time smoker.

"I distanced myself a lot from the family after the incident with the car, although I should have done so much earlier... I didn't dare. Sometimes when you're very young, you don't know that you can make your own decisions. Soon afterwards, my uncle sent him to a military academy in the United States. I don't remember what it was called. He was there for three years and on his return they put him in charge of an import company that was going bust. They practically gave it to him as a gift. He started making his own money and moved to his own apartment. It seems that as a businessman he is not so deficient. I suppose that by then the grandmother had lost her influence over him because of his age."

"Do you know if he followed any specialism in this military academy. Engineering? Economics or medical science?"

"I think it was an economic discipline. As I've told you, I lost contact but I think that Libia once told me he had studied something like business administration."

"What do you know about his private life, girlfriends, lovers?"

Lucrecia responded with a smile that spoke volumes. She bit her lower lip, a feminine gesture that often reflects a strong emotion, Morales thought. The gesture was followed by a long silence, which confirmed his perception.

"It's a bit delicate but since we've practically torn him to shreds, I have a friend who was his girlfriend and went out with him for six months. One day she told me that she had found it very difficult to get him into bed, he always invited her to places where there were lots of people and at parties he got so drunk he was capable of nothing more than dribbling down the front of his shirt. She said that when he finally agreed to go to bed with her, he went crazy, biting her and pinching her so much that he left her covered in bruises. Of course, she pushed him off her by hitting and punching him, and refused to have sex. Then, Bruno accused her of being frigid and things got more complicated so that in the end they broke up. I suspect he's impotent and that he does things to avoid anyone discovering his problem."

Seeing his glass was empty, Lucrecia insisted on offering him another beer. He looked at his notes while she served the drink and suddenly noticed that there was an important gap in his interrogation. What about the mother of the suspect? The boss had insisted on this point and it had somehow escaped him, as distracted as he was by many details, including the girl's legs and her smile.

"The woman was very busy," Lucrecia explained. "She would go out early in the morning and come back late at night. As she was surrounded by domestic servants, it was hard for her to have a direct link with her children. She would talk to them for a few minutes, give them a kiss and send them off to bed. Some weekends she and my uncle would take them to a country cabin near Puntarenas. More than once they invited me and I remember the house was always full of visitors, relatives, associates of my uncle, political hangers-on, but it was all the same to us. Despite Bruno's brutish behaviour, we had a lot of fun. However, looking back on the whole thing from an adult's perspective, I don't believe that my cousins had a sufficiently strong link with their parents."

"And your uncle. Was he the same?"

"Worse. My uncle never addressed them or came to see them unless it was to give orders: 'Silence', 'Get out of here', 'I am busy', 'Bring me my slippers', 'Turn down the volume on the TV'. Those were the phrases we heard when he was at home, which wasn't very often."

"And how do you think that this relationship with his parents could have affected Bruno?"

"When you are a child you get used to anything. What starts off as routine ends up being natural. They had the grandmother as the great figure, the one who always imposed authority and discipline. On the other hand, they – as much as we did – always got what they wanted in material terms."

The officer nodded. He looked at his notes under the enquiring gaze of Lucrecia Robledo. It seemed as if he had got answers to all his questions, although some were ambiguous.

"I think we have finished," he said. "At least, unless you want to add something that you consider important."

"How should I know?" she crossed her arms over her chest. "I thought that I could discover what this was about by following the thread of your questions, but I admit I'm more intrigued than I was at the beginning."

"We are working on an investigation into the crimes of the Psycho."

"What?" Lucrecia's eyes began to overflow. "Do you mean they suspect that my cousin is the one who killed those women?"

"Not exactly. As I said, the investigation could lead towards another person, but we have to discount some important signs."

"No, it can't be," Lucrecia laughed with a mixture of hilarity and nervousness. "The guy is awful, I know, but not that... please. He is an idiot, a yokel, whatever you want but... a disemboweller of women?"

22

That April afternoon when the bodies of the new victims appeared could not have been worse for Gustavo Cortés. Shortly before, he had said goodbye to Aurelia in the lift, the epilogue of a desolate meeting... two of the most bitter and confused hours that he remembered spending in his life. The woman looked as if she was in mourning, her eyes reddened and her dignity in tatters, although the last declaration she had made to Gustavo had been sincere: she was not bitter. She even gave him a last kiss on the cheek.

He had chosen a discreet café near the Los Yoses district and Aurelia accepted the invitation immediately because she already suspected the gist of what she was going to hear and she wanted to get it over with. Gustavo had been avoiding her for several weeks, his attitude was beginning to irritate her and, as a result, the best course of action was what she herself called 'dental therapy': an opportune extraction without further contemplation. However, she did not know that it would hurt her so much until she stood before him and heard his raw confession.

"When we started dating, I had already discounted that relationship," Gustavo said. "It all seemed clear. Moreover, I began to feel very comfortable in your company and I believed we had a future."

"Then?"

"Then... she appeared again. That was a possibility that I had contemplated in theory and I was sure that it would please me to reject her and tell her that I loved another woman. The problem is that sometimes one doesn't really know oneself... and one thinks that nothing is stronger than rationality, that to think and to want are the same thing. The point is, Aurelia, that I was mistaken. I had not stopped loving Maricruz however much I had tried."

Aurelia licked her lips lightly. The argument did not really convince her but she nodded because she was not in the mood for a debate. There was nothing she wanted less than a pathetic outburst, complete with a scene.

"It's not that I am in love," she argued. "But I must confess that I had started to get my hopes up."

Gustavo interrupted. "Like you, I was not in love but I also had hopes for us. I genuinely believed that what we had would develop into a beautiful relationship."

She smiled and wept simultaneously. Vanity and integrity on her lips, nostalgia and despair in her eyes. And Gustavo had the sudden wish to touch her skin, to explore her intense whiteness once more. Perhaps he was mistaken, perhaps he had begun to love her – but everything was confused.

"It's okay," said Aurelia, wiping her wet cheeks. "It was the best thing that could happen. After all, I'm a married woman and the truth is that before I get involved with someone else, I have to resolve my own situation. It's just that my pride has been hurt a little, but I don't feel any bitterness."

Gustavo had also wept while he was driving back. They were a couple of rebellious tears that escaped while he was thinking about that afternoon at the hotel with Aurelia and he began to feel grateful for the sense of vindication that her love had afforded him. He felt ashamed, not because he thought, as is the common perception, that machos don't cry, but because in that situation it seemed such an absurd reaction. He wiped his eyes with his shirtsleeve and, so as not to appear dramatic, made what he thought was an amusing comment.

He was still feeling unsettled when Officer Malcom Scott came to tell him the news. The bodies were found in a country house that belonged to a company in Lomas de Ayarco. The man, who was 30-something, had been executed inside his vehicle with a single shot to the temple and the woman, who was 28, had been dragged some distance, mutilated and executed in the same way as the previous victims.

"Fifteen deaths," the homicide chief calculated immediately.

This time he did not go to the crime scene, partly because he did not expect to find anything different, partly because the time and place of discovery indicated that it would be Aurelia who would be present. It would have been extremely difficult for him to meet her again and to pretend, for public consumption, that nothing had happened a few hours earlier.

Neither was he in the mood to discuss the case with his boss, from whom he had distanced himself in recent days. He decided to meet Officer Morales, to go over progress made in the investigation. Nevertheless, they told him that Morales had left early and that, on hearing the news, had decided to go directly to where the bodies were. Finally, he tried to call Maricruz but she was also unavailable. She had just left, they told him at the newspaper, to cover a last-minute story.

He ended up waiting for a call from the security minister, who politely and calmly expressed his utter consternation about the information he had just been given. Of course, he felt it necessary to express his concern about the impact this criminal saga was having on public opinion, that's to say, on the image of the authorities, judicial as well as administrative. Above all, he feared that in an election year the affair could be used to score political points and the issue of public security would be reduced to this single matter when there were so many other things to highlight, such as the important progress made by his administration. "Do I make myself clear?" The point was that they had to increase co-operation between the two police bodies to find the Psycho without delay. He had already broached the subject with

Don Jovel, who had very rightly indicated the need to talk to the homicide chief co-ordinating the investigation and with whom "I could come to an understanding".

Gustavo understood the message behind the phone call loud and clear. The minister was acting under orders, with the aim of pressuring him so that he would agree to take part in the farce that Don Jovel was proposing. However, he preferred not to show he was aware of these undercurrents but let it be known that he was working at full throttle on the case. He told him that he had important clues leading to the identification of the killer and that very soon they would have encouraging news.

After the call, Gustavo noticed that his feeling of impotence was reaching intolerable levels. If, in a reasonable space of time (two months maximum, he decided), he had not made significant progress, the best thing would be to find something else with which to amuse himself, as he had promised the director. However, the prospect of such a radical life change horrified him. What could he do? What did he know how to do that was beyond the funereal routine of this profession? He tried to picture himself with a helmet on his head, some boots and a tool belt, handling electric cables on a construction site, but the image was unimaginable.

That night he attempted to have a therapeutic chat with Maricruz, but such was her excitement about the day's news that she did not notice her lover's distress. She wanted information, details that Gustavo did not know and did not want to know. Sunk in despair, he sought refuge in the last 300 millilitres of whisky that he found in the sideboard and an hour and a half later he slipped into a comforting state of unconsciousness until the next morning.

That day began with a breath of optimism. At mid-morning, almost a week late, Officer Morales handed him a detailed report about the intimate and private life of Bruno Robledo, including the transcript of a long interview with his cousin Lucrecia. According to what he read, the homicide chief was growing stronger in his conviction that he had all the necessary keys to crack open the case. And it all fitted together much more than he had imagined possible scarcely a few hours before. It was not just the character and the personal history of the suspect that fitted like pieces of a jigsaw puzzle in the criminal profile, but material indications that had impressive certainty.

Gustavo meditated in the solitude of his office before taking the next step. He weighed up the risks from the perspective of his long experience and finally decided.

"Ask the judge to issue a detention order for Manuel Funes Sandoval, tell him that we need to apprehend him within 24 hours."

Juan José knew that she had returned but he considered it prudent to wait until she called him. He did not want to seem needy let alone anxious. The technique of the game, as he saw it, was not unlike that of fishing. Once you had thrown out the bait, you had to wait patiently until the fish bit, let out just enough line and then reel it in slowly and imperceptibly. Now he was in the third phase, that of floating the line, which in this case signified a certain amount of indifference.

"I've been here for 24 hours and you have not come to see me," Camila reproached him.

Juan José tried to make a gesture of uncertainty, of afflicted innocence.

"One supposes that the one who arrives is the one who does the greeting, the one who takes the initiative. It's something that we Ticos understand as a norm of courtesy."

"I am not Tico."

"Nor I Italian."

She shrugged. "The thing is that now I've come and I wanted us to talk a little."

"How is Bill?" asked Juan José, thinking that he was moved by a sincere concern for the health of his boss, although in recent days he had thought a lot about the possibility that he would stay mad forever and the idea did not repulse him. In fact, he found himself rather enjoying it.

Camila sighed, but who knows whether it was because she

was suffering from a similar inner conflict that was impossible to confess.

"Bad," she said. "The doctors say he is on a kind of journey. He is receiving some special treatment but they don't know how his mind is going to react. They say he could come back in a month, maybe two, in a year, two years or maybe never."

"I'm sorry," said Juan José, without realising that he was referring to the last and worst of the outcomes she had listed.

"The point is that I want to guarantee him the best medical treatment available and so I am going to leave him for a while in the United States. That means I'll be travelling a lot. I'm going to look for an administrator who will work very closely with me and will stand in for me when I am not here."

Juan José nodded without celebrating the irony, and went straight to the part that most interested him. "And the editorial operation?"

"That is where you come in," said Camila. "I think the natural thing would be for you to take over the editorial leadership."

The affirmation produced an impact that shocked the editor within, from the nerves of his brain to the last blood vessel of his big toes.

"Don't you like the idea?" she asked astonished. "I thought that was your dream."

"My dream has always been to be a good journalist, incisive and in-depth. The position from which I do it doesn't worry me so much."

"I am offering you a much higher salary, according to my calculations we can pay you 3,000 dollars a month. It's a lot more than you earn at the moment. Besides, I'll authorise you to use a company car. Meanwhile, if you want, you can use Bill's car."

Juan José studied the nails on his right hand unconsciously. Suddenly he realised that he had imitated a gesture of Mr Grey himself, and he felt a kind of terror.

"Let's understand each other," he spoke as calmly as possible. "What I don't want is to be director of a newspaper where I can't make any decisions about editorial strategy. Do I make myself clear? I don't want to be more of a puppet than I already am. If

I am not going to be autonomous, I'm prepared to stay where I am and let someone else have the title."

"What I'm talking about is you taking over editorial strategy. With Bill not here, who else is going to get involved in that? I am not fired up by news, what I am interested in is the contracts, the bills and the bank balances. That's what I understand. You'll deal with the rest."

"Do you mean that?"

"Completely. The editorial is yours on one condition: that you do no economic damage to the firm. You have to use your good judgment to ensure that your strategy doesn't lose us any advertising and that we continue to grow – because the worst disaster would be for all the journalists and all the staff to be out on the street. And I have Bill's spirit in fighting against adversity."

Juan José Montero could be temperamental and impulsive, occasionally a romantic, but he was never naïve. From the first moment he worked out what Camila was proposing, which was a hundred times more astute and dangerous than the gringo had offered during his long years in charge. She knew that the offer to lead the newspaper, without interference or apparent conditions, would be an enormous temptation for him. She probably counted on the fact that he could not turn it down, which was very close to the truth. But she was not presenting him with a gift. If he wanted to taste the fruits of power (which was the meaning of her proposal), he had to pay a price. And this was much more than a limitation, much more than an editorial line or a style of working.

She was demanding that he empty himself and adopt doctrines that he had never professed, to start being someone that it had never been in his plans to be, with the cold blooded attitude necessary to favour the business interest over the journalistic one. In addition, to be responsible for the working destiny of so many people, because a single mistake on his part could mess up the project. It was a difficult decision, far more than Camila could imagine.

"'In addition," she said. "You would have to be in charge of public relations. You know that my style is not very diplomatic."

"Neither is mine."

"But I have learned that you know how to pretend," she said with exquisite irony.

To her surprise, Juan José asked for a couple of days to think about his answer. She did not expect him to offer any resistance but neither did his response alarm her. She understood that between them there was a game whose rules were complicated and that she would have to learn them as she went along, before she mastered them.

"Let's accept it," Pedro proposed, "we are in the midst of a stinking pond. The whole country is a boiling pot of thieves and opportunists. From the most senior official to the humblest civil servant, from the most affluent businessman to the meanest contributor, you could uncover corruption scandals every day for years without needing to touch on the interests of the advertisers. Why should we worry about it? It's a technique that our competition has always used, with a lot of success."

"It's logical," Gabriel said. "We all know that a newspaper does not survive on advertising."

"But where does that leave the ideas about ethics that Juan José has taught us, that he has always defended?" Diana protested. "What you are proposing is an obscenity."

"Diana is right," said Maricruz, "we journalists don't have to take on this problem. That's why the firm has administrators."

"The problem is that the offer is integral, I can't accept just the attractive half. And, as I told you before, I am not prepared to take this on without your support," Juan José explained. "I don't want you to come to me afterwards to tell me that I'm a trickster, that I'd hardly been named director and then I turned into a reactionary, into an ally of the owners and stuff like that. I am leaving the decision in your hands, if you don't agree to back me, I'll simply thank the lady and I'll stay where I am, while I can."

"In that case," Pedro insisted, "they would hire someone else, someone we don't know and who, at the end of the day, might be worse than Mr Grey. On the other hand, if Juan José is director, we can have some influence. No one is giving us a newspaper so we can do what we like with it, it's about whether we are not such slaves as before."

"I prefer to carry on as a slave than become responsible for the manipulation of information by the company," Diana retorted. "And I'm even less disposed to do it for free… because they're not offering us a pay rise of even one *peso* or anything like that."

"If I've asked your opinion, it's to help me make a big decision, which is hopefully in your best interest."

"Well, I'll make your decision easy: I'm going," said Diana, getting up and collecting her belongings.

"Where are you going?" asked Juan José.

"To hell, where I can continue being a simple slave and where I don't have to wear chains to further the interests of the owner."

"Don't be so dramatic," said Gabriel. "Sit down."

"Don't worry guys, this is something I should have done a long time ago. Enjoy your independence," Diana left the meeting room with her arms held high.

Maricruz excused herself. "I am going to try to convince her to stay. But I know how I'm going to vote: I think we should allow Juan José the freedom to accept or reject the offer without it meaning either that we give him unconditional support or that we are going to boycott him from the outset."

After that meeting and before answering yes, Juan José Montero submitted his conscience to exhaustive scrutiny. To accept the leadership of the newspaper under the conditions that Camila demanded of him would represent his surrender. That was the only thing that, from the outset, was clear to him. It would be a surrender of certain principles that guided his professional life, which signified the largest part of his existence. What were those principles worth? Where did this character of absolute and unalterable truth come from, to which his conscience had to remain true? Why was it so hard for him to discount these principles or make them fit his needs? His father, a school caretaker, self-taught and a militant communist, had a powerful influence over him as he grew up and surely this particular itch came from him. He had taught him that a man must act in line with the dictates of his conscience. And that he should never move far away from values of justice, equality and honesty, which according to him were the essence of being human.

The old man had lived in accordance with such pronouncements and, perhaps because of that, he had died poor and disappointed, with a deep pessimism in his soul. "I don't regret anything I've done in these 78 years," he told Juan José, "but I wish that things had been different, that I had lived life a bit more comfortably, with a bit more freedom, I admit." Those words had such a profound impact on Juan José that he remembered them almost word-for-word. It had never occurred to him to stop and think if he himself would come to regret having lived with such rigidity. Was the sacrifice worth it? Did sticking to your principles provide happiness, some sensation of fullness, a spiritual abundance? In his case, at least, the question could not be answered entirely in the affirmative. At 45 he had accumulated a bundle of bitterness that did not allow him to feel comfortable with himself. His economic limitations annoyed him, his professional stagnation tormented him, his solitude hurt him, a solitude that, he had to admit once and for all, did not constitute a lifestyle that he had happily adopted but was the result of an exercise in methodical intolerance. He did not want to reach old age, like his father, sheltering in the room of a hostel, without possessions, without family or true friends, moaning that the world had not been compassionate. Throwing up tearful smoke-screens, he told himself, to hide the fact that I had not been capable of inserting myself in a creative way in a complex and changing reality, of learning how to get along in a scenario of bloody competition, even when I had the resources to do so. Now was not the time of the great social struggles, the banana strikes, the armed uprising and all the revolutionary illusions that had marked the life of his Papa. He had more than enough reasons to be the way he was, but Juan José Montero – in what age was he living? He did not even feel part of the revolutionary dream from which humanity was starting to awaken with the thunderous collapse of the Berlin Wall. He was nothing more than a man who was trying to make the world fit some inflexible values to which no one attributed any practical use.

On the other hand, it was not about converting himself into a cheap opportunist. He was not relinquishing his conscience, he thought, he was just accepting a decent job which implied certain compromises and responsibilities of a business nature. How bad could it be? Limitations? Yes, who did not have limitations in their work? Hadn't he had them for years while Bill Grey exercised his proprietor's rights in his tyrannical way? What genuine difference was there between a censorship imposed from outside and a self-consorship exercised with intelligence and practical sense?

At an age such as mine, when the senses begin to lose their original sharpness, a stirring of the heart is active. Something whose existence we sense but which does not have a name, allows us to perceive aspects of the reality beneath the skin of appearance with which reality usually presents itself. This is what happened that morning when Lidia returned to the newspaper. At first glance, nothing had changed, but in the kiss with which she greeted me, in her smile, in her tone of voice and crystalline eyes, there were troubling signs. I could not describe each one, but together they represented a reduction of several degrees in the temperature of her affection. Later, my initial perception proved correct. For several days I tried, vainly, to have a private conversation with her. The excuses rained down: she was behind with her work because of her long absence, family commitments, extreme fatigue, migraines, headaches. I waited patiently until she ran out of excuses and agreed to meet me outside the newspaper. We met, at dusk on a rainy afternoon, in a depressing café on the Paseo Colón. A friend had recommended it to me as the ideal place for a romantic meeting, perhaps with the innocent intention of pulling my leg and without knowing of the unhappy atmosphere that it contributed to that meeting, which already looked as if it would be gloomy.

Scarcely had she mentioned a couple of generalities about the trip; the voluptuousness of Paris, the serenity of the Swiss cities, the high culture of the Italians, aspects of the architecture, nuances of the meals, than she moved as abruptly and quickly as she could to the reality that interested her. She accused me of having pressured her, during those days after her return, in an unacceptable way. She didn't know if my new position was influencing this, she noted with infinite cruelty. She talked of the space that she needed for herself. She reminded me that she was a married woman, who at no moment had put her marriage on the line. She considered, she said, the possibility that we would never see each other again in any circumstance outside work, not because that was what she chose but because I had demonstrated that I was incapable of recognising my limits. I am noting the basic threads of her words, because my mind refused to retain the details of her multiple reproaches. Then I felt miserable, ridiculous, guilty, stupid and lonely to a superlative degree. Loneliness had never weighed as heavily on me as that night. At the time I felt so bewildered that I could not utter a single word in my defence. I asked forgiveness and begged her not to abandon me. I made vows of good behaviour and swore that I wanted to conserve the privilege, however small, of seeing her occasionally, talking with her, to know a little about how she was.

Some days later, as I go over her words and the tone of her accusations, I realise that I have never been blamed so unfairly. I think I did nothing other than react to the expectations that her behaviour had generated in me before her trip. Lidia often came looking for me. The nights that she spent alone, which I presume were not a few, she would call me at my apartment and we would talk for hours, she would fill me in on her past and make me part of her plans for the future, although I did not include myself in them, in such an enthusiastic way that I felt part of her life. The closeness between us was growing. I do not understand why now, after neither seeing nor hearing from her for several weeks, I should have guessed that she wanted to establish limits and distances that she had not proposed and understand that my interest in her could be interpreted as hateful harassment.

I have been informed of her wish, it's clear. But the situation crushes me because in reality I love her. I love her desperately, with a force and an intensity with which I have never loved any woman. I have confessed it in many ways, but she cannot believe me. She had advised me to try to control my feelings as she controls hers. I imagine that her love must be a small and inoffensive animal, nothing like the monster that is devouring me from within, eating my guts and threatening to destroy me bit by bit.

Of course, she didn't even bring me back what I had asked for, not because I like those shitty little towers, but because I wanted to have something for myself, however symbolic, from this time of her life. She denies me everything.

23

He was expecting neither a less sour expression nor a friendlier attitude from Don Jovel. Their relationship had cooled rapidly, to the point where now they no longer met one another even to deal with work matters. They had begun to communicate through memos, at first frequently and then more sporadically, and increasingly brief. And if he had asked for an appointment, it was not because he wanted to set things straight but because it was necessary to take important decisions that were not up to him.

The boss called him into the office in his rasping voice as he fixed him with a hard stare that would have discouraged anyone. Indeed, Gustavo felt an impulse to turn around, go back to his office and inform him about the situation in a 40-page memo. But he put his papers on Don Jovel's desk and made himself as comfortable as possible in the chair he was offered, ready for a long and eventful verbal duel.

"Go on," said the director in an offhand way.

"It seems to me we are at a critical point," Gustavo said.

"Yes?"

"Yes, I think that for the first time the investigation is on the right track. We have a lot of coherent evidence that points to a single suspect."

Don Jovel made no comment. He eyes remained fixed on the face of Gustavo Cortés. It was the look of a rattlesnake lying in wait, on the defensive and yet ready to attack. His body, although slouched in the chair, reflected the same mood.

"We have a fairly complete profile of Bruno Robledo, and we can ascertain that he's a 99 per cent match to Pedroso's profile."

The boss emitted an equivocal "Yes" between clenched teeth.

"Besides, there are clear elements that link this individual with others among those accused of the crime at La Cruz de Alajuelita, as well as convincing evidence that someone tried to divert attention with a false story about the crimes."

At his last words, Don Jovel swapped his somewhat scornful demeanour for a curious, anxious look, which Gustavo perceived immediately.

"Let's see... the details."

Gustavo smiled inwardly, opened a file and began to expound his thesis carefully, almost warily, conscious that it would encounter a resistance that was not easy to overcome.

"I am basing this literally on Pedroso's last document," he explained. "Let's consider the first element of the profile: 'The subject comes from the upper classes, and is linked either through himself or via his family to big business or politics.' In this case, Bruno Robledo complies with all the characteristics: his family has strong links to business and politics and he himself is a wealthy entrepreneur."

"That's obvious," Don Jovel shrugged his shoulders.

"As you will remember, the technique is based on narrowing the universe of possible suspects, and that's no more than the first delimitation."

"Go on then," said Don Jovel, rubbing his hands.

Gustavo went on: "'His residence must be located outside the triangle formed by the districts of Desamparados, Curridabat and the Unión'. Robledo lives in Escazú, at the other end of the city."

"Go on."

"Third: 'At some point in his life, the killer must have been linked to military activities. He could be an ex-policeman, but is more likely to be a member of a left or rightwing paramilitary group, owing to his obvious skill in moving stealthily in mountain areas without leaving any tracks.' Robledo attended a military academy in the United States, where he received a broad training in counter-insurgency tactics. That means he knows how to move around in mountain areas without leaving any trace."

"Many people in this country have had training in American military academies and there are also people involved with the rebels, but that doesn't turn them all into psychopaths," the boss presented an argument he believed to be very convincing, but Gustavo did not even bother to rebut it.

"'We have to look for a man whose temperament is unstable, who is prone to episodes of uncontrolled rage or euphoria, the son of a woman who is extremely dominant and aggressive with her children but who has rigid moral criteria'," the homicide chief read. "Here you have a transcript of our interview with Robledo's cousin, someone very close to his family nucleus. She described him as an obsessive type from a young age, with a particular skill for causing psychological pain. She recounts how he was about to run her over in a car he was driving at high speed simply because of an argument they had had about some trivial matter. She also recounts how the grandmother played the maternal role in Bruno's case, and that this woman was intransigent, highly religious, tyrannical and incapable of showing affection to the children."

"If I remember correctly, the gringo's report says that the suspect must have done some advanced medical studies."

Gustavo nodded. He had deliberately left this point until last in the knowledge that it would be a convincing argument.

"Exactly. For weeks that was the discordant note in the investigation, but I have resolved it," he said. "The answer lies in one of his frequent absences from Costa Rica. Around four years ago, during a stay in Miami, Bruno enrolled in a medical school and, oddly, spent six months or more studying anatomy. It was so hard for us to find this out because no one, neither relatives nor friends of the suspect, seemed to know about this episode. It does round out the profile that we're looking for, but the fact that he has kept it so secret is also very striking, don't you think? Apart from that, we have statements from two women who had intimate relations with him and who assure us that he did not show signs of being sexually adept, another characteristic that Pedroso suggested as highly likely."

Don Jovel arched an eyebrow, scratched his head as usual and stared at Gustavo in a way that no longer transmitted hostility but a kind of confusion. He tried to say something but only a strange rasping noise came out of his throat, as if someone was treading on eggshells.

"The only thing that does not fit in with the whole thing is that it seems Robledo smokes marijuana, but Pedroso's profile does not categorically exclude drug addiction, only considers it unlikely."

At last the director was able to speak, although his voice was oddly uneven. "Let's say that this guy does match the profile, we still can't go with this to the judge. We need incontrovertible material proof of his participation in the murders. We would have to find the weapon, to have identification. If not, we'd just make ourselves look ridiculous."

"It's highly likely that we'll find in his possession one of the M-3s that disappeared from the government storerooms... various members of his family have held positions of command in the security bodies, and it is well known that in his parents' house there is one of the biggest weapons collections in the country. On the other hand, some of the physical characteristics of the guy who stopped the couple in Tarbaca match those of the suspect: the height, the athletic build, at least what they were able to notice in those conditions. Do you remember?"

His boss nodded, not with enthusiasm but with growing concern.

"We have to be careful," he said. "You know that this family is very influential, an error of judgment on our part could be catastrophic."

"I know, but neither can we deceive ourselves. Everything that we investigate is strengthening the case in an astonishing way, which hardly ever happens."

"Exactly," warned Don Jovel. "Things that are easy can sometimes be deceptive."

"I didn't say that it has been easy and you yourself know that it hasn't. We have invested a lot of work and resources to come up with this report. What I'm saying is that the elements fit."

"And what do we do now, according to your plan? Because I imagine that you have one or you wouldn't have come to consult me."

Gustavo understood the message immediately. He himself, before Don Jovel insinuated it, had become convinced that he could go no further without support from his boss.

"I have asked for an order to detain Manuel Funes who, as you know, is Bruno Robledo's lackey."

"Why?"

"So he can explain why he was selling a false story about a terrorist conspiracy, so he can tell us that he was trying to divert attention and under whose orders. Apart from that, I would think about a raid on Robledo's property to seize material proof."

Don Jovel made a negative gesture.

'That's risky. If you hold Funes, it's going to put Robledo on the alert, if he really is the killer. If he's been so skilful so as not to leave any signs at the crime scene, neither is he going to make it easy for us to find clues at his apartment or office. I doubt that he leaves the machine-gun under his desk or anything like that."

"I don't see how else we could get hold of material proof. Well, we could put him under surveillance for a few days, find out which places he visits, his nocturnal habits, that kind of thing. That way, simultaneous raids on various places would be more effective."

"You haven't put him under surveillance?" Don Jovel exclaimed astounded, as if he had omitted something obvious.

"I thought that was the kind of action I had to get your approval for. If we mount an operation, it's highly likely that Robledo will detect us, not just because he's got experience of conspiracy activities, but because being the murderer he'll be alert to any abnormal situation."

Don Jovel gripped a pencil by the rubber on its end and jabbed it distractedly into his desk. He seemed worn out by his worries.

"I don't know why you insist on complicating things. If you had done as I asked and found a suspect from the underworld, someone who we can display publicly for a few days, we could throw up a smokescreen, make the real killer think that we are on the wrong track and lead him to drop his guard. Don't you realise? It would be a very smart tactic. On the other hand, if you go on with all this, making arrests, raiding Robledo's properties, we could lose the last chance to catch him if, as you say, all the signs stack up so clearly against him."

To get Gustavo off his guard was no easy thing. From very early on, in his youth, he had learned to master his impulses and, over time, this experience taught him that circumspection was a valuable weapon. He acted in moderation and in a calculated way even in the most unpredictable and awkward situations. However, this time he felt as if something was boiling up inside him, as if his arms and legs were moving of their own accord and obeying the will of an unknown man who lived within.

He stood up, put his documents under his arm and pointed his finger at Don Jovel's face.

"So that it's clear once and for all, sir, I am not going to take part in this immoral game. I don't care if you have political aspirations, or if there are powerful interests pressing you. I am not going to put an innocent guy in jail even for a day and neither am I going to abandon an investigation that's as promising as this one. Do you understand me?"

Don Jovel's features were contorted with rage although he tried to smile placatingly.

"Remember that I am the director of this case," he warned. "No one is going to make a mistake that's going to be regretted afterwards."

Gustavo did not respond. He turned, left the office and slammed the door.

His fish-like eyes stared unblinking at the mirrored window, defying those who (although he could not see them) were observing him from the other side like a strange insect.

After a 30-minute break that he used to have a cup of coffee and splash water over his face, Officer Scott came back into the small room, switched on the tape recorder and began to repeat the questions that he had asked again and again during two and a half hours, this time without much hope of an answer.

"Who are the leaders of the Clan? Why do you say they are responsible for the crimes attributed to the Psycho? Where do they meet? Does this organisation really exist? Why did you offer this story to *El Matutino*? Are you acting on somebody's orders? Do you know the pharmacist Don Vico? Have you ever taken part in a cult of the full moon?" The officer went over his questions. During all that time, Manuel Funes had repeated the same demand: I want my lawyer, and Scott thought there was no point in continuing with the same strategy. He switched off the tape recorder and gave him a long, incisive look.

"Let's be clear. We know you are not the killer of the women, but we can detain you as a suspect, we have all the evidence to justify the decision. We could put you in jail for several days, weeks or perhaps months until you decide to talk. And do you know what? I guarantee you that it is not going to be a pleasant experience because we're going to put you as near as possible to the relatives."

Manuel Funes smiled defiantly, for someone who was not Scott but an anonymous observer on the other side of the small window.

"Whose relatives?"

"Of the victims of Alajuelita," the officer said.

Funes smiled again and reiterated his demand: "I want a lawyer," but the policeman noticed the first crack in his fake veneer of control and self-sufficiency, a detail as small as a twitch, involuntary and repetitive, on the right side of his upper lip, which deformed his smile.

"You'll get one, but it won't be much use to you. There's heavy pressure from powerful people who want to find whoever is responsible, at least during the elections."

"You're trying to scare me," Funes said without looking at the police officer.

"If I were you, I'd be scared. This is not a game, you're in some pretty ugly shit."

"You can't hold me, you have nothing against me. You have to let me go."

"You're wrong, mate. Do you see what I have here?" he showed him an official paper folded in three. "It's the application to put you in jail that we took to the judge. It's all been discussed. We simply have to take you to make a statement and we'll make the order there and then. You wouldn't even have time to call your wife before going to La Reforma."

For the first time Funes took his eyes off the small window and looked at the floor. For the first time he blinked and a greasy sweat glistened on his forehead and nose.

"I have nothing to say," he insisted. "I want my lawyer."

"We'll make sure you get no special treatment, no protection, and we'll do that in the name of the 15 innocent victims whose killer you are protecting."

"I don't know what you're talking about, I'm not protecting anyone. I'm just defending my rights."

The officer rocked back and forth on the back legs of the chair. A nauseating smell told him that his tactic was getting results, the guy was not only sweating, not only had he lost his arrogant expression and self-assured body language, but he was on the point of shitting himself.

"You just have to answer my questions and you can go home peacefully. It's very simple."

"What you are asking of me is suicide," he said in a voice that was almost a sob.

"What you say here is confidential, no one apart from the investigating police will find out about it. No one knows at this moment that you are being held, no one will know that you spoke to us. If it turned out to be necessary, we would give you protection."

"I'd be a dead man," Funes shook his head.

"On the other hand, if you carry on like this, we're going to put you in jail, everyone will know and you're going to have two very serious problems. One with your friends at La Reforma and the other with your boss, who will have heard the rumours that you spoke to the pigs."

24

Today she told me that she's leaving. I noticed no sadness in her voice, rather happiness, excitement, she said, partly because of her pursuit of new personal goals. A better paid job although, however high it is, such a salary is just a bonus for someone who has so much money. A job with more social recognition, she said, nothwithstanding that her surname confers on her, automatically, all the prestige and status for which others would pledge their lives.

I don't want her to go, I told her, everything would dry up, lose all meaning for me. She responded to my moaning by saying that I am selfish and don't understand her position. It's difficult, she says, to try to be yourself when one is rich and everything is within reach. To be a hard worker, intelligent or kind is optional because everything is guaranteed – she explains to me – without it depending on personal qualities. One starts to tire of the ease with which people and things fall in your lap like fruit from the trees. And she doesn't want that. She is determined to study further and to make her fortune through her own efforts. She wants to be somebody, not just somebody's wife. I say that I have backed her up in her sentiments, that I am full of praise for her plan. But – what about us? What about us? She looks confused and she doesn't know what I mean by 'us'. We have had nothing together, she starts to say, I was just a close friend who offered her emotional support during a time of need. She is grateful to me for that. I must understand that I have no part in her plan for independence, that I was merely a fruit touched by her hand and now condemned to rot away in oblivion. I insist that I love her and that I cannot live without her, and she smiles. A compassionate smile, the kind of tender look an adult gives an innocent child. She assures me that she is also interested in me (she deliberately uses the low-key word 'interest'), but that she has decided to take control of her life, turn a blind eye to random feelings. It's time to impose rationality, she lectures me.

What can I do? Lidia is the only woman who has moved me in a long time. She caused tenderness and compassion to break out in a man who thought he was a stone, she disrupted my plans and she changed my life. And now, ignorant of what she has done, she is going to leave and never return, like someone who gets up and leaves behind an empty chair. I should cry, but I cannot. I must not. If I started now, I would not stop for decades.

"Will we see each other again?"

"Of course. Why not? Call me and we can get together for a coffee."

So, I've told myself that all is lost, that I must close this chapter of my life and go on as if nothing happened. I won't even have the consolation that someone will hear my moans.

This ending makes me sad but is far from surprising me. I sensed it from the beginning, I always knew that love is a merciless business in which there is at least one certain loser and I was sure that this role was the one I would play. The constant of my life has been defeat and even when I win, in any way, it is at the cost of a painful and irreparable loss. Sometimes I've asked myself if everyone shares my tragedy, if those whom the world identifies as 'winners' are not simply those who know how to hide their defeats, those who act out their lives and do so convincingly.

If recent events had been disturbing, what was now happening in Don Jovel's office was alarming. The man was pale, with bags under his eyes, his hands shook and it was difficult to follow the thread of his diatribe because his voice would dry up or change tone in a chaotic way. Gustavo stood listening to him, his arms crossed.

"You're crazy," the director was saying. "Do you know what you have done? You have destroyed any possibility of solving this case, ruined months of investigation and, by the way, you should forget your career. Yes sir, you'd better know it once and for all: you're finished with the police."

"It would be better if you explained," said Gustavo with a terrible urge to punch his boss in the face, pull out his hair and poke him in the eyes.

"Interrogating Manuel Funes, what you did put Robledo on his guard. If there existed any material proof of his involvement in the crimes, now he will have set light to it all, it will all be three metres below ground in a place that you and I are never going to know about. And the worst thing is that you did this without my consent, you went over my authority as if I was some figure of fun. You have made us look ridiculous, above all the institution."

"I only carried out a procedure that was essential. We're talking about a key witness, a determinant in any eventual judgment. Now, what will proceed is the raid. I already have the judicial orders…"

"You're not going to raid one square centimetre of anywhere," said Don Jovel clenching his teeth and pointing at Gustavo in a threatening way. "Absolutely nothing, did you hear me? Over my dead body."

Gustavo sighed deeply. He felt tired, almost without the strength to carry on with such an unequal battle, but something convinced him to stand his ground. He could not have explained what was driving him but it was something more than sense of duty or professional dignity. It was this absurd conviction that he carried a heavy load on his shoulders, this foolish feeling that he was responsible for the destiny of people, of a community, of being a key element in the future. An exotic case of the Messiah complex on the part of a public servant.

"I understand that you have political aspirations," he said, "but it would be an unpardonable crime to let someone continue killing innocent people. How could you... in all conscience?"

Gustavo's words inflamed Don Jovel even more. He seemed on the point of leaping on top of him, but kept his attack on the verbal level.

"Gustavo, you are talking and behaving like an idiot. I could toss my ambitions straight in the dustbin and it wouldn't change a thing. Don't you understand? You want to go in with hobnail boots against one of the most powerful families in the country, people with infinite amounts of money and with huge political influence in all spheres. Just one word and they could crush us like a couple of cockroaches."

"What about justice?" Gustavo protested.

"What justice, for God's sake? We're talking about your skin and mine. How do you want me to explain it? They are justice, only an idiot would imagine that he could beat them in a legal battle."

"In other words, you don't care about the success of the investigation but..."

"At last he starts to get it! Thank God!" Don Jovel said sarcastically.

The point, Gustavo thought, was that he had only half understood. He had thought that the reticence of his boss was due to a personal, transitory interest, the wish not to delay his own nomination to the Legislative Assembly, but there was something far bigger going on: Don Jovel was acting out of fear. Even so, he tried a last argument.

"And what happens if we collect all the evidence, if we find the weapon and other evidence in the possession of Robledo?"

"After you disobeyed my orders, that becomes difficult," Don Jovel replied. "But allow me to add something: with the proof that we've got we wouldn't even manage to sit this guy down in the judge's waiting room. Before that happens, before the press publishes a story implicating him in the murders, you and I will have disappeared. Think about whatever tragedy, whatever incident could occur, from a traffic accident to a fire at your home to an attack by a common criminal. Gustavo, I have received concrete threats."

"Threats? What sort of threats?"

"Death threats. Two telephone calls, one yesterday and another today, and they were directed against us and against two other officers. I don't know about you, but I am not prepared to turn myself into some anonymous hero."

"Let's make a public denunciation," Gustavo suggested.

Don Jovel smiled, a smile that contained both anger and sadness. He flopped down into the seat and filled his lungs before he went on.

"And what would we gain with that? We can't prove anything, we can't point the finger at the guilty. What do you want? That we end up making the Psycho responsible for whatever could happen to us, to us or our families. We would be a laughing stock from Peñas Blancas to Paso Canoas."

"What you're telling me is that I have to separate myself from the case because the other option, which is to fabricate some convenient story, is something I am not prepared to do, definitely not," Gustavo said.

Don Jovel scratched his bald head, took his eyes off Gustavo for the first time since the beginning of their conversation and diverted them to the first object that was between them: the telephone. He spoke weakly, in a voice without conviction but in a language that was clear and seemingly unwavering.

"No," he said. "What I am saying is that you are fired. There are two ways of doing it. Either I throw you out for insubordination or you, simply, avail yourself of the high turnover in the force and retire with a good economic compensation. You choose."

The most surprising thing about this statement was the internal effect it produced. First, a combination of rage and terror, followed by a feeling of relief. "Think about the date you go, it could be towards the end of the month," Don Jovel had said, but Gustavo told him that it would be that same afternoon even though he had not yet packed his belongings.

"I couldn't bear to meet you even in a casual way," he said to his face with impotent rage.

The director, who now seemed relieved of an annoying burden, shrugged his shoulders and his expression recovered its habitual serenity.

"As you like," he said.

For Gustavo, it was the moment in which his rage reached its peak but soon afterwards, while he was packing his books, his personal documents, his neckties, his coffee mug, the photo of Maricruz, his revolver, his medals, diplomas... his mood began to change. It still troubled him to wonder if there was a place in the outside world for a policeman (ex-policeman, he corrected himself) like him, a decent job, a group of friends, important work with which to fill his remaining time; he felt intimidated by the challenges of the street. However, nothing could be as gloomy as what he had experienced in the past few weeks. He gazed around the room and the atmosphere of the precinct revealed itself in all its opaqueness: a dozen or so officers shirking around, pretending to be busy with work, although he could, with a single look, tell who was doing the crossword or reading the latest instalment of the Condorito cartoon strip hidden beneath the covers of judicial forms, who was talking on the phone to their lover or counting the money from their bribes. All life was here: corrupt, miserable, some hard workers, honest and essentially decent policemen. But in all was a trace of decadence. He himself, he noted, must have this air of progressive ruin, of which he had been conscious almost since the beginning but which he always justified as a by-product of a dignified mission, of a noble service to society. Now, the myths had been crushed, of this world all that remained was deterioration. 'What have I really lost,' he asked himself, 'apart from the motive of addiction?' What has my police career been but a front for an uncontrollable vice?

Beyond the walls of his job, the world seemed hostile but now there was no going back. Besides, there was Maricruz. Her temperament had the virtue of dissolving obstacles, her vital energy was contagious and, inexplicably, next to her he felt light again. He only had to take her hand, one more time, and let himself be led to a world full of possibilities. The rest would just be extras.

As he left with his bundles of papers and cardboard boxes a group of officers surrounded him, alarmed. They wanted to know the reasons for his departure, details of his differences with the boss in the last few weeks, his plans for the future. But Gustavo did not want to recap a futile discussion, he just wanted to abandon ship and get as far away as fast as possible. He felt a complete disgust, bordering on contempt. Everything about the police, the crimes of the Psycho and Jovel Contreras was suddenly unbearable.

"Nothing, nothing," he told his curious colleagues. "I'm going because I've found a business that is a goldmine."

He picked up Maricruz at the newspaper and she managed to get time off until the weekend. They were in the apartment just long enough to pack underwear, stopped a few minutes at a supermarket to buy sunscreen and something to nibble on the journey, and rushed off in search of fresh air and warmth. They settled in a tavern with a view of the peaceful sea of Puntarenas, on the Paseo de los Turistas. In the recalcitrant atmosphere of the port, Gustavo began to feel different. Little by little, he became convinced that not only a geographical distance separated him from his previous job but that his psychological ties, strained under extreme tension, were beginning to break. They were violent ruptures, but with a certain musical resonance, like the snapping of a guitar string.

It was as if he had begun to emerge from a long nightmare.

"I wish I could erase my memory, live for the moment in the future, like a wise man," he told Maricruz, slightly tipsy from the alcohol, but more lucid than ever.

"You'll see that everything will work out," she said.

"Or not, but it no longer matters. I want to start my life again. I want to get to read Homer and Aeschylus and Aristophanes again without fear of anyone taking the piss out of me. I want to have many evenings and nights making love to you. I want to get drunk and throw up in the gutter and be ridiculous without thinking that I represent the dignity of an ancient institution and that I have to hide my emotions and cover up my instincts."

Maricruz leapt over the table, hugged him around the neck and kissed his ears.

"I want to be part of this disorder. Let's get married," she proposed.

For an instant he was petrified. Marriage was not in his plans, he hadn't even thought about it even though his love for Maricruz was growing each day amid the abundance and disorder of the tropical setting. He felt panic, not because of the proposal, but that the spell might break at any moment, that his sanity and equilibrium would return, that the carriages of his fantasies would be transformed into pumpkins.

"Wait here for me," he said.

"Where are you going?" she tried to stop him. "You haven't even answered me."

"I'll be right back."

He came back half an hour later accompanied by the first notary he found available. The man came bewildered, clutching his briefcase and convinced that something very serious must be happening for a senior police official (Gustavo had omitted to tell him he had quit) to summon him to accompany him, so urgently, on an errand.

"Let me introduce my fiancée, Miss Maricruz Miranda. I want you to marry us now," said Gustavo.

"What?" said Maricruz.

"How?" said the notary.

"As you heard. I promise to send you the necessary documents so that you can draw up the certificate next week, but I want you to perform the ceremony right now."

"But I would have to write down the proceeedings."

"We have time."

"We need witnesses."

Gustavo announced his intentions to the owner of the bar, who not only found it a great idea but offered himself and his wife – who worked on the till – as witnesses, and promised a small party, private, but at a reasonable price for which he would need no more than an hour to make preparations.

"And the rings?" the notary asked.

"I suppose that in some part of the city there must be a jeweller's. I'll bring them back in less time that it takes you to write the proceedings."

The lawyer shrugged his shoulders, but attempted one last argument.

"It will cost you more."

Maricruz entered the director's office. Everything had been put back in its original place: the documents in the files, the telephone on the table, Impressionist pictures on the wall. Apart from a few things that had been moved (the computer table pushed further back, the filing cabinet to the right and not at the left) one would have said that things were continuing as they always had and that there, on the other side of the desk, would sit Mr Grey smiling formally or devouring his fingernails. But it was Juan José who received her and asked her to come in.

"What can I do for you?" he asked.

Maricruz found the atmosphere strained. The voice belonged to Juan José Montero but she had the impression that it was being used by someone else. The gestures of authority did not suit those long extremities. The friendly treatment, which he seemed to be forcing, made him seem almost theatrical. However, she made a mental effort to overcome her displeasure and told herself that her prejudices might be affecting her perception. Perhaps she was exaggerating.

"I have the news of the year," the reporter said.

Juan José looked at her over his glasses, intrigued.

"What's it about?"

"The police already knows who the Psycho is and I am the only journalist who has the information," said Maricruz.

The director celebrated with several over-the-top expressions, "Fabulous", "Terrific", "Incredible", he repeated as he stood up, went over to her and lifted her a few centimetres off the gound in his enormous arms.

"Really? Are you sure that we're the only ones who have it? What news, Maricruz!"

"Yes, we could do a big report, a series of articles. I promise to get it done in three days. What do you think?"

"Fantastic, of course, but your face says that there is a 'But'."

"In a way," she said. "The suspect is Bruno Robledo."

Juan José sat down again. "I can't believe it."

Maricruz provided him with the details: the characteristics of the criminal profile, which Robledo fulfilled unquestionably; Funes's confession that his boss had dreamed up the story of the leftwing paramilitary group, as well as the idea of convincing *El Matutino* to publish it; the fabrication of supposed proof; the coincidences between the dates of the crimes and the suspect's migration records, among other things.

"Gustavo was convinced that they could find irrefutable material evidence against Robledo if they had permitted him to carry out the raids," she concluded.

"And what happened?"

"They didn't let him, they forced him to resign."

"Bloody hell," Juan José exclaimed.

"Gustavo is prepared to state how he was pressured to leave the case when he was on the point of solving it and that his refusal to do so cost him his job. It's the most important proof that we have that someone very powerful is behind all this. Don't you think? We could do a first report with this angle, then we could go on to reveal the evidence in chapters."

"What evidence?"

"The evidence I mentioned. It's circumstantial evidence but linked with everything…"

Juan José hesitated. "It's a great idea but the whole thing is pretty complicated, let me think about it for a while and I'll tell you later."

She waited in vain for two days for an answer, until she decided to go and get one. It was evident that Juan José was trying to avoid her so on the morning of the third day Maricruz appeared at the door of his office and marched straight in.

"I'm very sorry, but you can't…," said the director without even looking at her, before she could even formulate a reproach or a simple question.

"Why?"

"The Robledo family is very powerful, Maricruz, We can't accuse one of their members of being a monstrous killer and go unpunished, much less without having overwhelming proof."

"We don't have to state that he is the Psycho, we can say that in the course of the investigation, they found coincidences, indications. We can prove that. And we can also prove that the homicide chief was fired when he tried to take the investigation further. That is objective journalism, isn't it?"

"The practical effects would be the same," said Juan José. "They would simply destroy the firm and I cannot risk the jobs of 50 people. I would do it if it was only about my interests, you know me well, but now I have other responsibilities."

Maricruz looked at him confused and then, almost immediately, her face contorted in fury.

"No, Juan José, the truth is I don't know you well. I thought that you believed in journalism, that you were still guided by ethics. But now I see that they have managed to twist your arm, that they bought you off with a sweetener."

Juan José bit his lip. Anger, Maricruz supposed, must be consuming him inside, but now there was no threat that would manage to intimidate her. She had reached the point where her disillusionment was greater than her passion, which was saying a lot. She stood up, shot him another look, this time of scorn, and got ready to leave.

"Don't go," Juan José asked her in a humble voice, almost pleading. There was a brief but profound silence. Then Maricruz let out all her disappointment.

"What bothers me most is not that you put yourself on that side. In reality I didn't expect anything different, now you are the director, you represent the firm. Since you accepted the job, I knew you would have to change for the worse. What hurts me is the hypocrisy, invoking your love for slaves, adopting a mask of social sensibility to hide your own mean interests! That's the limit."

"You are being unfair," he told her.

"I don't believe so, on the contrary, I am talking about this in the most respectful way I can, but neither am I going to pretend to be happy with your reply. You are only defending your new position, that's the only thing that interests you."

Juan José nodded. He sank into his chair, and pressed his hands to his temples.

"You're right," he said. "I'm not being honest. Of course the other issues matter to me, but it is my situation that concerns me most. The truth, Maricruz, is that deep down I have always wanted this, although I know it's not much at all. Don't think that I think of myself as the great victor, I understand perfectly that I am nothing more than a puppet. But it's that I have never had anything. Since I was very small, life denied me the warmth of a true family... I didn't have affection, I didn't have resources. Through sheer balls I escaped the street, drugs, crime and through sheer balls I made of myself what you see now. It's little, very little, but it has not been easy for me."

"A few days ago you told me that the only thing you had was your dignity, that's another speech."

"I'm fighting to hold on to it and you don't know how much, but dignity doesn't feed you, or pay the rent. You see things from a different perspective. You are very young, starting your professional life, you have a world of opportunities ahead of you. I am going to turn 47, I can't go out tomorrow and ask for a job as a reporter, no one would give it to me. I can't say: here I'll start again, I am going to remake my life. Contrary to what you might think, experience does not add points on your curriculum vitae, instead it subtracts them. Media businesses don't want experienced people to write outstanding reports and earn a lot of money, they prefer kids who work for whatever pay and churn it out even if it is rubbish."

Those words did not relieve her bitterness but they calmed her rage and allowed her to see Juan José from a new angle: one of compassion. She had heard similar arguments before, but she never imagined that his survival was such a pressing concern for him. She believed that beyond all those uncertainties, there was a man of principles, an idealist and she wanted to confirm it.

"It seems to me you are exaggerating, I don't believe that a journalist like you can't get a decent job that would allow you to survive."

Juan José smiled, stood up and walked silently around the office. He stopped behind the back of the chair where Maricruz sat and he put his hands on her shoulders affectionately.

"To survive," he repeated. "That is such a relative concept. For a beggar it means not starving to death, for someone else it is to conserve the hundreds of millions that they have in the bank, to maintain the position of command from which they view the world."

"And for you?"

"My personal situation has improved in various ways, Maricruz. I can't deny it. I earn more money, that allowed me to get out of the shit hole where I was living and rent a comfortable apartment, in a modern area. Now I can have friends round to my house, invite them to have a drink and listen to good music. That makes me feel less isolated. Being the director of a national newspaper, although it's not the number one, has opened up a world of new relationships. I feel that I am more respected, inside and outside the firm. It's true that some relationships with very dear friends, like you and Diana, have cooled, but it's not me who has distanced myself but you."

"But you have a rich lover, that makes up for it."

Juan José returned to his executive chair and for a moment relaxed in the sensation of firmness and softness afforded by its cushions. It had belonged Mr Grey, like everything else that he was enjoying, including the lover to whom Maricruz had referred with such brutal sarcasm.

"I want to tell you a secret," he added, "just for you. Agreed? In the last few months I've had a romantic relationship with Lidia?"

"What?" exclaimed Maricruz. "That girl who does the culture stuff? Are you mad?"

"Yes, I was mad about her, so completely infatuated that I was capable of giving up everything, my job, journalism, the little that I have."

"But isn't she married?"

"Wrong thing to say," Juan José replied. "I've already told you it's a secret and I hope it stays that way. The point is that I started thinking that love had come into my life, that for the first time I was going to be completely happy. One day she came and told me that that was it, that she wanted to preserve her marriage and continue her life as before. She thanked me for being kind during a difficult time."

Maricruz looked at him now with renewed sympathy. The story kept the idealist afloat because every idealist is deluded.

"If you had told me before, I would have told you how it would turn out. It was predictable."

"But I wanted to have the chance to dream, even if only a little. The problem is that these kinds of dreams leave scars. My entire love life has been that, one wound after another. Now I have a lover who is not only rich but who is also the owner of the company where I work. It's very convenient. Don't you think? Well, yes it is. But she's also a woman, she shows me affection, she puts up with me, she even finds me handsome. I realised that I also need some of this, and so I took it. I know that I am a figure of fun, that they're talking behind my back and that some of them are calling me *Mister Montero*. I don't care, it's a subject that I try to reconcile with my conscience, without being dependent on what this person and that thinks, for the first time in my life I am doing something myself for myself."

"Don't you feel like you're stealing the shirt off a dead man?"

"Not at all. I haven't even felt bad for wishing that Bill Grey is lost in his madness forever. One day I will go my own way and Camila, *El Matutino* and all the mediocre people who criticise me will be a thing of the past."

Maricruz suddenly felt lost, she did not know what to think or say. Perhaps the affair was much more complicated that she had imagined and could not be resolved by taking principled positions. Perhaps her friends had the right to be imperfect, weak and even corruptible, but at that moment she felt overwhelmed by an irredeemable sense of loss.

That afternoon she called her friend the money lender and

secured a promise of credit for the necessary sum, at a ridiculous interest rate and in exchange for nothing. He only wanted to know, he told her, that one day he had been useful to the woman of his dreams.

Epilogue

"Tilín never decided to sell me La Villa, but we found this bar and, at the end of the day, we liked it better, we had to invest a bit in renovating it, but it is free from a leftwing history and we have a good clientele."

"And don't you miss the newspaper?"

"I miss journalism. You know I am addicted to adrenalin, but you can't swim against the tide. To be in it you have to give up too much, you end up being a docile operative, producing and packaging lies every day. Or half-truths, which amounts to the same."

"And this satisifies you in some way?"

"There is no great excitement here. I am a bit of a slave to the drunkards, as you can see, but at least I am earning money."

"A lot?"

"More or less, enough to live off and to put some aside. If we carry on working, perhaps one day I'll be able to set up my own newspaper."

"Hope is the last thing to be lost," said Pedro ironically. "But the truth is I admire your character. I, on the other hand, sometimes feel that I am stagnating in that newspaper, that my life is going by with no meaning and I carry on doing the same thing. Imagine – I will have been there for nine years."

"Time flies," Maricruz sighed. "It's seven years since I left and it seems like only yesterday."

"Nine years," Pedro said again, not losing the thread of his lament. "I should be doing something better but I can't find anything that's either nobler or more profitable."

"It's not so bad," said Maricruz trying to console him. "What you do is different. The society pages are lightweight and don't compromise you. I, on the other hand, felt that I had no choice, look for something to do or become a depressed hack. Besides, Gustavo's decision to leave the police spurred me on."

"I imagine it was hard, especially at the beginning."

"We were both without work and we had taken up a serious financial commitment. I felt sad at leaving journalism and Gustavo was tormented by the rumours that they started about him to ruin his image. They said they had had to get rid of him because he was in a deep depression, that the story with the Psycho was driving him mad, that he had turned into a fantasist. Can you imagine how angry he was?"

At that moment a ranchero song changed the rhythm. '*Me cansé de rogarle, me cansé de decirle que yo sin ella de pena muero...ya no quiso escucharme...*' sang Chavela Vargas.

"By the way, how are things at the paper?"

"There have been a lot of changes. Many people have gone and others have replaced them. There are new computers, at last they fixed the air conditioning, they made some changes to the building. It seems that the financial situation has improved a lot, because they publish a lot more adverts. But it's not as exciting as before. I think that Juan José does his job well but he has become a serious man, very quiet and formal. Now he comes to work dressed in a suit most of the time. Diana is still there but Gabriel left a couple of years ago, but they make a great couple."

"What happened with Mr Grey and the Italian?"

"They brought Mr Grey back a while ago but he's not the same. They say that it's as if he had a lobotomy, he's without his own will. He is at home being looked after by a nurse while Juan José and Camila are screwing each other madly, going here and there, visiting different countries. That's life, you never know who you are working for."

Pedro drained the glass and there was a trace of a sad smile. It was not his customary smile nor his confident demeanour, nor did those troubled eyes lost beneath a veil of insecurity belong to him. Maricruz noticed it right away. It was a vague, imprecise perception, but nonetheless real. We all change with the passage of time, she tried to explain to herself.

"Something's going on with you," she said at last. "I can feel it."

Pedro knew what she was referring to. He should have realised that with her it would be different, that he would not be able to hide his distress however much he tried, because between them there was an intangible bridge that connected them beyond words.

"I am ill," he said.

The expression alarmed Maricruz.

"What is it?" she asked.

"Have you heard of that auto-immune whatever disease?"

"That can't be. This is a joke, right?" Maricruz exclaimed.

"I'm not ill, just seropositive, but it's the same to all intents and purposes."

The news produced in her an inner turmoil, a sudden collapse that froze her in internal turmoil and left her in utter silence, incapable of articulating a thought, much less a word.

"If I had told you that I had cancer, hepatitis or some other thing, it would not hit you like this. Cheer up, there are millions of us and there will be a lot more in the years to come," he tried to say ironically, but it didn't work.

"But... how could it happen?"

"I made a mistake one night, after a lot of drinks, I slipped up in what seemed a harmless way. They say that it can take up to seven years for the illness to manifest itself, adding it up I think I've got two years left of fun. But there is always hope. Today there is medicine that can keep you alive, perhaps until they find a vaccine and within time this fuck-up will be nothing more than an anecdote. I've always been lucky until now."

The meeting had been transformed into a mesh of embarrassing silences and half uttered words, confused thoughts, chaotic feelings. Customers started to arrive and Maricruz seized the chance to flee, feeling pangs of remorse and surprised by her own weakness. She would have liked to embrace Pedro tenderly, kiss him to show him how strong their friendship was and how unimportant this new situation was to her, but she couldn't do anything at all. She did not know what to say or how to behave. Pedro shrugged off her confusion with perfect aplomb. He finished his beer and said goodbye with a meagre kiss and a promise to return one of these days.

When he left the bar, it was 10.30pm and it had started to rain again. It was the closing stages of a wet October. Pedro reached his old car with rain pouring down his face (he always forgot his umbrella) and on turning the key he felt a shooting pain in his chest. He had difficulty breathing and his hands were shaking. Pneumonia, sudden lung cancer, he thought. He started the car and after a few minutes was no longer anxious. It was merely, he said, the price of a mouthful of chickpeas and pork. A warm sensation of weakness invaded his body: now there was no pain or tiredness just a profound relaxation. He closed his eyes for a few moments and imagined that the passage to death would be like this state of abandonment and total indifference.

In just seven years, his single grey hairs multiplied at breakneck speed until his head had been turned into a symbol of respectable whiteness. As for the rest, he did not seem to have undergone transformations of any significance: he still had his easy-going manner, abundant moustache and corpulent physique. However, he had changed. However humble and reasonable one is, a person changes inside when he begins to issue the orders that he had previously received and criticised (although the inverse does not always happen). And so it was with Marco Aurelio Morales. The huge officer occupied the position that Don Jovel had left vacant a few months before when he finally achieved his precious dream of becoming a parliamentarian. Until then, Morales had spent two years as sub-director and gained a law degree which he obtained with a lot of sacrifice of his free hours and which hung on the wall behind him in a luxurious frame. Gustavo was so pleased to hear the news of his appointment that he was on the point of sending a telegram to congratulate him, but he had not had a chance to greet him in this manner when he received a telephone call from his friend that sounded of extreme, anxious urgency.

Morales welcomed him with the unrestricted warmth that is permitted only between equals, but he did not look like a satisfied man. Anxiety was eating him up and he could not hide it.

"It's a pleasure to come into this office and find a true friend," said Gustavo. "How's it going?"

"It was going very well until a few hours ago," he replied.

"Has something bad happened?"

"Did you hear about the disappearance of a couple about four days ago?"

"It can't be," Gustavo interrupted. "Is it what I am thinking?"

"No more, no less. The Psycho again."

Gustavo sighed deeply. Since the day when a small item in the newspaper had mentioned the disappearance of a young couple, his mind had begun to whirl around, at frenetic speed, the suspicion that was relentlessly urging itself on him. The following day, the press revealed the place where the police found the man's empty car, in a solitary street in Patarrá. He knew the area well, so well that he was tempted to call his old friends (but he didn't) to tell them where to look: a desolate cliff less than a kilometre away. He supposed that the killer made them walk to the perfect spot for the sacrifice. He knew how the Psycho would have killed each one and how their bodies would be found under a covering of earth and few handfuls of stone, which was abundant in the area. He even predicted that he would have been wearing jeans and the striped T-shirt that the witnesses had seen on the murderer the last time, the night on which they had decided to go off the road home towards the deserted spot where they met with death. She was naked and her body had been mutilated. The moon was full. The fatal shots in the left temple, the absence of other tracks apart from those of the victims, the total lack of witnesses, of someone who remembered hearing a gun go off or who had seen some suspicious movement.

He heard the version of events from Morales with a sensation that he was listening to himself. Only one detail surprised him: the officers took four days to find the bodies in spite of the fact that the killer had indicated, strangely, the way towards the improvised tomb with a piece of black insulation tape of the kind that electricians use, which went from the side of the road to the bodies of the victims (the bread crumbs in the story of Hansel and Gretel, a similar story of terror, although the other way around).

He was not surprised by the police incompetence but it seemed to him a new element in the Psycho's behaviour. His sarcastic animosity, his defiant streak had grown. And it was not enough to kill and disembowel the victims, now he wanted to show evidence of how stupid his pursuers were – establish the extremes of his own audacity. The killer knew beforehand that the investigators were going to search every millimetre for two hundred metres around for a trail and he also knew that their work would not come up with anything more than some limestone dust or the shit of an invertebrate.

"When did they find them?"

"Two and a half hours ago? I called for the utmost discretion with the press, while I decide how we are going to present this publicly, but you know that those bastards monitor our communications. I don't think we can keep the secret for long."

"It might seem unbelievable," Gustavo said, "but I imagined everything that would happen as soon as I heard the news of their disappearance. I was about to call you to tell you about my suspicions, but I thought it might seem impertinent."

Morales patted him on the back as if to show that he appreciated his scruples.

"I know it doesn't surprise you. There is no policeman in this country with such good intuition, that's why I called you."

"Really?"

"I need you to come back."

"To the force?"

"I assure you I'm not going to let myself be intimidated. We will go as far as we need to solve this case. What do you say?"

It was music to Gustavo's ears but he closed his eyes and clung to his bad memories, as if to a flagpole that could save him, until it stopped and his sanity returned.

"I'm sorry," he said. "But I can't. That for me is history."

"It wouldn't be like before, I..."

"It's not about that," said Gustavo. "It's that now I have other interests. I am involved in a project with my wife, I have finally returned to my studies of classical literature and I swear to you that I really enjoy my new life. But the solution to this is more than easy. You know where to direct the investigation."

"That's the problem Gustavo," Morales tugged at his moustache nervously. "We don't."

"You yourself found the clue that led us to Robledo."

"Since the couple disappeared, I ordered an investigation of Robledo. The guy has been in Miami for a month."

"Are you sure?"

"I have the forms from the migration department here."

"It could be a trick. Haven't you thought about that? It's fairly simple. He goes out in a legal way and comes back in a clandestine way, over land."

Morales sighed and shook his head.

"I don't know, it seems a bit difficult. From the start we asked for help from Interpol and they located him there, the identification is positive."

"An imitator?"

"Difficult," said Morales, "very difficult. The crime is a perfect replica of the earlier ones. The experts say there can't be two guys with these skills. So the hypothesis that it's Robledo has gone up in smoke...unless..."

There was silence for a few moments while Morales stroked his beard thoughtfully.

"Unless what?"

"Two things. One that this is a sinister, complicated scheme that has been woven to protect Robledo's skin. But I wonder what would be the point if the case was practically closed, if it had not occurred to anyone to disturb the hornets' nest. And how do you explain a gap of seven years between the activities of the killer? Is it possible that a mind like that of the Psycho's can be liberated from its obsession and then succumb to it again seven years later, so suddenly?"

"You said two things."

"The other is that the case is linked to Funes."

"Funes," Gustavo said between his teeth, bewildered.

"It's like looking at the investigation in reverse. In the last few days people here have been talking about a theory that maybe the guy is not so innocent, that maybe he played a much more active part in the crimes than we thought."

"How?" Gustavo's ears were burning.

"As an accessory. It's a possibi'   but it's worth analysing. It turns out that, investigating case   ve have found that with some serial killers they had a kind of lackey who found the victims for them, collected information and helped them to construct alibis etcetera. Some even helped their masters at the crime scene. If we analyse Funes, we arrive at the conclusion that he fits the characteristics of the lapdog. And if he tried to trick us with the story of the political conspiracy, what else might he have done to please his boss?"

"What's the idea?"

"What if Funes was with his master at the disembowelments of the first era, learned the procedures and then decided to launch out on his own."

"It's no more than speculation," said Gustavo.

"That's why I need your help."

"No."

"As an assistant, perhaps?"

Gustavo shook his head. And yet he wanted to. The last seven years at Maricruz's side had been unbeatable. To live for himself, to enjoy free time, to construct a world for him and the person he loved, was much more than he had dreamed possible. Besides, everything seemed to be easy, it flowed from him so naturally that at times he thought it was amazing, because beforehand he had believed himself made of cardboard, with almost no feelings.

No, he was not prepared to renounce his new life, nor do anything to endanger it. But in spite of the arguments with which he tried to convince himself, there was a part of Gustavo Cortés that had remained anchored to nostalgia. A small degree of suffering that at times he refused to recognise. It stopped him being entirely happy. 'But no one is entirely happy,' he would tell himself.

"If I went back, everything that I have built until now would start to be destroyed," Gustavo tried to explain.

"It would only be for a few weeks, perhaps a few months," Morales insisted. "Afterwards you could return to your business."

"It's not the business that worries me. If I come back, I don't know if I'll be able to leave again. I'm an addict. Do you understand? If I drink from this cup again I might not be able to stop."

"I promise that once the case is resolved, I'll send you away without thinking about it, you wouldn't have a way to stay."

"Alright, six months but not a day more."

It was not difficult to convince Maricruz. It was enough for her to hear the theory about Sandoval's possible role for her to get carried away and start trying to tie up the loose ends. She went on to explain why Sandoval had spent so much energy trying to convince her who was behind the political conspiracy. Doing so was in the interests of his boss but above all for the sake of his own repugnant skin. It was practically proven that the man who had taken part in Don Vico's ceremony, whom she had recognised, could be no other than Sandoval. She had always known it because there could not be two people with that look. If Sandoval was directly linked with these murders and if these had, as it seemed, an element associated with a ritual of the full moon, wasn't it then coherent to presume he was involved? Gustavo had to stop her when she suggested the possibility of renting out the bar, or if that didn't work, finding a manager so that she could also dedicate herself to the investigation. She was dreaming whether some newspaper would accept her services, even as a freelancer.

"This is getting dangerous," Gustavo objected. "The truth is I think he is more dangerous than ever, and if I agree to get myself involved in the investigation again, it's with the security and support that the organisation can give me. You're not going to have that protection and I don't want you to run unnecessary risks."

"So I have to stay like this, watching the bulls from behind the fence. You can't decide for me, you know that, don't you?"

"I know that very well. But if you insist on getting involved, I will call Morales and tell him that I have thought more about it and that it's not going to work. I also have the right to decide and I decide that I am not going to work on this if it puts you at risk."

For the next two days the debate continued intensely. On the third day a telephone call ended it abruptly, and forever. It was Morales. He told Gustavo that he was sorry but he had made a stupid mistake by supposing he could decide he would be contracted without consulting the administration. There weren't resources for him, but they would put it in the budget at the first opportunity if the case did not resolve itself. He was grateful for his willingness, etcetera.

"Tell me the truth," said Gustavo.

"Mate, it's what I told you," muttered the chief of police.

"I have many faults Marco, but being an idiot is not one of them. Tell me the truth."

Morales opened his mouth and shut it for a few seconds, indecisive.

At last he said: "As you can imagine. As soon as I opened my mouth and announced that I planned to bring the investigation to closure, the pressure started."

"From who?"

"I can't tell you and definitely not by phone, it's not worth it."

"So, there is no investigation."

"We'll keep it going but with another hypothesis."

Gustavo did not want to hear anymore. To a certain extent, the news was a relief because it resolved a difficult dilemma. On the other hand, it saddened him to think that perhaps he would never find out the truth. More than the enigma itself, he was tormented by the thought of the earlier and future victims (because without doubt there would be more); he imagined all the suffering that the killer had left in his wake and would add to.

"Do you think we'll ever find out for certain who the killer is?" Maricruz asked, disappointed.

"Perhaps," said Gustavo. "Perhaps in 80 or 100 years it will occur to some historian or novelist to dust off some old documents and reconstruct the events. Perhaps those who are alive then will know of a name but this will be history or literature, and we know that history and literature never offer you concrete knowledge but one among many possible outcomes. When the killer or killers die, there will be no one left who knows the truth."

"Only the full moon," murmured Maricruz.

"Yes, it is a mystery of the cadence of the moon," Gustavo said, and switched off the light.